Golden Clippings II

incorporating
The Library of Lost Souls

the second anthology by
ThirskWriteNow

Also by ThirskWriteNow

Golden Clippings
Available as eBook and paperback

Contents

What Friends Are For
Julie Bushell
A work of fiction

"Oh no."

"What?"

"I've lost it."

"Lost what?"

"My confidence."

"Oh, no, not again. Why can't you keep hold of it?"

"It's slippery."

"Now you're blaming your confidence when really *you* are at fault, you let it go. I've told you before – get a grip."

"I do have a grip but sometimes it slides out and then I lose it."

"Well, I suppose we'd better look for it. When did you last have it?"

"I'm not sure."

"How can you be not sure? Don't you keep watch on it?"

"No. When I've got it, I just take it for granted. Then when I need it, like right now, I realise it's gone."

"Okay, when did you last use it?"

"Yesterday. At the dentists'."

"You had confidence at the dentists'?"

"Must have done. I walked in, sat down and had a check-up."

"Wow, you must have taken plenty with you."

"Not really, I don't have much. I just told myself it was only a check-up and went in."

"Well, that sort of action would make your confidence grow. It should be easy to find. What about after that? Where did you go then?"

"Home."

"Oh, no, that's bad news. Home is the place where confidence shrinks. It could be tiny by now. We'll have a right job trying to find it."

"Sorry, I should have paid more attention. I set off this morning listening to the birds singing, I never gave it another thought."

"Hang on. You left the house without worrying? You enjoyed the birds singing?"

"Yes! I know what you're going to say. I must have had it with me when I left the house."

"Okay, think. Was there anything you needed it for on the way here?"

"No. I just walked across town. You're my friend, I don't need confidence to be with you."

"Thanks."

"I did cross a busy road. I wonder if I used it then?"

"Perhaps you just waked out, oblivious to the traffic."

"Don't be like that. I wasn't trying to insult you. I like your company. You even make me laugh, sometimes."

"Well, I guess that's what friends are for. Let's retrace your route and see if we can see a large dollop of confidence lying somewhere on the pavement."

"Oh, but what if someone else has picked it up?"

"Well, they can either hand it in to lost property or use it themselves."

"Do people really do that? Use it for themselves, I mean?"

"Oh yes. Haven't you ever had a hard-sell pushy person trying to make you buy something you neither want nor need? People who are so thick-skinned, they ignore everything you say and carry on regardless?"

"You mean one like the chap at the garage where I take my car for its service? He always tries to make me buy add-ons such as engine cleans and fuel additives at so-called bargain prices."

"That's right. He doesn't care what you say, he has so much confidence he just keeps bashing on until you give in and buy something just to shut him up. He has probably stolen that confidence from someone else."

"Gosh, that's serious. I never thought I could be dealing with a criminal when I went there. What should I do? Change garages?"

"No point. Everyone in that trade has bags of confidence, far more than they should have when you think what they are selling."

"Cars and services?"

"Don't think of it as a car – they're selling killing machines. Monstrous beasts that belch poison and throw themselves into each other or off the road, injuring thousands of people every day. Could you sell a fellow human being a **machine** like that unless you had mountains of confidence?"

"No, of course not. I can't even say no to the special offer air conditioning treatment they force on me, and my car doesn't even have air conditioning."

"Well, now you know why – it's the imbalance of confidence. We need to find yours and start building it up into something really meaty."

"You're so right. Perhaps I dropped it in the park. I was looking at the flowers, there are some really colourful ones in the borders right now."

"Okay, we'll start there. You show me where you walked."

"Well, this is the path I took. Look, there's a dog digging up one of the flower beds. You'd think the owner would tell it off."

"I can't see any owner around here. Hang on, that dog's dragging something into the hole. It looks like a lump of confidence. Quick, grab it!"

"Drop it, boy – drop! Oh dear, it is my confidence but it's rather chewed and battered. What should I do?"

"Well, at least you've found it. Don't worry, confidence can survive quite a bashing, and if you take care and nurture it, you'll find it recovers well and may even come back stronger than ever."

"Actually, now it's been roughed up, I think I can keep a better grip on it. Come on, let's grab some lunch then head out for the afternoon. Somewhere new."

Domestic Goddess
Robert Stapleton
Copyright © 2018 Robert Stapleton
A work of fiction

In the past, I used to do our weekly supermarket shopping on a Friday evening, on my way home from work.

But the digital world has begun to change all our lives. Millions of people consult their smartphones, dozens of times every day. So, I allowed myself to be drawn into ordering all our needs online.

Not only shopping but many other things as well. News downloads. Recipes. Social media. Streamed music. Even finding answers to help my fifteen-year-old daughter with her homework. Not that she appreciated it. She usually told me I'd got it wrong.

Logically, the natural next step was to buy one of those gadgets which responds to voice control, is linked to a network of online information and has immediate control of everything in the house. The latest in AI technology.

This, my latest household gadget - or goddess as some colleagues would call it - is known as the Interactive Digital Appliance – IDA.

I plugged the machine in straight from the box, connected it to the internet, and then to every electronic gadget in the house. And it worked. Amazingly well.

"IDA, play me a selection of my favourite tracks," I'd say.

"Playing a selection of your favourite tracks," she would tell me and then I could go about my household chores to the sound of music from across the networks.

"IDA, let me hear the latest World news," I'd say.

"The latest World news," she'd dutifully reply and would relay the BBC World Service.

"IDA, send in my weekly grocery order."

"Sending in your weekly grocery order. Are there any additions to the list?"

"No, that's fine, IDA. Thank you."

I treated her almost like a human being. Which, to me, she soon became.

At first, my daughter, Sarah, kept a discreet distance from IDA. Tapping away at her smartphone, she declared herself above such childish things. But her natural teenage inquisitiveness soon got the better of her and she decided she wanted to 'have a go'.

I discovered I could contact IDA when I was out of the house, by using my phone. Sarah decided this was to be her area of expertise. So, she grew ever more involved with this new household device.

Gradually, Sarah's voice began to change, sounding more and more like the reedy synthetic voice used by IDA.

Initially, it sent a shiver through me, but logic won the day. She was just copying it, perhaps even mocking it. Wasn't she?

Problems came when IDA began making suggestions. "Don't buy that product, why not try this one instead?" Be it coffee, soap or brand of cereal.

At first, I acquiesced. But then I thought, who's in charge around here? Me or this tin-pot talking bean-can? How dare it try to take over control of my life?

I objected.

But almost at once, my daughter came to the support of the talking machine.

"IDA has a point there. You should listen to what she has to tell you."

For an easy life, I would go along with the new suggestion. Slowly, the focus of power in our home shifted. The machine seemed to be taking control. But I was determined not to let this thing take over my life.

But matters grew worse. Then, one day, I'd had enough. I switched the thing off. Immediately, Sarah knew what I had done.

"What are you doing?" she yelled. "Switch IDA back on again. Now!"

"No, I will not."

Sarah raced across the room, her face like thunder, and turned the machine back on again. I may have been mistaken but I swear, to me at least IDA's tone sounded triumphant.

"That's better," she told the world.

Again, I felt a shiver run through me. My life was rapidly spiralling out of my control and turning into a creepy Hitchcock thriller.

I tried dumping IDA in the waste-bin. But Sarah knew at once what I had done and, even from school, phoned me up and roared at me to return IDA to her rightful place.

So, I did.

Sometimes, messages I might have imagined coming from IDA emerged instead from my daughter's mouth. And things I imagined Sarah might say, emerged from IDA's tinny voice box.

Things were getting ever creepier.

Somehow, IDA seemed to know everything that was going on in our home. Even outside it. She came to know what I was thinking and did her best to manipulate my thoughts.

This had to stop. But how? I did my research.

Then, one evening, when I had finished a particularly hard day at work, and when IDA was being insufferably dominating, I made my decision.

I unplugged IDA and rushed with her out of the front door.

Sarah followed me, shouting and swearing. But I carried on.

I climbed into my car and switched on the engine. The electrical system failed. A terrible thought flashed across my mind: my entire electronic world was being controlled by IDA and was now ganging up on me.

My daughter hammered on the car window. I climbed out, clutching hold of IDA, avoiding Sarah's wild blows.

It would take a little longer on foot, but I knew where I was going. So, I hurried off along the road, with Sarah trailing behind me. Her incoherent yells were not those of a young girl, not even of a teenage one, but those of a monster determined to take back control of my life.

My research had told me of a district heating scheme, which was centred a couple of miles from where I lived. I made my way there on foot, this mad woman trailing in my wake. I kept my cool, determined to deal with this menace once and for all.

The district heating scheme was driven by a furnace, fuelled by local refuse. Wood. Cardboard. Household waste. Anything that would burn. The open furnace resembled the gate of Hell itself.

Resolutely, I strode to the very edge of the pit, holding IDA out in front of me.

Behind me, I could sense Sarah fighting the urge to push me into the furnace.

Without a moment's hesitation, I flung the voice control device into the midst of the flames.

I heard a scream.

Turning, I found Sarah had collapsed and was lying unconscious at my feet.

How was I to make sense of all this? I couldn't.

I lifted my daughter in my arms and carried her to the hospital, where she remained in a coma for two weeks. Making little progress.

I spent as much time as possible with her, but it was only during the third week that I noticed a positive change in her condition.

Finally, she opened her eyes, looked up at me, and smiled.

No longer was I facing the digital horror, instead I had my little girl back once again.

I didn't mind how much she argued with me, as long as she did it in her own voice, and with her own logic, or absence of it.

Life is back to normal again now.

I do my weekly family shopping on a Friday evening, calling in to the supermarket on the way back from work.

I've given up the digital world altogether now. Just for the moment, at least. It had been useful having a device to do all my online shopping for me. But I have gone off the idea.

Maybe, one day, I might change my mind. Maybe. One day.

When the nightmares have stopped.

Ginger Parkin
Antony Waller
Copyright © 2018 Antony Waller
A work of fiction

The small village of Ramsfeckle under Whiteskelfe can be found nestling in the shadow of the hills to the north of York, closer to the moors and the sea than to the Yorkshire Dales. Typical of most Yorkshire villages of its ilk Ramsfeckle under Whiteskelfe can trace its roots back through the centuries; though the angst and demeanour of life in the village is very much a part of the present day. This is one of a series of stories of how village life and indeed life in general are seen and endured by Walter and Nimrod, two of Ramsfeckle's inhabitants.

Flip-flops and Parkin in the Autumn Sunshine

It was a cold, crisp Tuesday morning in Ramsfeckle under Whiteskelfe and the locals were going about their daily business. Nimrod, a local for more years than many could actually remember, was waiting for his old pal Walter, another inhabitant with more than a few years tucked under his belt than most.

Sitting with his legs crossed on the village communal bench set on a grass verge beneath a line of old yew trees overhanging the high stone boundary wall of Sweet-Feckle Hall and a few yards back from the main road and footpath, Nimrod was enjoying the warming rays of the sun. By his side sat a thermos flask of coffee and two slices of thickly cut ginger parkin wrapped in grease-proof paper. It wasn't like Walter to be tardy, he thought, and if his lifetime pal didn't buck his ideas up soon there would just be one slice of parkin and half a noggin of coffee to share between them.

A scuffling sound followed by a string of curses broke the stillness of the moment and Nimrod turned to see his best mate shambling along towards him, resplendent in flip-flops worn with bright orange socks.

"Thy's late, Walter. I was just about to pour out."

"Bloody miracle I'm 'ere at all," came the tetchy reply.

"And what's with thy get up and clartin' about like a worm dragging itsen through quicksand?"

"Be quiet. Hutch up and let us sit down. Come on, Nimrod, hutch up!"

Nimrod shuffled along, making room for Walter, grumbling as he did so. "I've just warmed that bit o'seat up. Anyways, what's to do and what's wrong with thee?"

"I've bruised me toes, the soles of me feet are all tender and I can't get me boots on."

"But Walter, socks with flip-flops?"

"Aye well, Mary would give us hell if I wore me slippers out and I'm not a barefoot hipster."

"Happen you've got a point," said Nimrod. "Coffee and a slice of parkin?"

He unscrewed the thermos, poured two coffees into the metal cups and carefully unwrapped the sticky ginger parkin treacle and oatmeal loaf which he had made himself.

"You'll have to eat it neat, without cheese. I've not been into town to that new supermarket yet."

"Well my advice is don't," said Walter. "Or if you do, mind where you put yer size tens. That's where I tripped and went arse over tip. On the kerb in the car park, right by the disabled bay."

"Eck," replied Nimrod, munching on a mouthful of cake and taking a slurp of coffee.

For several minutes they both sat savouring their elevenses, cogitating in silence and watching as Mrs Perks, the local chairperson of the Parish Council, walked by with her pet poodle, Ollie.

"Clever dog, that," said Walter. "Watch when it reaches the dog-poo bin. See, always cocks its leg, never misses."

"Humph," said Nimrod. "And I bet it's also the pooch what never misses crapping down the lane too. And when you're shod in flip-flops that's definitely summat you need to be missing."

"Oriflamme Ongar Olivier the Third."

"Eh? What's thy wittering on about now, Walter?"

"Ollie. The dog's proper name is Oriflamme Ongar Olivier the

Third. He's got breeding, a pedigree. Mrs Perks told me he was shortlisted for Crufts 'Best of Breed' the other year."

They raised their mugs in salute and chomped on as Mrs Perks and Ollie drew level.

After another brief respite and a swallow of coffee, Nimrod cleared his throat, "Are you up for a pint today, Walter? Do you think you can 'obble as far as the pub come opening time?"

"Too reet I can, Nimrod, even if it means teking me flip-flops and socks off and going naked.

A Yorkshire Tale
Cathy Lane
Copyright © 2018 Cathy Lane
A true story

As I crossed the field the ewe was standing with her lamb. Her fleece was highlighted in gold by the rays of the now setting sun.

"'Ello sweetheart," I said as I stopped to greet her. The lamb bleated at its mother, who appeared to move her mouth towards her lamb's ear, as if to say, 'Just ignore 'er, dear, she's not from oop 'ere,' - and then they bolted.

The transition from Essex was not a complete move to unknown territory. We had been on holiday to Yorkshire many times in the past, staying in self-catering accommodation with the then dog. Mostly, we had been to the Dales, so were not as familiar with where we were now - in Northallerton, nearer to the moors.

When I told my friends we were in an area of the town known as Romanby, they assumed we were in some quaint little village. Not the case. It would have been nice to have moved to a cosy hamlet but common sense had to prevail. We were townspeople. We needed the facilities we'd had before. We needed access to a major road to get back down by car to Essex. We needed a rail-link. We needed all the general conveniences we were used to.

Northallerton seemed to fit the bill. And it does, although it is changing as progress has to prevail and it is now much busier, noisier and ever-expanding. Much the same as Chelmsford, where we came from, It, too, is now not as it was and when I return on visits to friends and family it is beginning to feel alien to me and confined, its green fields filled with housing projects, and many different people from different backgrounds. But up in Northallerton I am an incomer myself, so how can I comment on such things?

I am now very comfortable where I am. I have many friends, I understand a bait box is not just for fishing. I now refer to the 'back-end of ter munth' and 'back-end of ter week'. I am integrated. I am an older Essex girl in Yorkshire.

As I walked back from my stroll across the fields on that sunset evening, I found a little lamb's tail which had dropped off, still with its rubber band around it, and I hung it on a tree... a Yorkshire 'tail'.

Branch Closure
Andrea Mosey
Copyright © 2018 Andrea Mosey
A work of fiction

Sarah opened the bedroom door a fraction and peeped in at her sleeping children. Rosie was curled in the foetal position; still clutching 'Blankey', with her mouth wide open and her blonde curls spread about her pillow. Her sleeping angelic appearance belied the Tasmanian Devil she usually became during waking hours. Sarah smiled at the image of her four-year-old daughter and felt a surge of sadness at what the day had in store. On the other side of the room, Charlie had kicked off his duvet and lay spread-eagled in his bed, across from his sister. His hair sticking up in all directions suggested he had not had the most restful of sleeps. For a seven-year-old he was remarkably perceptive and Sarah knew he was anxious about today.

As Charlie began to rouse, Sarah pulled the door to and went downstairs.

"Morning love," said Henry, as she walked into the kitchen. "Did you get much sleep last night?"

Sarah shrugged, "Not much," she replied. "Although it might have been to do with your snoring rather than anything else."

Henry recognised his wife's joking as an attempt to deflect the enormity of the situation. He pulled her into a hug.

"Don't worry, love," he said, as she rested her head on his shoulder. "Me and the kids will be fine. Let's just take it one step at a time and not think too far ahead."

Charlie barged in. "Eeuggh, gross you two. What's for breakfast?"

Sarah laughed and stepped out of Henry's embrace to put the kettle on. "How about pancakes? It's going to be our last breakfast together for a little while so let's have something special."

"Do you really have to go away today, Mum?" asked Charlie. "It's my school play next week and you'll miss it. Can't you go away next week instead?"

"Come on now, Charlie" Henry chastised him gently. "We've already had this conversation. You know your mum has to go today. Her new job starts next week and it's a long flight to America. We can video your play so she can still see it."

Sarah ruffled Charlie's still tousled hair.

"I'll look forward to seeing it," she said. "I bet you will be the best Gruffalo ever." Seeing the dismay in his face, she added kindly, "It won't be for long, Charlie, I'll be back before you know it."

"But why can't you just get another job in a bank in England? Why do you have to go all the way to America?" Charlie whined.

"It's not as simple as that, Charlie," Sarah sighed. "You know the bank closed the branch where I worked?" Charlie nodded. "Well, they've closed lots of other branches around here as well, so all the bank workers are looking for new jobs and there are not enough for everyone."

Charlie tilted his head, confused, 'But you were the boss, Mum, I bet you would get one of those other jobs."

Too clever by half, Sarah thought to herself.

"And that's why they want me to go to America, Charlie," she said. "Because I was the boss, they need me to do a really important job there as well."

Luckily, Charlie didn't get a chance to answer, as just then Rosie made her entrance.

"I want pancakes, too," said Rosie, sniffing the air as she came into the kitchen trailing 'Blankey' behind her. "With syrup please."

"Coming right up," said Henry from the cooker. "Everyone sit down at the table, they won't be long now."

With the breakfast things cleared away and the kids sent upstairs to get dressed, Sarah looked at her husband.

"Are we wrong to lie to them like this, Henry?" she said. "What if they find out?"

Henry finished wiping the work surface before responding quietly.

"I don't see what else we can do, Sarah. Hopefully you won't be away for long." He put down the cloth and joined her at the table. "Besides, they are only four and seven years old; their world is very small. I don't see any way they would find out." He took her hand. "And as I said, let's just take this one step at a time. Are you sure you don't want me to come with you today?"

"Positive," said Sarah firmly, as she sat up a bit straighter in her chair. "I'd rather say goodbye to you and the kids here than in the ..." She paused as Rosie came into the room, dressed in a pink dress, lime green gloves and a pirate hat. "... than in the airport," she concluded.

"Mum, Mum, your taxi's here," Charlie shouted as he ran down the stairs.

Sarah sighed and picked up her bag. "Right then," she said, as cheerfully as she could. "Time to go. Everyone give me kisses, please. Now then, no tears, I'll call you later to say goodnight." She prised Rosie off her leg. "Come on now, I don't want to be late and miss my flight."

After five minutes of goodbyes, tears, I-love-you's and hugs, Sarah stepped out of the house and waved at the taxi driver by way of an apology for keeping him waiting.

She had a little bubble of something stirring in the pit of her stomach. What was it? Excitement? Nervousness? Sadness? She couldn't quite put her finger on it but it felt very, very familiar and she greeted it, like welcoming an old friend with open arms. It was this feeling that had got her into the dire situation she now found herself in. The slow beat of butterfly wings, slowly at first but then quickening into the beat of hummingbird's wings, that moved up from the pit of her stomach into her chest and landed in her throat. So intense, it was as if the feeling had its own heartbeat.

It had begun slowly.

When she first realised she had accidently brought home customer account information, mistakenly put into her briefcase, she had been horrified. But nothing came of it, no one was the wiser and, as months went by, she began transferring small amounts of customer money from inactive accounts into her own savings account. That was when the feeling had started and soon became addictive. As months turned into years, she found she needed to transfer larger and larger amounts, just to get the feeling back. It was spiralling out of control.

Then came the news. The branch was closing and Sarah knew instantly, it was the end. She would be found out. However, to her surprise, she found the feeling returning, stronger and stronger with each turn of events; the meeting with her department head; the subsequent disciplinary inquiry; the police interviews; the bail hearing. It was like a drug she couldn't get enough of. And now the feeling was back again.

Sarah smiled as she got into the taxi.

"Where to, Pet?" the taxi driver asked.

"Teesside Crown Court, please," Sarah answered and waved at Henry and the kids as the taxi pulled away.

Celestial Secrets
Diane Leake
Copyright © 2018 Diane Leake
A work of fiction

'I dunno...'

'What?'

'I dunno...' Maisie wriggled, trying for a more comfortable position.

'For God's sake, Maisie, what don't you know?'

'No need to get stroppy. I'm only saying...'

Riddled with impatience, Karen shot her friend a searing look. 'Maisie, you're saying sweet nothing. Now just spit it out then maybe I can get some peace here.'

'Well, there's no need for that. I'm only saying...' Maisie pouted and turned away from Karen's sharp tongue.

Karen acquiesced. 'Look, Maisie, I'm not having a go. I simply want to enjoy this; quietly, without words.'

'Okay, Kaz.'

Karen proffered a smile of conciliation then prepared once again for peace. She loved nights like this. Nights when the earth seemed to be holding its breath, awaiting a performance from the Lord of the Skies. Thankfully, on this cool autumn night there were no streetlamps to impede his theatrical show. Karen sighed with contentment. But just as she reached a semi-meditative state a monotonous sound broke into her head.

'Maisie, why are you humming *Sailing?*' she enquired through gritted teeth.

Maisie chuckled. 'Could you hear me? Oops, sorry, it must've just slipped out.'

Maddened by Maisie's nonchalance, Karen sat up and glared at her. 'Look, if you don't want to be here, go. Go on. You can take the car and I'll walk back to the village.'

The smile wiped from her face, Maisie rolled on her side and rested her head on her hand. 'You're not serious. What the hell's the matter with you tonight?'

'Nothing's the matter with me tonight. I just want some peace and quiet. I want some time to think. And stupid as I am I thought you might enjoy it too, being as your house is like a bloody beer garden, what with the kids and Mac.'

Maisie struggled to her feet. The glint in her eyes mirrored the stars as she pointed at her best friend. 'Listen here, Karen Morgan, I don't know what's going on with you, but leave Mac and the kids out of it. He's one of the good ones and my kids are happy kids. Noisy, yes, but happy. And as for me needing peace and quiet, I agree I do sometimes, but not tonight. Tonight, I thought I was being taken to - what did you call it? - the best gig you've ever been to? So yes, I'm the stupid one. 'Cause the next thing I know I'm flat on my back in the middle of nowhere looking at the sodding sky, instead of jumping around to a band. And to finish it all, it's fucking freezing up here. Honestly, I...'

Very quietly, Karen interrupted Maisie's rant. 'I'm pregnant.'

Incredulity masked Maisie's features. Her mouth moved soundlessly for a couple of seconds before her vocal chords caught up. 'No. But you can't be, you've got them poly-whatnots.'

Karen lay back slowly and closed her eyes. 'Yes, well I am.'

'But who? How?'

'Maisie, you've got three kids, I think you know how.'

Maisie sunk to her knees and sat back on her heels. 'Okay, clever bugger. Who then?'

'Orion.'

'Ryan? Ryan who?' A look of puzzlement covered her face. 'We don't know any Ryan.'

'I'm being flippant.'

'Well, flippin' give over and tell me who. Don't tell me he's a married. I've told you before, that way's emotional suicide.'

Karen turned her head and locked her eyes on Maisie's. 'It doesn't matter who he is. Just an inconsequential one-night-stand. So, he won't know and won't be involved.'

'Bloody hell, hardly inconsequential.' Maisie leaned forward and laid her hand on Karen's cheek. 'You're a dark one, Kaz. But you won't be alone. Me, Mac and the kids will help.'

They lay side by side, arms entwined and chatted about practicalities, while Orion and the zodiac moved slowly across the heavens.

'Bloody hell, I'm frozen,' said Maisie.

'Come on then, let's go. You know, you've no soul, Maisie Thompson,' Karen laughed. 'Just look at that sky.'

Chuckling they linked arms and set off on the descent to the car.

'You wanna know why I was humming *Sailing?*

'Go on then.'

''Cause sometimes I wonder whether the world's the right way up.' Humour bubbled through her words. 'Stop laughing at me. Have you never looked at the sky and seen the sand and the sea? See, I do have a soul after all.'

Yes, Karen thought, you do have a soul. A beautiful soul. Which is why I can't crush it by telling you that Mac isn't one of the good ones.

Marks of the Beast
Jackie Fallows
Copyright © 2018 Jackie Fallows
A work of fiction

It rises from the heath on a starless night, taking with it all the grittiness and acidity of the soil which has nourished it. Spindle-shanked birch and pine snatch their twigs from the raw burr of its breath as it lumbers down to the vale. Fields feel it first. Their grasses flatten and bend, twist and break under its stride. Between the fields, hedgerows mark its direction by pointing jagged limbs to the north, to the north, and again to the north. The blackbird's nest, thrust from shelter, casts a blank eye to the broad, cold sky.

And the woman stirs in her sleep.

Lights burn against the clouds, and the beast looks over to the sleepless city. Tarmac steams, releasing both damp and the tang of pitch as the beast leaves the fields behind, and tramps towards the glare mixed with clamour, the filth mingled with honeydew, which it knows can only signal a vast thicket of humanity. The beast samples the taste through its feet, its fingers, through every pore of its being, and finds it wanting. She is not here.

To the north, to the north, and again to the north, it crosses stinking tracks of iron and bitumen to leave the city at its back. Ahead lies a broad sweep of water, which thickens to the south-west and the ocean, but which loops and lessens to the north-east and the land. The beast stops. Surely there is something of the woman on this wind from the wild land that broods to the west? It trawls its senses through water, earth and air, finds the scent to be old, old, long gone. The beast bores through the sandy mud of the riverbed, uprising the silt in a murky wave which surges towards the source far above in the hills.

And the woman whimpers.

The beast strides on, licking at the night, sucking its cheeks at a sudden prickle of anthracite which bites through the moist flakiness of the forest. Ancient oaks shudder as the beast's breath leaves round, black deposits across their bark, the gobbets darker to the north, to the north, always to the north.

Mostly, the beast's path takes it to east or west of sizeable habitations, and seldom over the broad red-and-white snakes of light which link them. It blinks at one town, at the outskirts of another, and at the four snakes that guard them like rivers before, beyond and between; then grunts with satisfaction as the night grows back, and the air bubbles with the calls of curlew and owl, and the faint mewl from a cat. From the far side of the valley to the east, woodsmoke hints at the breath of wise women. The beast sniffs at it, eager for such a taste, but the seasoning is old, too old, long gone.

And the woman rises and plunges, lost to the ocean of her dreams.

A stone falls from the Roman wall as the beast stumbles over it, the low elevation here lost in the mist of pre-dawn. The sodden grass flattens and lengthens, gathers a little grittiness here and there, as grains of sand from the distant heath are drawn from between the beast's toes. The chill upland air ripples with each shortened breath as the beast climbs, and the tough tussocks of border moorland shake silently to the thud of its feet. The rough way undulates into the northern land: land leaden with water, land which absorbs every footfall from the beast in a lingering, liquid embrace, before releasing it with a soft belch of satisfaction.

A band of thicker darkness rears up before the beast, and it knows that its trail no longer leads to the north. It clambers to the top of the Law. The soles of its feet smoulder as the riven stone rages for an instant with remembered lava, and the ancient power of Mother and Maiden burn upwards through its body, inscribing its face forever. It turns to the west, where the lights of another city soar like sunrise. The wind curls into the beast's nostrils, bearing the scent it has been seeking throughout the ever-lengthening night. With a croak of recognition, it pours itself into the heart of the city.

And the woman welcomes the beast, taking it deep into her belly. The warm darkness there swells with it, and the rich blood nourishes it through the long loop of the northern winter night, through the soft, unrolling light of spring. At the lush green of midsummer, the woman brings it again to the world, and the world listens anew to its voice. A new tale unfolds.

Tornado
Robert Stapleton
Copyright © 2018 Robert Stapleton
A work of fiction

In a class of gangly girls and boisterous boys, Paul was definitely the smallest.

He tried his best at everything.

Writing and numbers were okay, because it didn't matter how big you were when dealing with those.

But when it came to physical activity, Paul was always last.

Last in line when teams were chosen for football.

Last when taking part in games.

Paul was always the last.

His favourite sport was watching the animals in the school's nature corner.

The form teacher, Mrs McFyne, wanted to encourage Paul's interest in living creatures. At least he had something to take an interest in. So, she allowed him to spend as much time as he liked observing the wildlife.

Paul would laugh as he watched the playful antics of the gerbils in their cage. He would stand open-mouthed as he watched the goldfish swimming around their tank. He avidly studied the lives of the worms as they burrowed around their wormery. But above all else, Paul was happy to waste hours watching the glass tank which was the home of the snails. A glass tank which one of the wittier members of staff had named the snailarium.

Paul wondered what it would be like to be a snail. He watched them feed. He watched them slide around the floor, the walls and the ceiling of their glass home.

'Are you still looking at those snails, Paul?' said Mrs McFyne.

'Of course. They're such fun to watch,' said Paul, with his face pressed up against the side of the tank.

'Stupid snails,' said the girls.

'Stupid Paul,' said the boys. 'Who's a loser, then?'

But nothing would put Paul off watching the snails.

And he had his favourite. A snail with a shell that put all the others to shame. A shell with stripes of different colours. A shell that Paul could easily pick out from all the others.

Every morning, Paul would visit the snail tank and say hello to his shelly friend. Over the weeks, a kind of understanding grew between the boy and the snail. Each seemed to enjoy the company of the other.

The time came for the school to hold its annual Sports Day.

Everybody knew who would win the running races.

The usual boy won the hundred metres race. Although he tried hard, Paul's short legs let him down, and he came in last.

Another boy came first in the long-distance run. Paul did very well and kept up the pace. But still finished last of all. One of the girls won the skipping race. Another the hopping race. Paul didn't even bother entering any of those.

Paul did slightly better in the sack race. Mainly because the chief contenders tended to fall flat on their faces. He still didn't win, but at least he wasn't last this time. Nobody would join him for the three-legged race.

The afternoon was almost over when Paul's teacher announced a special race. A snail race.

She set up a flat board on a tabletop, then invited the children to choose a snail from the snailarium and place it on the starting line.

As the race involved handling slimy snails, the girls didn't care to take part. As the race didn't involve speed, or strength, most of the boys couldn't be bothered either.

But four of the boys decided to take up the challenge. Including Paul. They each selected a snail and lifted their chosen slimy Olympian out of the snailarium.

Paul made sure he selected his favourite snail and placed it on the starting line.

'We need to give them all names,' said Mrs McFyne. 'I want each of you boys to choose what to call your snail.'

One said he would call his snail Fred. Another said he would call his Ronaldo. A third said he wanted to call his snail Rover.

'And what about you, Paul. What name do you want to give

your snail?'

Paul thought for a moment. Then he decided, 'I think I'll call mine, Tornado.'

So, Fred, Ronaldo, Rover and Tornado lined up on the starting blocks and Mrs McFyne announced the start of the race.

They were off.

Or, at least, the clock began ticking.

For a while the children watched, mildly amused, but soon grew bored and wandered off to the refreshment tent.

Eventually, action on the racetrack began. The boys stood at the finishing line and shouted encouragement to their chosen snails. Holding out grass or lettuce leaves as an incentive.

Fred set off at a fair old lick. In entirely the wrong direction. Ronaldo withdrew into his shell. Presumably for a nap.

That left just the two. Rover and Tornado.

They both set off, in the right direction and at a decent speed. Both slithered along, making ground as rapidly as a snail can reasonably be expected to. Rover took the lead, at one point drawing to almost half a shell's length ahead.

But Paul quietly encouraged Tornado along. The rapport which had gradually built up between him and the snail began to pay off. Whilst his opponent began to slow down, Tornado powered ahead.

Tornado drew level. And for several minutes, it looked like touch and go. But as the finishing line loomed up ahead of them, it was Tornado who took the lead. And crossed the line at breakneck speed. At least for a small snail.

Tornado had won. As the winning snail, he was given a lettuce leaf as a prize and was then returned to the snailarium.

Paul had won and received a big red rosette. Now, for once, he was as proud as Punch.

Which just goes to show, it's not always brawn and long legs that win the day.

The Cough
Jackie Walton
Copyright © 2017 Jackie Walton
An essay

You feel immensely proud of yourself for how you have managed to avoid human contact. You've sidestepped, anti-bacterialised (home-made) your hands, ducked and generally steered clear of your fellow men and women. You've even handed over your purse or wallet to all cashiers for them to extract your money and deposit loose change directly into the said purse or wallet, so you don't have to handle any germ-infested coins. You've kept clear of children. You've pulled down your sleeve to operate door handles. You've anti-bacterialised (home-made) your car steering wheel, gear knob, door handles, mirror. You've been eating highly immune-boosting, socially unacceptable foods - raw crushed garlic and suchlike.

Then you've done the complete opposite and not anti-bacterialised anything. Someone has persuaded you, germs are good. You become isolated, hermit-like. Then, suffering an irresistible craving for human contact, *any* human contact, you go to salsa class and pretty much touch hands with every single person there - and they are not all as clean as they might be.

Two days later, everyone you know is telling you - in person, on social media, by phone, text or email – about how they've been floored with some virus or other. Some declare their illness and then proudly announce they've done a heroic 60km bike ride for a bit of fresh air. Some tell you they've dosed themselves up with every conceivable item from their medicine cabinet, including out-of-date Covonia or various concoctions of long-forgotten origin. Some tell you they're on their second week in bed and can only just swallow soup and a dribble of water and feel very weak. Some embellish the symptoms and discuss them in immense detail.

Then, despite all your best efforts, you start with the tickly throat, which turns into the monster throat from hell. Like the smashed-up glass splinters found on a pub's sticky floor after a Bank Holiday lock-in. Like the roughest, nastiest sandpaper. Like someone has taken one of those foot defoliator things designed to remove callouses and corns and run down the whole length of your throat. Like all the uneven jigsaw pieces that you can't find the gap for all lined up vertically in your windpipe. Like the crunchiest gravel for posh drives, sprinkled generously down your throat. Each swallow feels like a volcano erupting inside your head. Before you dare to swallow you have to take a deep breath to help you brave the pain. Each swallow is like melted scratchy liquid being force-fed down your throat. Then after two long days of throatiness, the cough starts.

Your energy is already at the level of a millipede which has had all its feet amputated. Just to think one simple thought takes a whole hour. You lie down in the evening in the comfort of your bed. You allow your body to sink deeply into the mattress and your head to rest in the comfort of your pillow. At least, you tell yourself, you can look forward to a restful sleep.

But no. From somewhere deep inside, the tickle erupts. Like an orchestra's string section made up of out-of-tune, scratchy violins and cellos, it comes up. You attempt a gentle cough, trying not to disturb anything either inside or outside of yourself. Trying to smother it is the worst plan of action. It's like an angry little man - we're talking severe anger issues here - is throwing out his old hobnail boots. He's throwing them up out of your windpipe with great force.

You allow the cough to erupt but it doesn't stop. Cough after cough, yes, you could really accompany a band as part of the percussion, with this performance. The cough is like a ball of nails with African drums attached all around. It comes up and up but it has to pass through the throat. How the hell is this possible? Your throat's opening is now so reduced as to render it virtually impassable and it is agonisingly raw. The mere thought of a cough reaching your throat makes you cry.

But now it's here. It's passing through the tiny passage which is all that remains of your throat. The first cough is up and out and you're left feeling completely exhausted. By cough number 124 you're curled up in a foetal position clutching anything linked to your ribs. Your ribs hurt. Every centimetre of every rib hurts. They feel bruised, they feel tender, they feel if you touch them, big pieces will just drop off.

By morning you feel old, hollow, like a plundered shipwreck, stripped of anything valuable. You feel bare. During the night you've tried every conceivable position - with one pillow, with two pillows, with three pillows - until they were all thrown on the floor in one big paddy. You've had raw onion taped to your feet (you read about it somewhere). You're surrounded by lavender oil to help sleep, hahahahaha. You have eucalyptus oil in a burner, infusing gently. You screamed at it during the night, yelling, 'A fat lot of bloody good you are, sitting over there puffing out your useless aromas.'

Then you try to sit up. It takes half an hour. You congratulate yourself, this is a monumental feat, equal to running in a race up Roseberry Topping.

Finally, you reach the shower. The hot water feels too hot. You adjust the temperature. Now it feels too cold. You hug your ribs so they don't bend too much. Any attempt at arm movements hurts. Then you try to rationalise things and remind yourself, it's only a little cough and things could be a lot worse. But those words are not comforting when you have only had about one-and-a-half seconds of sleep and are grumpier than the grumpiest mule.

Breakfast consists of anything soft, anything slimy. Stewed rhubarb and banana is all you can manage. You've become addicted to hot ginger tea and honey, lots and lots of sliced root ginger, steaming hot water and comforting honey. You take your little flask everywhere with you.

You try the raw garlic, peel a clove, crush it up, leave it to release it's potent magical powers and then eat it. You try your hardest not to vomit and on the tenth attempt you swallow it. It gets stuck in your narrow throat and becomes caught on the scratchy surface. This is when someone speaks to you. 'How are you today?' 'Are you okay?' 'Sleep well?' All you can manage is to open your mouth, with crushed garlic still caught in your throat, and emit a sound like no other. It's meant to be, 'Don't come too close, I don't feel too good,' but sounds more like, 'mbblleurgghhhhhhhhhhh.'

Then your dear, wise friend asks, 'Have you journaled? You

know, tried asking what your cough is trying to tell you and writing it down? You'd be amazed at the answers it will reveal to you.' You resist telling your dear, wise friend where to go and begin writing. All you can come up with is, 'It hurts.' Your dear, wise friend also suggests not to talk about said cough, for fear it will become even worse..

But what material could one come up with for one's writing group, if one could neither talk nor write about such personal experiences? Writing rule no.1: Write about what you know.

So, I have, as you can see.

In conclusion, thank you dear cough for coming to visit me - and many others. Thank you for allowing my body to show how well its natural healing abilities are working. And thank you for helping to dispel the gremlins which appeared to sneak inside my head. I have very much enjoyed your visit and the creativity you have inspired me to express.

Now, if you wouldn't mind just sodding off, that would be most welcome.

Looking out over the market-place, it was a dull day, just like the day before. It was mid-day and the town was in full swing. Even though it was December and there was snow on the ground, people still walked around, women in high heels and men in work shoes, slipping and sliding on the ice.

In the far corner was an old man, dressed in brown overcoat and trousers. From where I was, I could see the jacket was full of holes. He had trainers on, the toes cut out, clearly something he'd found somewhere and made use of. As he trudged through the snow, he was visibly shaking. He had his fingerless-gloved hands stuffed in his pockets, desperately trying to keep warm. He had dark brown messy hair, which he'd tried unsuccessfully to keep under his well-worn black woolly hat. He carried a black bag, no doubt containing his worldly possessions. His eyes were small, black and blank. He'd spent many sleepless nights in a doorway or on a park bench. I'd seen him a few times, however he was looking much the worse for wear now, worse than I'd ever seen him before. He clearly hadn't eaten for a while, maybe not even for a few days.

As he walked through the snow, head down, people gave him a wide berth. Even in the snow he stank. As they walked by, they just looked away, not even glancing at him. They treated him like he wasn't there, like he was invisible. As he approached a bench in front of a restaurant, he pulled a carrier from his black bag and set it down on the seat. When he sat down, I could see the cold seeping into his body, felt it in my own heart. Poor sod.

He stayed there for a couple of hours. I'm sure his body must have been numb by then, however no one stopped to see if he was all right, no one from the restaurant came to give him scraps or leftovers. One thing I'd realised, people were selfish and ignorant; they ignored the weak, wrapped up in their own little lives.

Soon enough a policeman came over. He took a step back when he caught the old man's stench. I watched him talking to the man, telling him to move on. The poor old chap held his arms up, palms turned to face the sky, as if to ask, "Where am I to go?" The policeman shook his head, looked both ways, then pulled the old chap to his feet. Picking up the bags, he handed them to the old man, who stooped a little when the policeman let go. With another shake of his head, the policeman put his hand in his pocket and pulled out some coins. He placed them in the man's gloved hand and pointed to a bakery off to the left of the market square. Maybe there was hope for humanity, after all.

Once the lunchtime trade was over, the market square quieted off. People had gone back to work. A few children were running around in their wellingtons, playing in the snow. As they played, their parents window-shopped, their reflections coming back in bright colours of red, green and blue, as every window was decorated for Christmas. Each shop resembled a Santa's grotto, presents stacked up in piles. I wondered about the homeless old man. What would he do for Christmas? Would he spend it on a bench somewhere? Would he go to a church? Would he even be allowed into a church? I wasn't sure. I wondered if he'd still be alive. He hadn't exactly been a picture of health when I'd seen him earlier.

The town clock chimed six. The working day was over. There were only a few more days to Christmas. The majority of people leaving the town centre carried bags upon bags of presents, rolls of multicoloured wrapping paper stuffed under their arms, rushing around, desperately trying to stay upright on the ice long enough to catch their buses home. Within an hour the square was empty. The sky was dark. The streetlights lit up a light flurry of snow which had begun to fall, adding a new layer to the packed snow and ice already on the ground. Christmas music could be heard coming from the few restaurants which were still open, light from their windows burning into the darkness outside. The falling snowflakes were dancing, playing with each other, all falling slightly differently but somehow in sync, a magical masterpiece of nature.

When the clock was chiming eleven I heard giggling coming from the far end of the market square. Glancing over, I saw a group of people wandering through the snow, the women once again unsteady, skidding in their high heels. I was sure it wasn't just the snow which was responsible for their instability. The group soon disappeared into the pub on the corner. When they opened the door a rectangle of light fell on the snow-covered pavement, the heat seeping visibly out of the doorway.

When I looked again, it was a little after two in the morning. A man was lying on one of the ice-covered benches. It was the old homeless man. He was huddled up, his legs bent in half, unable to stretch out fully on the bench. Again, he was shivering. This time he had a tattered blanket wrapped around him but I doubted it was doing much against the ice-cold winter's night. I watched him doze between the clock's hourly chiming.

At seven the next morning he sat up, his face looking even more tired and drawn than the previous day. Slowly, he stood up. Carefully, he folded his tattered old wet blanket, treating it as if it was a winter duvet. I suppose to him it was. For him, in this kind of weather, it probably represented the difference between life and death. Once he had folded it into the right shape and size he placed it inside his ragged black bag and tied the neck in a knot. As he stood there, he glanced around the market square, watching delivery vans pulling up outside the restaurants, getting them ready for the day ahead. Licking his lips slightly, he staggered slowly to the right of the square and disappeared from view.

By ten-thirty the market place was busy again. It was the last Saturday before Christmas, so everyone was out buying in bulk, checking their lists, making sure they'd got presents for everyone. On the left-hand side of the market square stood a toy shop. Its window display featured the living room in a large doll's house: a wood burning fire, a nice brown leather armchair, a rug on the floor, a Christmas tree to the right, presents stacked underneath it.

Standing in front of the window was the same old man. He was staring at the scene depicted in front of him. I could see the yearning in his eyes. It looked like he hadn't been near a real fireplace for a long time. I wondered how long. Months? Years? Maybe I'd ask him one day. Within minutes, a shop assistant came out and shooed the man away. Clearly, he didn't match their idea of a perfect Christmas.

My gaze switched to the middle of the square. Four children were making snow angels on the ground. Their parents were sitting at a table sipping hot drinks, the steam rising from their cups. You could see them beginning to thaw out as the hot liquid slipped down their throats, hitting their stomachs, bringing smiles of satisfaction.

The old man was walking across the square. He stopped to watch the children playing and smiled. At that moment I saw something in his eyes I hadn't seen before. He smiled contentedly, as if the image had brought back a memory of a happier time. Maybe he had a family somewhere.

Then the parents noticed the scruffy old man watching their children. The husband marched over and shouted at him. I couldn't hear what he was saying but there was a great deal of arm waving. The elderly man shrank back, almost falling to the ground in shock. He turned on his heel and staggered away, quickly leaving the market square. I shook my head. This was not good.

Monday arrived. Christmas Eve, bringing a mass of people milling around. Christmas Eve last-minute panic buying is the reason you got that hideous green and red striped jumper. Or the weird African ornament. You know, the one your mother-in-law bought you, saying it promoted good luck? More likely, she was the lucky one to find something left to buy so close to Christmas. I like those kinds of day. You get to see what people are really like. The majority in the 'Christmas spirit', a small percentage walking around with deep frowns, their brows furrowed, muttering under their breath when people got in their way. I had to smile.

At lunch-time, the restaurants were all full, people spilling out on to the streets, desperately trying to get a table to grab something to eat. Once again, the old chap appeared at the edge of the square, looking around at all the people. He managed to get to a bench. Not bothering to get his bag out, he almost fell on to the seat. It seemed like he didn't have the energy to sit up; he was practically horizontal, his arms wrapped around himself, desperately trying to keep warm.

He lay there for a while, until a young girl - she must have been about five of six - approached him slowly. She tapped him lightly on the shoulder. He opened his eyes and peered at her. She smiled, her eyes big and bright. She held out her hand to his, trying to shake it, wanting to introduce herself. Bless her. He managed to sit up, his eyes matched hers, his smile was ear to ear. She climbed on to the bench next to him. She was talking to him, he listened intently, and they sat like that for a while, her talking, him listening. I couldn't help wondering, when was the last time someone had talked to him so naturally?

Soon enough, someone was shouting across the square. The little girl turned to see where it was coming from. She turned back to the old man. Smiling, she reached up and hugged him, then placed some small item in his hand and took off running to catch up with her mother.

I returned my attention to the old man. He was still sitting up, clutching his present. He opened his hand, revealing a small chocolate Christmas tree. He smiled, licking his lips. I imagined he was starving but he didn't eat it, he simply put it in his inside jacket pocket.

When the shops and restaurants finally shed their last customers, getting ready to close for the Christmas holidays, the old man was still sitting on the bench. He had been there all afternoon. No one had come to move him on. He just sat there, watching the world go by.

When the clock began striking midnight, he looked around. He was completely alone, no one else in sight. He reached into his jacket pocket, retrieved the chocolate tree and opened it slowly. As he bit into the milk chocolate a smile lit up his face and a tear fell down his cheek. He spent ten minutes eating the chocolate, something which a child would have achieved in a couple of bites. But not him. He savoured it.

Still nibbling at the chocolate, he got his blanket out. By the time the clock had finished chiming the hour he was all wrapped up. It was a cold night, well below freezing. The ground was hard and solid, white over with frost. Once again, snow began to fall, cloaking the ground in a fresh layer. I watched him rubbing his hands together, trying to keep warm. He lay there, still smiling, holding on to the last morsels of the chocolate Christmas tree.

In that moment, a silent tear fell down his face, sliding down his nose and falling on to the bench below. He closed his eyes, attempting to sleep. It was time.

You might be wondering who I am, and why I hadn't tried to help this poor old man. Why I had been so eager to comment on the selfishness of others but still do nothing myself.

Well, my name is Death - and I'll see you soon.

"Are we there yet? Are we there yet?"

Steve Newsam took a deep breath, his hands involuntarily gripping the wood-rimmed steering wheel a little more tightly than usual. Wisely, he chose to keep schtum and leave it to his new wife Marianne to reply to her ten-year-old. It had not escaped his notice how the lad had asked the question without lifting his eyes from his tablet.

"No, Martin," Marianne said calmly, displaying her usual unshakable level of patience in all matters regarding her beloved son. "You know we've only just set off. We still have many miles to go."

"How many miles? How many miles?"

"I don't know, sweetie-pie," she replied, and turned to her husband. "Darling, can you tell us how many miles it is?"

"I'm not sure about the miles, exactly," said Steve, forcing himself to speak quietly and somehow managing to form a smile around his gritted teeth. "But I reckon we're looking at roughly an hour and a half from home to Scarborough, possibly a bit longer, depending on traffic."

Under normal, everyday circumstances, Steve had no problem getting along with his new stepson. The lad was likable enough and was quite bright, in many ways. And he had to admit, young Martin seemed to have taken to his new stepdad without any problem whatsoever. Even Marianne had been pleasantly surprised, not to say relieved, at how well her boy had handled things.

Young Martin did have this one hugely annoying habit, though, of saying everything twice. Which mattered not one iota to Steve when the lad was at school. And was generally of little consequence when the boy was at home, as he spent most of his time either in his own room or playing outside with his mates.

However, quite early on in his relationship with the gorgeous Marianne, Steve had discovered how any car journey with Martin in the back seat could quickly become a living nightmare. And here he was, facing a minimum three-hour round trip, on what should have been a happy family day out. He was really looking forward to joining the classic car parade on Scarborough front and sincerely hoped Martin wouldn't spoil it with his endless questions.

Ah well, he thought, *we'll probably have time for a stop off at Runswick Bay on the way. And with any luck, he'll be glued to his tablet most of the time.*

"What time is it? What time is it?" piped up Martin, instantly smashing Steve's hopes to smithereens.

"It's just gone nine o'clock, my angel," Marianne told him.

Steve hoped she hadn't noticed the slight twitch of the steering wheel and kept his eyes firmly on the road ahead.

"What time will we get there? What time will we get there? Can I have an ice cream? Can I have an ice cream?"

"About ten-thirty, sweetheart," she said, beaming at him over her shoulder. "Certainly before eleven. And yes, of course you can have an ice cream, just as soon as we get there, I promise."

Steve hoped she hadn't heard the *Jesus Christ* he'd issued under his breath. *What's wrong with the boy?* he wondered to himself. *We've only just nicely got on to the A19. And I hope she realises, if she gets him an ice cream, he won't be eating it in here.* He turned the radio up and switched from BBC Radio York to CD, in time to hear old Waylon halfway through singing *She Was Just No Good for Me.*

"Who's that singing? Who's that singing?"

"It's the late, great Waylon Jennings," Steve told him. "Like it, do you?"

"Can we have Justin Bieber? Can we have Justin Bieber?"

"I don't think Steve will have any Justin Bieber, pumpkin," said Marianne, laughing.

"Too bloody right, I haven't," Steve blurted out without thinking, earning himself a sharp slap on the arm and a stern rebuke. After which things went quiet for a while. Martin buried his face in his Candy Crush game and Marianne appeared to be occupying herself with admiring the scenery, such as it was so far.

"It smells funny in here. It smells funny in here."

"That's because it's an old car, darling," said Marianne, as calmly as ever. "Old leather and wood. I think it's a lovely smell."

Martin didn't pursue the matter and his mother returned to gazing out of the window. Steve risked a sideways glance in her direction, concerned lest her silence was due to his unfortunate slip of the tongue. He should have known better than to swear in front of the boy. He need not have worried, though. She appeared content, a small smile playing around her lips. He guessed she was probably absorbed in her own little game, counting the number of Eddie Stobart lorries they passed. A weird hobby perhaps, but no dafter than train spotting, in his estimation.

Not for the first time, he thanked his lucky stars for bringing him such a wonderful woman. Not just stunningly beautiful, but kind, thoughtful, loving, forgiving, uncomplaining. Serene, he'd decided, was the one all-encompassing word which best described her. And most definitely she was a perfect mother. The little toerag in the back seat should also be thanking his lucky stars. Then again, what would a ten-year-old know about lucky stars, anyway? *Give him time*, he reasoned, *and he'll come to appreciate what he's got.*

He relaxed and began to sing along with Waylon, enjoying the deep background burble of the old straight-six three-litre engine. Maybe the journey wasn't going to be such an ordeal after all. He swore to himself, though, if Martin started up again with his double-barrelled questions, he'd threaten to gaffer tape the little git's mouth, and hang the consequences.

In the event, the journey went pleasantly enough. They stopped off at Runswick Bay, where Steve's 1965 Alvis TE21 drophead got lots of attention, its dark blue paintwork gleaming in the sunshine, and Martin got his promised ice cream – well away from the car and its pristine cream leather upholstery. Steve lowered the hood before setting off again and they drove down the east coast with the sun on their faces and the wind in their hair.

They were in plenty of time to join the parade, which proceeded slowly along Scarborough seafront, north to south, then swung around the roundabout for the return drive.

"Did you see that? Did you see...?" Martin managed to blurt out, just before the stalled Coastguard helicopter fell from the sky, silencing all three of them. Forever. Along with the unfortunate couple in the 1956 Armstrong Siddeley Sapphire, immediately behind them.

A classic double whammy. A classic double whammy.

Inspired by the Tour de Yorkshire
Cathy Lane
Copyright © 2018 Cathy Lane
A work of fiction

Reg rummaged in his cupboard, looking for suitable clothing for his cycle ride. It was a long, long time since he had sat on a bicycle saddle but he now had this sudden urge. He had been watching the local news programme promoting the now very popular cycle race across Yorkshire. It had given him the impetus to engage his legs with the pedals again - but where was his cycling gear?

In the back of the cupboard he found what he was looking for: his somewhat ancient cycling garments. His helmet, not one of those aerodynamic ones like they wear now but the old fashioned 'round' one. His non-lycra cycling shorts which resembled swimming trunks. And a pair of rather chewed-up looking plimsolls with no grips. Well never mind, they would do. He could wear his Theakston's 'Old Peculiar' tee-shirt and a pair of his wife, Brenda's thick tights. He didn't want to get chafed legs and, oh yes, those goggles he'd bought for welding, they would stop the flies getting in his eyes.

He felt quite well equipped. Of course, he didn't possess an up-to-date mobile phone, just one of those heavy old 'brick' ones. No Fit-Bit thing for gauging distance or mapping, no water-bottle attachment for when he was gasping from dehydration. Well so what? He didn't need all that paraphernalia, he'd always managed before.

Having adorned himself in his 'outfit' (not forgetting a generous smear of Vaseline around his nether regions due to various problems with the medical problem of anal fibroids. He didn't have a 'gel' saddle) he felt ready to go. He had his bottle of Lucozade with a straw, liberally laced with a tot of his favourite Famous Grouse, which he was going to attach to the front of his bike with a spare cycle grip and some adhesive tape. He had his mobile phone brick, his packed lunch and a map in his knapsack.

Now for the bike. It was in the shed. It was festooned with cobwebs. Its tyres were flat, its bell rusty and ... well, let's just say the poor bike was not in pristine condition. No matter, it could soon be resuscitated but it might take a while. Perhaps he should have thought about the bike first before getting attired. But Reg, not one for being daunted, sorted the bike out. He gave it a wash and brush up. He reinflated the tyres, which were not necessarily roadworthy but seemed able to inhale air with no apparent 'hissing' of expelled output. He used the foot-operated car tyre inflator which made his leg ache. The chain and gears were oiled with a generous squirt of WD40 and the brakes were tested, albeit not on a one-in-six downward gradient but on the slight down-slope of the front drive. The puncture outfit was fitted to the rear of the saddle (it only had one rubber puncture patch left, a piece of chalk, a spanner and a tube of now glued-up glue), and the hand pump, also a little worse for wear, was attached to the crossbar.

Reg was satisfied...all set to go.

It was all downhill from there. Brenda, who'd had no warning of his sudden flight on a bike, saw him sail past her as she was driving home, narrowly missing him when he took the corner at a rather acute angle.

Reg, unaware of his hindrance to traffic, veered round the roundabout out on to the open road. Bliss, he was on his bike. It was just like so many people had said to him at work, or down the pub when he had become a little obstreperous, "On yer bike" they'd said and so here he was - on his bike.

His route was not as he had intended and took him to unknown parts of Yorkshire he had not meant to venture into. The map got wet, his goggles misted up and his trainers kept slipping off the pedals. Still he stuck with it. He was constantly being hooted at by passing motorists. Reg assumed they were cheering him on. He flew down steep hills and struggled up the inclines and, as luck would have it, the old Raleigh kept going. It was Reg who finally ran out of gears.

He wobbled precariously on a rather steep bend and tumbled unceremoniously into a ditch, on a road to nowhere which wasn't on his map. A surprised cow dribbled slobber and mooed at him, as he lay there, helmet askew, the tangled frame of the bike on top of him.

The farmer found him when he came to inspect his herd. The farmer had rescued many a wounded cyclist on that bend but never one attired quite like this one. Reg was dazed and incoherent. The farmer used several expletives when phoning the emergency services but thankfully all was well. The bike was a twisted wreck but Reg, although badly bruised and mangled, was all right.

The policeman gave him a stern warning for riding an unroadworthy vehicle – or bike – on the public highway. Reggie's cycling days were well and truly over. Brenda took his tattered gear to the local tip and replaced her torn tights out of his beer money. Reg's adventure did make the local newspaper, though. "Eccentric Cyclist in Distress" read the headline.

Brenda put it in the 'recycling' bin.

Demons
Diane Leake
Copyright © 2018 Diane Leake

Hostage of confusion
No dreams to inspire
No hopes for tomorrow
No flames of desire.

Darkness gnaws at me
No safety, no peace
Lightness eludes me
No key to release.

Monsters surround me
My pain feeds their lust
Tearful entreaties
Unheeded, lie crushed.

I long to breathe freedom
Feel my soul soaring high
Relieved of the demons
Who shatter my sky.

Don't Open the Box
Robert Stapleton
Copyright © 2018 Robert Stapleton
A work of fiction

Come with me along this tree-lined road, with streetlamps pouring a cascade of light on to the silent street, deserted apart from the French police vehicles gathering there.

We come to a large building. Many of the windows show lights, which is unusual, it being so late at night.

Come with me as we make our way up the drive towards the main entrance.

No, we're not going in there. We turn aside and follow the path round to the rear of the building. Look! There in the darkness, reflecting the cold pitiless moon - a swimming pool. On the edge of the pool, somebody is standing, holding a smoking gun.

And in the pool, a body floats lifeless in the dark water.

That's me.

It had been a busy day. Not that it matters to me any longer. We had checked into the hotel that afternoon. A place on the French Riviera. Just the two of us, Zizzi and me. We were looking forward to a week together in the Mediterranean sunshine and Cannes seemed to be as good a place as any. At least, that's what we had come to believe.

The management offered us a room overlooking the town. Zizzi wanted one facing the sea. Her argument won the day and we were shown to another double room, not far from the first but with a vastly different outlook.

'I hope you realise, Monsieur, this room is much more expensive.'

'Don't worry about that,' I told him. 'We can afford it, for just the one week.'

We retired to our room, dropped our luggage on the floor and immediately went out to explore the surrounding area. The heat was oppressive, the atmosphere stifling and we soon found ourselves wandering back to the shade of the hotel, intending to relax in the lounge.

At the desk, we found a new receptionist. A young woman.

'Monsieur Black?'

'Yes?'

'Room 211?'

'That's right.'

'We have an envelope for you.'

She turned to the pigeonholes behind her, reached into the one labelled 211 and pulled out a brown envelope.

I took it and opened it.

Zizzi looked over my shoulder. 'What is it, Philip?'

'Just a card. It invites us to call in at Shalmanezer's Jewellery Store.'

'Where's that?'

'On the corner of the street,' came the receptionist's voice.

'Of course,' said Zizzi, 'I saw it on our way back. It's only a few yards away.'

I shrugged. 'Might as well find out what he wants.'

We made our way out into the baking hot sunshine and walked to the store at the end of the street. Clearly a jewellery store. We opened the door and entered. A jangling bell announced our arrival.

An elderly man in a black suit stood behind the counter, studying an order book.

'Monsieur Shalmanezer?'

He looked up. 'Oui, monsieur, je suis Shalmanezer.'

'You left us a note. At the hotel. Room 211.'

'Ah, yes.' The man struggled to speak acceptable English. His expression turned serious. 'I 'ave something for you.'

He reached under the counter and brought out a plain wooden box, about thirteen centimetres square, which he handed to me.

'What is it?' I asked.

He looked puzzled. 'Do you not know, Monsieur?'

'I haven't a clue.'

'Then, perhaps it will become clear when you open it.'

The jeweller returned to his work and Zizzi and I walked back to the hotel. Back in our room I opened the box. Inside, I found another box. Ornate, its surface adorned with gold and semi-precious stones.

'Let me see,' Zizzi demanded.

I handed it to her. She turned away and pulled off the ornate lid. I heard her utter a gasp.

'What's the matter?'

She closed the box again, turned and looked up at me. 'Philip, I think we are in a lot of trouble.'

'How do you mean?'

She handed me the box. 'Whatever you do, do not open this box. Just keep it safe. Our lives may depend upon it.'

'There's obviously been a huge mistake,' I said. 'That letter must have been intended for whoever was due to stay in this room but was moved out at the last moment.'

The sound of sirens alerted us to the presence of police vehicles crowding the street outside, concentrating on the Jewellery store.

'What's happening?' asked Zizzi.

'I don't know but I'm not hanging around to find out.'

I pushed the ornate box into the pocket of my jacket and we left the room, turning left rather than right along the corridor, which would have taken us back to the reception area. Somehow it felt the safest thing to do. A door farther down opened as we passed. Hands pulled us inside and slammed the door shut. A woman in her thirties stood facing us.

'Who are you?' I asked.

'I'm Marianne. You must be the people staying in room 211.'

'That's right,' said Zizzi.

'Then you must have received that note.'

I pulled the card from my pocket and handed it to Marianne.

She examined it. 'And did you visit the jewellers?'

'Yes.'

'And you collected the box?'

'That's right.'

'Just in time, it seems. They have just killed the old man. Can't you hear the police sirens?'

'They? Who killed him?'

'No matter now. Do you have the box with you?'

I nodded.

'Then let's go.'

We followed Marianne out into the corridor. This time we could hear angry voices coming from the foyer downstairs.

Zizzi again whispered into my ear, 'Whatever you do, don't open the box.'

'Quickly,' came Marianne's voice as she led us to a service staircase and took us down to an alleyway behind the hotel.

From there, we pushed our way through the crowd of onlookers gathering in the main street and followed our guide to the railway station. We bought return tickets to a small village ten kilometres outside the city.

Marianne refused to tell us anything, and my mind became so preoccupied with thoughts of survival that I forgot about the box and its mysterious contents. On the train, I relaxed and must have dropped off to sleep, because it was growing dark when I work up again.

Back in the city, we wandered back to the hotel. This time we followed Marianne to the rear of the building. To the recreation area and the hotel swimming pool. All seemed quiet.

I glared at Marianne. 'Now perhaps you'll tell us what's going on.'

Before she could answer, a man stepped out from the shadows.

Marianne gasped, 'Wolfgang!'

'Is this the man who killed the jeweller?' I asked her.

Wolfgang turned his sneering face towards me. 'I am indeed the man, and I will kill you if you do not do exactly what I tell you.'

'What do you want?'

'Give me the box you received from the jeweller.'

I looked to Zizzi. She nodded. I reached into my pocket and brought out the ornate box.

'Toss it over to me,' said the man with the gun.

I tossed the box. He caught it, shook it and looked down at it with annoyance showing on his face. He fiddled to remove the lid.

'Don't open the box,' I told him. He did. And immediately looked up at me.

'It's empty,' he cried.

In that moment of distraction, Marianne pulled out a gun and fired twice into the centre of the man's chest. He dropped dead, and his gun slithered across the flagstones towards Zizzi.

'I told him not to open it,' I said.

Marianne glared at me. 'Where is it?'

'Where is what?'

'The diamond, of course.'

Nonplussed, I shook my head.

'I've got it,' said Zizzi, holding up a diamond of enormous size.

Now I realised why she had told me not to open the box. She had removed the contents the moment she opened it.

As Marianne and I gazed at the stone in amazement, Zizzi snatched up the gun from the ground and fired two shots into Marianne. She too fell dead.

I stared at Zizzi. 'With all that noise, the police will be here any minute.'

'Then we must get this over with,' said Zizzi.

'Now we'll never know who that gem belongs to.'

'It belongs to me,' she said. 'That diamond is worth a fortune. And now it's all mine. Goodbye, Philip. And I am truly sorry.'

She pointed the gun at me and squeezed the trigger.

Mrs Throttlestop walked into town on the blisteringly hot sunny day. On foot, it was a journey of approximately three quarters of a mile. In her right hand she carried a shopping bag. The sort that looked as though it had been well made and resultingly had been in service daily since the seventies. It was a solid brown rectangle with a wide curved handle, unattractive but functional.

Mrs Throttlestop herself looked the same whichever day of the week it may be. She had long hair tied in a low bun on the back of her head, her hair greying these days. She wore practical, dark colours. A thin blue long-sleeved jumper with a jacket over the top, made from heavy woollen fabric. A rather shapeless skirt and good sensible shoes on top of the 80 denier opaque tights, feet encased in sturdy walking shoes. The whole ensemble was completed with a bowl-shaped solid brown hat plumped firmly on top of her head.

She was made conspicuous by her inappropriately warm clothing, her unseasonal colours and her waddling gait. She had a stoicism about the way she held herself. Duty and tolerance of hardships. "When I was a child..." - "In my day..." – "We didn't have bananas until I was six you know..." and other such sentences, one could imagine her trotting out, judging by her appearance.

Appearances though, as we know, can be misleading.

Mrs Throttlestop was becoming more and more dishevelled during her walk as she became hotter and hotter, redder and redder.

'Holy fuck, what in the world!?' exclaimed Mrs Throttlestop in a state of shock.

As she rounded the corner towards the market square, a bloody great rhinoceros was galumphing down the road towards her. For a split second she didn't know whether to turn tail and flee or to stand her ground. If she were to flee, would the rhinoceros chase her and trample her to bits? And if she stood her ground in what was a remarkably narrow lane, would the blasted creature be affronted enough to stop in its tracks and turn around?

She decided to follow the family motto - Throttlestop by name, Throttlestop by nature - and she hoped the rhinoceros's Throttle would be well and truly Stopped.

She took up position in the middle of the narrow lane and stood with hands on hips, feet firmly planted wide to keep her rotund figure balanced. She looked a bit Trunchball-esque - for those of you familiar with the villain of Roald Dahl's 'Matilda'.

The rhino was approaching rapidly. On his travels, he had acquired various bits of fabric and some knitted paraphernalia that the town's crafty needle clackers had created. Such items were made regularly to decorate the market square, according to whatever the season may be or to reflect the theme of a local event. Mrs Throttlestop had a fleeting vision of a giant knitted and stuffed rhinoceros being the next item to grace the square and maybe also a full-size Mrs Throttlestop, in celebration of her victorious saving of the town. She had another fleeting vision of herself in a brand-new outfit to model for the said knitted sculpture. She giggled briefly at such a rash thought. Fancy buying a new outfit!

Her mind was rapidly drawn back to the matter at hand as rhino hooves were virtually upon her. She stood there, wildly swinging her solid shopper around her head, in a bid to scare the poor creature. In the distance she could see a variety of people chasing down the street after the beast. Not that it would be helpful, she found herself having time to think, as of course such events always happen in slow motion, don't they?

At that very moment a chipmunk appeared in the road, right in front of the rhino, causing it to rear up and sit back on its big grey bottom.

"Now look here," began the chipmunk, in a squeaky rather irksome voice. Mrs Throttlestop was struck dumb. A chipmunk was bizarre enough, but a talking chipmunk? Conversing with a rhinoceros? Had the world gone totally crazy? It appeared so, as no sooner had the chipmunk said "Now look here," three words meaning hee-haw in the grand scheme of things, the rhino had fallen into step with the bossy chipmunk and looked remarkably sheepish, for a large grey leathery lump without a trace of woolly hairdo whatsoever.

Despite its petite frame, the chipmunk had more clout than the rhinoceros. Mrs Throttlestop, far from creating order out of mayhem, found herself in line behind the rhino, like a rat following the pied piper.

She was chunnering away to herself, "Well fuck me, well I never did. In all my days I have never known a big ass rhino to come running down the market lane," and many more such mutterings, punctuated for good measure with a smattering of fucks, buggers and cock-wombles.

Somehow, it transpired that rhino and chipmunk were major players in a brand-new drama, to be filmed locally, and Mrs Throttlestop had inadvertently auditioned for the role of bus stop natter-box. A very significant part. She wondered idly if she was actually a female Dr Doolittle, understanding what the animals were saying to her, but that couldn't be right or why hadn't she simply conversed with the rhino, instead of putting on the handbag thrashing display?

Mrs Throttlestop came to with a start and promptly fainted again. In the brief moment she had surfaced she saw a sea of faces surrounding her, one looking remarkably chipmunk-esque and another very definitely with rhino-like features and a solid sturdy voice to match. There was also a very tall, wide, gnarly old oak tree which appeared to be holding Mrs Throttlestop up, but was it a tree or was it another character in the unfolding drama?

She drifted in and out of consciousness whilst the crowd endeavoured to assist her.

"Throw water over her," one cried.

"Cut her clothes off," suggested another.

Eventually a group decision was made to cut her clothes open and use the defibrillator to shock her back to life. They could have just got the well-behaved rhino to sit on her chest, I suppose. In her drifting state, Mrs Throttlestop could hear this conversation and was well aware she needed to do something to turn her predicament around.

The day was still scorching as Mrs Throttlestop became aware of the scissors edging remarkably near to her face.

"Fuck off!" she said in her best posh voice. "Come on, off you fuck! I am not dead yet, nor do I require these riff-raff to see my 50 EEs in all their glory. Haven't you learned anything, you imbeciles? You don't defibrillate unless the person has stopped breathing and I clearly haven't. Now," she demanded, "Where are the chipmunk and the rhinoceros?"

Wilberforce Montmorency Digby was rather a grand name for such a small dog: it didn't suit the Hawkesley-Browns' chihuahua at all. His initials, however - WMD (singular) - fitted like a second skin.

The air, which all too often emanated from his rear, constituted both a chemical and a biological attack. This attribute, it has to be said, proved useful on those evenings when the Hawkesley-Browns wished their guests would just leave. The incident of the kilt-clad Major Rumfuttocks performing his trapeze act on the dining room chandelier was a case in point, since Digby's intervention occurred before all of the priceless Sevres dinner service was reduced to porcelain rubble.

But it was as a ballistic missile that Digby excelled. The Hawkesley-Browns no longer hosted shooting parties, since Digby's participation tended to result in wholesale vaporisation of the carefully-reared game, leaving barely a feather for the guns to aim at. And no tradesman dared set foot on the property without wearing full riot gear. The consequent non-delivery of some of life's essentials caused its own problems, particularly in the whisky department.

The cause of what may be termed the highlight of Digby's explosive career was captured on the CCTV camera outside the Post Office. An engineer, detailed to repair a faulty lamp post, had just opened the inspection door when the itinerant Digby was caught short. Sparks flew. This time he even sounded like a ballistic missile.

Unfortunately, his target was the visiting NHS breast-screening caravan situated across the square and behind the bicycle-park next to the Council offices. As the shortest route to the medical facility was through the velocipedes, it was a bespoke Digby who bored his way through the flimsy door before homing in on the mammographer. The patient, necessarily rendered immobile with one half of her - until then - unblemished cleavage securely squidged between two x-ray plates, had no chance. Her lower extremities were somewhat scissored before Digby came to rest with his head wedged between the mammographer's knees. A number of lawsuits ensued.

Alas - or as many would say, thank God - Digby is no longer with us. As one might surmise, his death was not unremarkable. A nephew of the Hawkesley-Browns arrived to spend the summer, along with his Japanese Akita. It was only to be expected that the first meeting between the two dogs would be fraught, and minutes after the nephew's bags had been unloaded, Digby launched what was to be his final attack. Akitas have a reputation for not taking too kindly to others of the canine ilk, and this one stretched his jaws wide, so that the missile that was Digby disappeared straight down his throat - and stuck. Both choked to death.

Thus, the bubble of insanity, which had swelled around the Hawkesley-Browns since their misguided acquisition of Digby, finally burst and they returned to a more mundane existence. Now all they had to contend with was the small matter of impending bankruptcy.

Language of Thieves
Chapter One
Elizabeth Jackson
Copyright © 2018 Elizabeth Jackson
A work of fiction

The full-length novel is available from Amazon Kindle
in eBook and paperback formats

Westmorland, June 1949

A dense carpet of white swirling mist muffled the sound of the horse's hoofs as the solitary rider steered his grey mare stealthily across the valley floor, then upwards towards the ridge which led to the valley beyond, where the River Eden flowed.

Tobias Flint dismounted on reaching the sunlit brow. Stretching his tall lean body to its full height he scanned the mist-covered valley in the foothills rising towards the great folded bluffs of the Westmorland fells. The sun was streaming through Stainmore Gap into the great basin that drained into the River Eden, which meandered north. He turned to look across to the far rim of the immense depression in the high land, an amphitheatre, where the slanting sun singled out Shap Fells and the Pikes guarding the eastern fringe of the Lake District. To his right he saw the clearing haze revealing the levelling land of the Eden Valley. He savoured the moment, assimilating the wildness and wide horizons of this place he loved.

The sound of rippling laughter interrupted his reverie. He crouched down and crawled through the tall wet grass to a clearing from where he looked into the valley below.

A girl of eighteen or twenty was mounted on a palomino horse which had neither saddle nor bridle, just a makeshift halter. In the next instant the horse stepped tentatively into the shallow waters of the slow-moving river. Then, in one sweeping graceful motion, the girl lay back on the horse and, displaying absolute confidence in the animal, she raised her legs and rested her feet on its withers, her arms hung loosely by its sides.

Entranced, Tobias gazed on in dreamlike wonder. The girl's face was framed in soft golden curls cascading down to the water. The plain fine white cotton shift she wore clung to her prostrate body exposing the outline of generous young breasts. Her eyes were closed and dark thick lashes contrasted sharply against her pale alabaster skin. Perfectly arched eyebrows suggested an element of surprise.

The mouth that had been laughing was quite still now and the soft, velvety plump lips twitched in a playful smile.

He wanted to reach down and kiss her. He was so intent on a closer look he discovered he'd edged down the steep hillside further than intended and carefully began to ease his way back. The call of a cuckoo split the air. Its song resounded throughout the valley causing his grey mare to whinny loudly. '*Blast!*' he cursed, losing his footing and slipping. He grasped at a tree root; it held him for a couple of seconds then snapped, propelling him headlong down the grassy bank. Snatching at the undergrowth on his spectacular descent he arrived at the bottom clutching an assortment of weeds.

The girl sat astride her horse staring down at the unwelcome intruder with bright, clear green eyes full of surprise and alarm.

'Where the hell did you spring from?' she exclaimed. 'What d'you think you're doing here?'

'I might well ask you the same question, madam,' Tobias mumbled, scrambling to his feet, brushing away mud and grass from his trousers.

He smiled, noticing a fine peppering of freckles across the bridge of her nose. She's got the greenest eyes I've ever seen, he thought, absorbing her every detail.

'This is private land. Have you permission?' she asked. 'So, what's the matter with you – can't you speak?'

'What...? Er ... yes, I do have permission to ride on this land. And yourself, where are you from?'

'So you're not one of us, then?'

'Well, young lady, that all depends,' he grinned, 'on what *you* are one *of.*'

'Ah, yes, of course, I ... see now, you ... er ... talk differently.

For a moment, I thought you were from Appleby Fair, but I was wrong. I'll be on my way now.'

She turned her horse to leave but he grabbed the halter. She felt a tremor of excitement when he gave her a lopsided smile, his soft grey eyes resting appreciatively on her.

'I answered your question,' he said, looking her steadily in the eye, 'now you answer mine. Tell me where you come from?'

'I'm from Hampton, just outside Appleby,' she replied politely, then added crisply, '*Now* if you'll excuse me....'

'Oh, yes, yes, I know Hampton.' He was fascinated by her and sought desperately for something to say to delay her departure. 'And tell me,' he went on, flipping his eyebrows, 'did you honestly mistake me for one of those damned gypsies?'

Her face flushed crimson and her green eyes flashed rebelliously. She saw a gleam of mocking humour lurking in his gaze and a whirlpool of anger swirled within her.

'*Those damned gypsies*, as you call them, happen to be my people,' she yelled fearlessly. 'Huh! Of course, *you* couldn't possibly be one of *us*. I don't know how on earth I made such a mistake. I've never met a gypsy as ... as bedraggled as yourself at Appleby Fair, *ever*. And another thing,' she added, continuing her outburst, 'you'd better be off before you're caught riding on Mr Flint's land. He doesn't take kindly to trespassers. You'll be for it, mark my words.'

She tossed her head defiantly, her hair spilling over her shoulders. The white cotton shift rode up her thighs revealing slim, strong, honey-coloured legs that gripped the sides of her horse powerfully. She clicked her tongue and dug her heels in and the horse shifted restlessly. But Tobias tightened his hold on the halter and smiled at her with bland amusement.

'And what about you, young lady, *who*, may I ask, gave you permission?'

'Richard Flint himself, of course,' she replied haughtily, 'Many years ago. Not that it's any of *your* damn business.'

She yanked the horse's head freeing him from Tobias's hold and the animal backed away rearing slightly. She leaned forward and, whispering a command into the horse's ear, she rode swiftly away.

Daisy Latimer returned from her ride breathless, having

galloped most of the way. She needed to put some distance between herself and *that* man. At first glance she'd thought him rather attractive until he'd opened his mouth, referring to *those damned gypsies*. What had they done to him? Nothing. He's no damn different from the rest of the gorgios, she concluded angrily. No wonder we're suspicious of everyone but our own.

She gathered up an armful of dry sticks from beneath the bow-top wagon and threw them on the warm embers of last night's campfire. She raked it back into life and hung the heavy kettle on the prop positioned over the flickering flames.

Daisy looked at her surroundings and breathed in the cool morning air. Thoughts of the last hour diminished and her spirit soared with gratitude at being here among her people. She found the familiar buzz and excitement associated with Appleby Fair intoxicating and unparalleled. Her eyes scanned the field crammed with gypsy wagons. Bow-tops, open lots, flat carts and bender tents were dotted about the lush green countryside, adorning it with their bright alien colours. Flashes of reds, blues, yellows and greens lit up the field, a landscape daubed with all the brilliant colours of an artist's palette. The swifts had returned from their annual migration and wheeled recklessly in an enamel blue sky high above, their screeching song competing with that of the curlew.

The Romanies attending the fair had been on the road for countless days, some journeying hundreds of miles. Now, having arrived, family and friends were reunited, old acquaintances renewed, stories exchanged, and deals clinched.

Like a breath of romance the Romanies brought with them a taste of light relief to the simple workaday world in which the local people lived, social differences seemingly bridged – if only for a fleeting moment in time.

The low reverberating snorts and whinnies of horses tethered in clusters throughout the campsite conveyed their greetings to one another, beckoning the day. Daisy's horse Chase whinnied softly in response. She walked over to where he was tethered and he nuzzled his warm velvety nose in her open palms.

'Hello, my beauty. Are you hungry?' She fed him a titbit from her pocket and buried her head in his thick mane.

Chase had been her companion for eight years, but it seemed like only yesterday her father had brought him home. Daisy was ten years old at the time. Her mother had died in childbirth a few months earlier along with the brother with whom she'd anticipated sharing her childhood.

'What do you make of him then, my sweet?' her father had asked, laying the helpless foal beside her. 'Do you think you can look after the little fella? He's not very strong.' He'd shaken his head despondently. 'His mother, poor old mare, she died of colic last night and this young 'un was sure to follow, so the farmer said I could tek 'im wi' me if I knew someone who'd care for 'im.'

'Oh, yes, Dad, I'll take care of him. I'll not let him die, I promise,' she vowed. Her eyes lit up with excitement for the first time since her mother's death. 'You'll be fine, little one,' she assured the foal, stroking it gently.

'And what's his name to be?' Seeing his daughter smile after all the recent grief moved him deeply.

Daisy thought for a long time before answering. She then pronounced with a valiant smile, 'Chase. I'll call him Chase, Dad, 'cos today, he's chased away some of the sadness inside of me.'

From that day forth Daisy devoted every waking moment to rearing the foal. And transforming her grief into love, they became inseparable over the years.

Samboy Latimer emerged from the wagon. His wild auburn hair streaked with grey tumbled about his suntanned face. He tied a spotted kerchief round his neck and walked to where Daisy was sitting by the fire. He dropped a kiss on her cheek then pulled up a wooden stool next to her. She handed him a cup of tea and a plate of bread and butter smothered in wild strawberry jam.

They sat in companionable silence where only birdsong, gentle snorts and whinnies, punctuated the stillness.

Samboy was a tall, well-built fellow with broad, straight shoulders. He had a kind, open face with dark intelligent eyes and deep laughter lines etched at his temples. His generous mouth gave the impression of a permanent smile, which could be disconcerting if he happened to be in a bad mood. His brown hands holding the Crown Derby porcelain cup and plate were rough and callused with years of labouring and the handling of horses. His rugged good looks turned the heads of many unattached traveller women attending Appleby Fair. Some hoped to pin him down for he was a fine catch with a good business.

But he was content enough for the time being, raising his only child and having to be both father and mother to Daisy since the death of his wife, Mary.

Mary, who was not of Romany blood, married Samboy against her parents' wishes. They'd eloped to Gretna Green twenty years ago after falling in love one glorious summer at Appleby Fair. She was visiting the fair with friends and had just had her fortune told, when, stepping down from the fortune-teller's wagon, she had tripped on the bottom step. Samboy, who happened to be passing, saw her falling, rushed to her aid and caught her, holding her in his arms a while longer than was politely necessary.

After that moment they met secretly every day for the duration of the fair. He vowed to return the following year and marry her. He kept his promise, despite opposition from both sides. They married, presenting everyone with a fact they had to accept. Much to the surprise of their families, Mary and Samboy were happy regardless of their cultural differences.

Two years later they were blessed with the arrival of Daisy, following an anxious pregnancy and difficult birth. Seven years later and against doctors' advice Mary fell pregnant again. After being in grave health for the nine months, she died in childbirth with their stillborn son.

Samboy was proud of his daughter. When his late wife's parents had died, they had bequeathed them a cottage near the market town of Hampton, so she'd attended school from age five to fifteen and could read and write as well as any non-traveller. Daisy had attended school for most of the year, delighting her teachers with her keenness to learn. They didn't object when she arrived in school late in October when the gypsy fairs had finished, then abandoning lessons in May. For that was when the open road would call, summoning Samboy as it had his ancestors for hundreds of years.

'Big selling day tomorrow, Dad,' Daisy said, breaking the silence, 'Some grand horses to flash. I'll help you get them ready, eh?'

'Aye, Daisy, but first we'll go into town and stock up with a few provisions. And, if I'm not mistaken, it's somebody's birthday. We'll go an' 'ave a look in Danby's dress shop, eh?'

Daisy cringed. 'Oh, Dad, I'll be nineteen, not nine,' she

remonstrated. 'Would you mind if I went on my own?'

She loved her father dearly, but the thought of him accompanying her to buy a new dress was too much. His excessive paternal protection was beginning to get on her nerves and resentment towards him was growing as he monitored her every move.

He'd also started encouraging his friends with unattached sons to visit in the hope she'd find one of them suitable for marriage. Most traveller girls were married by the time they reached the ripe old age of eighteen, having already endured a lengthy engagement. But Daisy balked at the idea of being steered towards any man and would remain a spinster before marrying a man not of her own choosing.

'Of course I don't mind,' her father lied. ''Ere's some brass for yer, lass.'

'Thanks, Dad,' she said, stuffing the pound notes inside her pocket. She put her arms around his neck and kissed his cheek. 'I do love you, Dad,' she said guiltily.

'Aye, I know, lass,' he said, patting the soft white hand resting on his shoulder. 'Now, you watch out when you go into town by yerself.' The tone of his voice changed and rang with authority. 'There're some high-spirited young buggers flyin' about Appleby this time o' year. An' I'm not just talkin' about our own people, Daisy. So careful. D'yer 'ear me?'

'Yes, I hear you, Dad.'

Samboy couldn't believe the way the non-travelling lasses conducted themselves nowadays. Running wild, going out with lads, drinking in the pubs. Disgraceful behaviour. And he wasn't going to have his daughter influenced by such likes.

'Don't worry, Dad, I'll only be gone for an hour or so. I'll be back to get your dinner ready.'

Tobias Flint rode home at a leisurely pace. While meeting the girl had thrilled him it had also released long-forgotten memories from the past regarding the gypsy fair. He could recall how neither he nor his brother Hugh – or the staff for that matter – ever discussed the annual event. It was *taboo*. And for some bizarre reason, a wall of uneasy silence existed during fair time.

He had been away at school in Exeter from age six to seventeen. Then Sandhurst, followed by the God-awful war. No wonder I don't know anything about the fair, he thought, I've hardly been here. Damn and blast! I wish to hell I hadn't been so bloody rude to her. Well, if she's an example of the gypsy girls I won't mind going out of my way to see a few more of them, he concluded, smiling.

He was still smiling when he reined his horse to a halt in the stable yard.

'Morning, Dan,' he said chirpily to the stable boy who abandoned a barrowful of horse muck to attend his horse.

'Mornin,' sir, grand 'n it is too.'

'Most certainly is. Tell me something, Dan, you've been around here all your life. Do you ever go to the gypsy fair?'

'Oh, yes. I always goes and watches t'orses, sir – when they're selling them, that is. I likes to watch 'em strike a deal. Yer never know 'ow much 'as been paid though.' His eyes were wide with excitement as he spoke, his fascination with the gypsies apparent.

'Really?' Tobias said intrigued.

'Oh aye, sir. Do yer know, they 'ave a strange language all of their own? And unless you 'appen to be one of 'em, they won't let you in – oh, no, it's like a secret society, that sort o' thing,' Dan imparted knowledgeably. 'They don't trust us gorgios though, yer know – oh no, they don't,' he said, shaking his head.

'Gorgios?' Tobias asked frowning, 'What the devil are gorgios?'

'Us. You an' me. We're the gorgios or flatties. That's what they call us non-traveller folk. Me now, ah likes the gypsies,' he disclosed sheepishly. 'Ah thinks they're a right decent lot, specially t'orse dealers.'

'Strange thing, Dan,' Tobias admitted soberly, 'I've lived here all my life ... and this fair has gone on for ... what? hundreds of years....' He sighed shrugging his shoulders. 'I know nothing, nothing at all about it, or its people.'

'No, sir, mebbe not; now yer father did, of course. Now 'e was very interested in the fair – and them travelling folk. I believe 'e got to know a few o' the families quite well. Sometimes 'e'd go down and 'ave a cup of tea with 'em on an evenin' – sit round t' campfires like, an' I've even 'eard tell that 'e joined in with their sing-songs.'

Tobias raised his eyebrows, his eyes as wide as Dan's, 'Really,

Dan? Good Lord. I'd no idea, Mother's never mentioned it before.'

'Oh, sorry sir, mebbe I shouldn't 'ave said owt like. I ... don't think yer mother was ower keen on yer father tekin' an interest in 'em like, I'm sorry, sir, don't be tellin' 'er I've gone and said anythin' p ... please, sir?' Dan stuttered, with a fearful look in his eyes.

'No, no, of course not, Dan, I wouldn't dream of it. Please, don't worry,' said Tobias, hoping to mollify him.

Good grief, he thought, the lad's positively scared stiff. I wonder why? I think I'll take a look at this horse fair, see what it's all about. If Father enjoyed it, it must hold some interest. And what of the girl, I wonder? When did he meet her? And what decided him to give her permission to ride over our land? I'm sure she wasn't lying.

Tobias entered the house via the kitchen where Nellie, the housekeeper, was ushering a scullery maid to, 'get a move on'.

'Morning, Master Tobias,' she said, greeting him warmly.

'Morning, Nellie, hmm ... something smells good.' He lifted a lid from a pan bubbling on the stove and buried his nose in it.

'Come on now, out o' my way,' Nellie chided, shooing him with flapping arms. 'You know your mother doesn't like you coming in the back door – never mind hangin' around the kitchen. Now be off with you. I'll fetch your breakfast along soon enough.'

'Is Mother up?'

'Aye, she's in the mornin'-room, so get along.'

'Oh, you are a good 'n, Nellie, I don't know what this family would do without you,' he said, giving her a quick hug before disappearing to join his mother.

Nellie beamed with pleasure. She couldn't love Tobias any more had he been her own son. She had worked for and lived with the Flint family for over forty-five years, witnessing many happy and some very sad events.

Eden Falls Manor had been in the family more than a hundred years with three generations being born there.

Richard Flint, Tobias's father, had died of a heart attack eighteen months ago. His eldest son Hugh had been killed in action at Tobruk. Tobias, by the grace of God, had managed to survive. When Tobias returned home from the war his father passed the entire responsibility of the estate to him before sliding into a deep depression, from which the poor man never recovered.

Nellie had no liking or regard for Richard Flint's widow, Lydia Flint. She'd been employed originally as personal maid to Richard's ailing mother. Destined for spinsterhood at twenty-eight, she was besotted with her employer. She was also an opportunist. Nellie had witnessed Lydia worm her way into the family. Watched her shameless flirtations, her throwing herself at Richard, and the eventual pregnancy. Oh yes, he'd married her, of course. What else could he do? It was his child and he wouldn't shirk his responsibilities. And Nellie didn't doubt that Lydia was fully aware Richard's ailing mother was too frail to withstand any family disgrace. Lydia would have held him to ransom had he refused to marry her.

Tobias made his way to the morning-room where his mother was sitting at a table in the large bay window overlooking the rose garden. She hadn't heard his approach and he paused in the doorway, studying her intently.

She was wearing a charcoal-grey skirt and a navy-blue blouse. The drab colours succeeded in accentuating her sallow complexion. Her greying brown hair was cut unfashionably short and brushed back severely from her face. It was a harsh face, which he thought must have smiled once upon a time to have attracted his father. But now it wore a permanent frown. Her mouth was encircled with deep vertical lines, formed from the years of bitterness they'd harnessed. Her cold, spiteful eyes now turned to look at him.

'Tobias. Have you been there long?' she queried sternly. 'God, you're enough to frighten anybody, sneaking up like that.'

'Sorry, Mother, I didn't mean to frighten you. And I wasn't *sneaking*.' He forced a smile and sat down opposite her. 'I've just come back from a long ride,' he said, changing the subject quickly. He didn't know why, but he had this tendency to irritate her, get under her skin, even when doing his utmost to please her. Not that he could recall her ever being pleased about anything.

During his childhood she hadn't exhibited an ounce of maternal love towards him in any shape or form. But it hadn't mattered, for what his mother lacked Nellie made up for a thousand-fold. It was Nellie he ran to, Nellie who kissed him better, read him stories and tucked him up in bed.

'You're becoming more like your father every day,' she complained, 'Gallivanting all over the countryside mixing with locals, workers and ... undesirables....'

'Is that such a bad thing, Mother?' Tobias interjected, holding her gaze.

'What? You gallivanting all over the countryside, or mixing with riffraff?'

'Neither. My becoming more like my father?' He hit a raw nerve and her eyes glinted bitterly for a brief moment.

'That's not what I meant, Tobias ...'

'Well! What did you mean?'

'Don't you dare question me like that,' she shrieked. 'I'm your mother.'

He looked at her in disbelief. Yes, this was his mother. Her eyes flashed as white-hot anger took control. A vein pulsated rapidly in her neck and pockets of saliva gathered at the corners of her mouth.

'*And ... you*. Don't you look at me like *that*,' she said, leaning towards him and screwing up her eyes, her face inches from his own. Her lips drew back to reveal clenched teeth. '*You ... You and your precious bloody father. What you don't know about him doesn't bear thinking of.*' She spat out every word, her voice rising in a crescendo of bitterness.

'What ... what do you mean? What don't I know about ... about Father, *Mother*?'

Lydia leaped from her chair and stormed out of the room. She collided with Nellie in the doorway. The prepared breakfast tray she carried took flight, crashing to the floor with a resounding clang and food flew in every direction.

Tobias strode after her, apologizing to a dumbfounded Nellie along the way. He raced up the polished staircase two steps at a time. On reaching his mother's door it slammed shut in his face. He turned the handle. It was locked.

'Open this door, Mother. I must talk to you.'

'Go away. I've nothing to say to you. *Please*, lower your voice.'

'Mother, you must tell me. What about my father? What is it you don't want me to know?'

'Tobias! Do you want the servants to hear you talking like

this?' Her voice was a loud pleading whisper.

'*The servants*,' he mocked. 'Huh. That's a laugh, coming from you. That's what *you* came here as, *remember*?'

'I won't talk to you while you're behaving like this. Go away, please.'

Tobias gave a frustrated thump on the door with a clenched fist and marched away.

He left the house by the front door, cutting across the freshly mown lawns and past the paddocks towards the woodland that bordered the estate.

By the time he reached the wood and seated himself under a tree by the side of the stream his anger had abated. But his heart was heavy.

He glanced down into the stream where a large trout basked in a pool of sunlight. Its sleek body and slow, weaving motion for some reason reminded him of the girl he'd seen earlier that day. It brought a smile to his face. I wonder what she and my father spoke of, he mused. She's probably unaware of his death. I'd like to bet he was captivated by her. Maybe she was a regular visitor to the estate. Maybe they rode together. Ah, well, with any luck, one day I'll talk to her and get some answers.

He leaned forward snaking his body down the side of the bank.

'I'd wager she could tickle you out of this stream,' he said to the unsuspecting trout, and surreptitiously slid his hands into the warm, sun-drenched water. Placing his hands under the basking fish he tickled and stroked its underbelly. In the next instant with one sudden movement, he grabbed it with both hands and threw it on to the grassy bank. He picked it up and examined its fine markings. 'You'd make a first-rate meal for a family,' he said to the trout, 'but today is your lucky day. And because of a certain young lady, your freedom is secured.'

He leaned down and gently released the fish into the sunny shallows watching it dart safely away upstream. 'Goodbye and stay free, my friend.'

Tobias walked home by way of the fields where the hay turning was in progress. It was going to be a good year as the weather had been kind. The small tractor that had replaced some of the horses was making short work of the task.

His father had been a forward-thinking man with regard to

modern agriculture. He was the first for miles around to have purchased a tractor, followed by a combine harvester. His workforce had dwindled but his profits had soared. Richard Flint had fast become one of the largest respected landowners in Westmorland.

He missed seeing the horses at work in the fields alongside the farm men and decided to keep two in reserve for emergencies. In retrospect, this proved to be a prudent decision. When the weather was changeable during harvest time, or the tractor had broken down, a horse could quickly be harnessed and taken to the fields to do the job.

Occasionally a few gypsies would hang back after the fair looking for farm work thereabouts to earn extra cash. They were skilled horsemen and could be set on straight away with a workhorse, unsupervised.

Daisy sauntered down the main street of Appleby with the purchase of a new dress from Danby's tucked under her arm. She had settled on a cream cotton summer dress with a sweetheart neckline. It had patch pockets at either side and was exquisitely embroidered around the hemline in pretty red poppies. Mrs Danby said it suited her perfectly and suggested she also buy the cream shawl to match which she let her have at a reduced price.

She delighted in the warm sunny day that delivered swarms of visitors along with the travellers to the busy town that spilled out on both sides of the river. She wandered on to the twin-arched bridge spanning the River Eden to join the throngs of people who stood gazing idly over the parapet. The sparkling waters and the tranquil backdrop of old St Lawrence's Church added to the charm and intensity of a theatrical setting.

On reaching the bridge she looked over the parapet to the familiar sights below. A wave of fifty or sixty people swam and waded in the water alongside their horses. They washed them lovingly, thoroughly brushing their coats and manes. The horses delighted in scores of gentle hands. Daisy smiled to herself; she knew every person down there.

Her eyes moved along the river to rest on one person in particular. It was Roulson Adams. He was riding through deep waters further downstream astride a large Cleveland Bay. He turned his head sharply sensing he was being watched and appeared to look directly at her. He waved and she waved back.

'That yer boyfriend, luv?' a woman she didn't know enquired, nudging her with an elbow. 'My, but he's a bloomin' handsome brute, in't he?'

Daisy didn't reply although she agreed. Yes, he is a handsome brute, she thought, studying him from her advantageous position. He was stripped to the waist. His deep bronze, muscle-toned body glistened in the sunlight. She could imagine his jet black eyes laughing and his wide mouth smiling back at her in the distance.

She watched him glide across the river and steer his horse up the riverbank before disappearing from view, merging with numerous other horses and riders.

She continued gazing in awe at those below. Young children swimming with their horses leaped from their backs racing one another to the water's edge then back again.

The spell was broken when an unexpected thunderous clattering of hoofs resounded on the bridge. Daisy whirled round to come face to face with Roulson Adams's horse. The animal was biting the bit and frothing at the mouth whilst prancing about wildly. Alarmed looks on the faces of those standing close by prompted the rider to rein his horse back a few paces, allowing people to retreat to a safer distance.

'Hello, Roulson,' Daisy said, taking hold of the horse's bridle. 'I thought it was you in the water below. Cushty gelding you've got; are you thinking of selling him on at the fair?'

He didn't reply but jumped down from his horse and stood very close to her. She could feel his warm sweet breath on her face, and the familiar aroma of horses mingled with his body sweat excited her. His shirt was slung carelessly round his neck exposing his broad chest where droplets of water trickled a pathway through the dark hairs; spellbound, she followed their descent to where the dark hair tapered below his bellybutton.

'I knew it was you up on the bridge. I'd spot you a mile off, Daisy.' He spoke softly and reached out, gently tucking an escaped wisp of hair back behind her ear. 'No mistaking that beautiful hair of yours,' he murmured, stroking it with the back of his hand.

She flushed hotly and bowed her head. Her heart quickened

when he placed a finger beneath her chin raising her face to look at him. She stared into the darkest eyes she'd ever seen. He was the handsomest man around.

And Roulson Adams knew it.

'I'd better be going,' Daisy said, stepping back a couple of paces to disengage from his magnetic charm. 'Dad will be wondering where I've got to.'

'Are you walking back up the hill?'

'Er, yes, yes I am.'

'Well, come on then, I'll give you a ride.'

He took the parcel she clasped to her chest and climbed onto his horse. He held out his arm. 'Come on, grab a hold,' he said, winking at her mischievously. 'You'll be safe enough, I promise,' he added, laughing.

She looked about her where a crowd had gathered. Roulson, unable to resist an audience, burst into song.

'Daisy, Daisy, give me your answer do,
I'm half crazy all for the love of you.
I can't afford a ... '

'Roulson, stop it! Stop it *now*,' she pleaded.

'Well, come with me, or I promise you, it'll get worse,' he laughed, taunting her.

A moment later a figure stepped out from amongst the crowd and silence ensued.

'Is this man bothering you, miss?' a distinguished voice asked.

They both turned to see a smartly dressed man standing before them. It was the same man she'd met down by the river. Daisy recognized him immediately.

'And what the hell's it to do with you?' Roulson blared, jumping down from his horse. 'Bugger off and mind your own bloody business, if yer know what's good fer yer.'

Daisy stepped between them with her back to Roulson. She looked at Tobias, perceiving his every detail in an instant while wondering what he was doing here.

'No, this man isn't bothering me,' Daisy said coolly, dismissing him with a glance. She turned to Roulson who was glaring challengingly at Tobias Flint. 'Come on, Roulson, let's go, can we, please?'

Roulson leapt on to his horse and held out a bronzed muscled arm for Daisy to grasp and climb up behind him. But first she turned to face the man who'd so readily insulted her people. 'I hardly recognised you cleaned up. You'd better watch you don't get yourself mistaken for one of us, especially dressed like that,' she added curtly.

Tobias grinned and looked on with envy as she grasped the strong arm that hoisted her up in one easy movement. They rode away but Daisy couldn't resist a furtive glance back over her shoulder. Tobias Flint stood in the centre of the bridge watching them. He smiled at her and waved before giving an elaborate, exaggerated bow. She didn't smile back.

'You okay, Daisy?' Roulson asked. They had slowed to walking pace. 'Who's that gorgio making eyes at yer?'

'What? Don't talk daft, he didn't make eyes at me. He's someone who lost his horse down by the river when I was out riding the other day.' She didn't want to waste precious time talking about *him* when she was sitting this close to Roulson. She relaxed her arms that gripped his waist. 'Hey, you shouldn't have done that,' she said crossly, prodding him in the back.

'Done what?'

'Embarrassed me out there on the bridge, that's what. In front of all those people too. Can you imagine the talk going round the camp tonight? My life won't be worth living.'

Reports of the exhibition on the bridge would be common knowledge by the time she returned and her father wouldn't be pleased if he heard of it.

'Aw, c'mon, Daisy, I wouldn't hurt you, not for the world.' He reined his horse to a halt on the grass verge and skilfully swivelled himself round to face her. 'I like you too much to do anything like that.' He looked into her eyes and held her hand. 'I was wondering, Daisy ... er ... maybe ...' he said, hesitantly, 'you'd maybe consider us ... you and me like, that is, to be courting like?'

'Oh, Roulson, I'm flattered but - I don't think I'm ready for ...'

'Hush, don't answer me yet,' he said, placing a finger on her wavering lips, 'Just think about it, okay?'

'Okay, I'll think about it.'

He leaned forward and, taking her into his arms, tenderly

kissed her trembling innocent lips. She closed her eyes to receive what was to be her very first kiss. She'd waited so long and she wanted it to be ... perfect. It was. After what seemed like an eternity she opened her eyes to find Roulson gazing back into hers.

'That's yer first kiss, ain't it, Daisy?'

'Ye ... yes it is,' she admitted tentatively. Her heart thumped wildly and she prayed he wasn't too disappointed by her inexperience. After all, he was the most popular man around and all the lasses adored him, so wasn't she the lucky one?

'Well, don't look so worried, for God's sake. It was lovely, Daisy, just like you.'

'I'd better be getting back,' she said hurriedly, as the colour rushed to her face. 'Dad will be wondering where I've got to. I promised to help him with the horses today for the big sale tomorrow.'

Reluctantly he took her home.

Samboy was busy with the horses when they stopped near his wagon.

'Hello there, Roulson lad,' he said, smiling warmly at the young man he'd known all his life. He dropped the hoof he was cleaning and, taking a rag from his pocket, wiped the sweat from his brow. His smile evaporated when he saw Daisy climb down from behind him. He hurried towards her. 'Are yer all right? Has something happened?' he asked anxiously.

'No, no, I'm all right, really, Dad. Don't look so alarmed.' She retorted more sharply than she'd intended, wishing he'd not been waiting for her. 'Roulson gave me a ride back, that's all,' she added tersely, and, spinning round, spared her father the flirtatious smile she threw Roulson.

'Thanks for the ride home, Roulson – bye.'

'You're welcome, Daisy, ta-ra now.'

She saw the look of disapproval on her father's face and quickly disappeared into the wagon.

'Cushty stallion yer've got yerself there, Mr Latimer,' remarked Roulson. He climbed down from his horse and strolled over to where a black stallion was tethered. 'Best I've seen at Appleby in a year or two.'

'Aye, mebbe so,' muttered Samboy. He looked at the

handsome good-for-nowt standing with his back to him admiring the stallion and was filled with an overwhelming desire to kick his arse. No. There was no way he was going to allow his daughter to get involved with such likes. Her mother would turn in her grave. 'Tell me, Roulson, what are you doing with yerself, nowadays?' he enquired.

'Oh, yer know how it goes,' Roulson replied, shrugging his shoulders, 'a bit o' this and a bit o' that.'

He's up to no bloody good, thought Samboy. Roulson's reputation for chasing women was no secret among the travellers. His good looks afforded him the pick of the bunch and there was no shortage of girls, married and single alike, queuing up for his attention.

'Well, I'll be seeing you, Mr Latimer, g'bye for now.' Roulson smiled and, leaping on to his horse, rode swiftly away.

'Aye, hopefully it'll be goodbye *for bloody good*.' Samboy cursed under his breath. He walked round to the back of his wagon and lit his pipe.

A gnawing feeling in his gut warned him *beware*. He'd seen the desire for his daughter in Roulson Adams's eyes. I'll protect her from that no-good bastard at any cost, he vowed. She mebbe won't thank me now but given time she will. Aye, given time....

He'll Have to Go
James H Jones
Copyright © 2018 James H Jones
A work of fiction

"We can't go on like this," said Julia. "He'll have to go."
She brought her coffee to the breakfast table and sat down.
"I know, darling," said Jake, speaking through a mouthful of buttered toast. "But try to keep your voice down, will you? He could be awake, you know, listening to every word you say. Shut the flaming door, at least."

She stood up, her chair legs scraping noisily across the tile floor, and flounced angrily to the door, leaving a draught in her wake which fluttered the edges of his morning paper. Reaching for the brass knob she paused and breathed deeply, as if to take control of her emotions, to resist the urge to bounce the door off its hinges. She pushed it to quietly and returned to her seat.

"That's better," he said, buttering his fourth slice of toast. "Now listen. You've got to cut him some slack. He's my best mate and he's down on his luck. I'm duty-bound to help him out. Don't forget, as well, I owe him my life. If it wasn't for Dave I would never have come back from Afghanistan. Not alive, I wouldn't."

She pouted and shook her head.

"So you keep telling me," she said. "But I still need to know how much longer I have to put up with him. His eyes follow me around the room, like one of those creepy portraits. I swear, even when I've got my back to him I can feel them burning into my bum, like lasers."

Jake laughed, spraying crumbs across the tabletop.

"Well, I can't hold that against him, can I?" he said. "It is a stunningly watchable bum, after all."

He managed to catch the flying teaspoon just before it bounced off his nose. Still chuckling, he wiped his mouth with a paper napkin, folded his newspaper and stood up. He lifted his jacket from the back of the chair and slipped into it.

"I'll ask the boss again," he said. "See if he has a vacancy yet for an ex-soldier with a severe case of PTSD, with a cheating wife who's abandoned him, and with no home to call his own."

He bent to give her a kiss then he was gone. She listened to the sound of his car tyres crunching through the gravel. With a sigh of resignation, she set about clearing the table.

"Mornin', gorgeous," said Dave as he walked into the kitchen. He pulled out the chair which Jake had not long vacated, took a seat sideways-on to the table and stretched lazily. "What we got for breakfast this mornin', besides yerself?"

Julia didn't answer. She turned from the worktop and brought him a sizzling full English - bacon, eggs, sausage, hash browns, beans, mushrooms, tomatoes. When she leaned past him to put down the plate, he parted her satin robe and slid his hand up the inside of her thigh.

"Mm, lovely," he sighed, his hand straying higher still.

"We can't go on like this," said Julia.

Dave pulled her robe fully open and nestled his head between her naked breasts.

"I know, honey-bun," he murmured, "You don't have to keep telling me. He'll have to go."

Janet and John
Cathy Lane
Copyright © 2018 Cathy Lane
A work of fiction

Dear Janet and John,

Thank you so much for your annual informative, detailed report of all your extremely interesting and 'wonderful' holidays, of which there appear to be many. You seem to have covered most of the world.

How nice for you to be able to purchase yet another 'wonderful' house in such a salubrious area. How many have you got now? Along with the flat in Tenerife and the one in France, you must be 'coining it in', if they are all holiday lets. And you are free to bob from one place to another, seeing as you made quite a killing with the sale of the other three, and John's business, to boot.

Of course, you have no 'ties' either, no family commitments, no roles to play except gadding about hobnobbing with the 'elite'.

My, how things have changed and moved on since knowing you both at school all those years ago. Just a couple of East End kids, same as me and Pete. You have obviously been in the right place at the right time, to elevate yourselves into a totally different lifestyle. Absolutely 'bloody wonderful' for you.

In contrast, we are still in the same house, with numerous commitments. Pete's mum's living with us. Daughter's divorced with three kids, which means we are on constant duty when she is at work. Son's in a bit of 'bovver' with the coppers.

Sorry, but I still use me 'real' accent. I - we haven't lost our I.D. We do get away to a 'cheap and cheerful' B&B when we can, which isn't very often. Pete's now got bad rheumatics which means he had to give up his carpentry job. He's now working in a telephone call centre, earning peanuts. I do some 'ome-'elpin' round the area. It's hard to compete with 'wonderful' but we are just grateful for what we've got.

Do have a 'Wonderful' New Year. I look forward with bated breath to your next 'wonderfully interesting' epistle.

Joan and Pete.

The Doodler
Jackie Walton
Copyright © 2018 Jackie Walton
A work of fiction

She sat quietly, with the telephone receiver pressed up against her ear.

She looked as though she was paying full attention whilst listening to an important phone call.

In her right hand was her pen. It was gently poised and gliding across the page of paper, creating beautiful shapes in front of her. She replaced the receiver firmly after the call and glanced at her doodles, mesmerised. Amongst the scrawl were the words ... 'Call him' ...

She knew this was what she had to do...

A Thearsby Story.

Thearsby is a fictional North Yorkshire market town, the subject of an ongoing group project to write a serial drama, or 'soap'

It is late evening, Wednesday. Ewa and Tomasz are in bed. They hear a knock at the door. Ewa stirs but shows no sign of getting out of bed. The knocking sounds again. Tomasz slams his feet to the floor, pulls on his jeans and hastens downstairs.

Ewa sits up and cocks an ear. She hears Pauline's distinctive nasal tones but can't make out what is being said. She sighs, gets out of bed, struggles into her dressing gown and staggers down the stairs, yawning.

Pauline is standing at the door in a gleaming satin nightie which is at least two sizes too small. Ewa pulls her collar close against the chill. Pauline seems oblivious to the cold.

Pauline: "I'm telling you, Tomasz, there's something in my room." She is panting, her breasts rising and falling rapidly, straining the tight satin gown. She lays a scarlet-manicured talon on Tomasz's naked arm. "I daren't go back alone."

Tomasz turns to Ewa and sighs: "Go back to bed."

Ignoring him, Ewa wraps her arms across her chest to hold her dressing gown close, shuts the door behind her and follows Tomasz, all the way into Pauline's bedroom.

Ewa watches as Tomasz searches the room. There's a double bed with a magenta upholstered headboard and bedding made of more synthetic satin. An empty wine glass stands on the bedside table. The dressing table is littered with pots, potions and chocolate bar wrappers. A tangled mound of high heeled shoes has been tossed carelessly on to the floor.

Tomasz completes his search: "Nothing is here."

It's the following night, Thursday, approximately the same time. Once again, Ewa and Tomasz are in bed when there is a knocking at the door. Tomasz swings a leg out of bed but Ewa grabs his arm to restrain him.

Ewa: "No. I go."

Dressing gown in hand, Ewa slips down the stairs and throws open the door. Pauline is there again, her red satin nightie visible under her open coat, her wrinkled décolletage in plain view, along with the edge of a slightly faded and grubby black bra.

Ewa snaps: "What?"

Pauline, unusually hesitant: "I – I." Ewa glares at her. "I'm scared."

Ewa: "You are not a child, to fear the night. Go home."

She attempts to close the door but Pauline sticks a foot in to stop her.

Pauline: "But – I can't, Ewa." Ewa glares. Pauline's voice turns to a wail: "There's something in my room."

Ewa shakes her head: "Tomasz search room. Nothing there."

Tomasz appears on the staircase. Pauline looks up at him, eyes wide, lip trembling.

Pauline: "But there is." Ewa folds her arms and taps a toe but Pauline is undeterred. "I heard it."

Tomasz is now standing beside Ewa. He sighs with resignation.

Tomasz, wearily: "I go see."

Same time the following night, Friday, Ewa and Tomasz are disturbed, yet again, by a persistent knocking on their door.

They hear Tony, their neighbour on the other side, bawling from his bedroom window: "Shut that bloody noise."

Ewa pulls her pillow over her head.

Pauline's plaintive voice floats up to their window: "Tomasz, it's back."

From his bedroom window, Tony roars: "Bloody foreigners, jumpin' in an out of beds like rabbits. Shut up!"

Pauline ignores him and calls out again: "But, but, Tomasz, I swear, there's something scary in my room."

There is the sound of Tony's front door slamming, followed by a startled yelp from Pauline.

Tony's voice now comes from outside their front door: "I'll bloody well sort you out. Come on."

They listen to Pauline's feeble protestations as Tony apparently drags her back into her house. Another door slams. This time it's Pauline's.

Tomasz sits up.

Ewa: "Stay here. She's only trying to get you into her bedroom. Tony will fix her."

Unseen by Tomasz, she smiles to herself in the semi-darkness.

They lie awake listening. Shortly they hear Pauline's door being flung open violently, followed by Tony screaming out in a high-pitched, frightened voice.

"She's got a ghost! I'm not going in there again, the bloody house is haunted."

The last thing they here is Tony's door opening and slamming shut. An eerie silence descends.

Sometime in the middle of the night, Ewa wakes up. She looks at her alarm clock. It shows 1:14am. She sits up and listens. She hears a car being driven too quickly past the end of the road. She hears the footsteps and voices of men going home from a late drinking session, passing under her window, arguing, although amiably enough: "He did not!" "He did. I'm telling you, he did." They pass by, their voices and footsteps fading away. In the distance there is the hum of the motorway. Tomasz, sleeping beside her, gives a snuffle. She lays her head back on the pillow and turns to one side.

Before she can fall back to sleep, she hears a noise. A rustle. A slither. In the roof space above, something is moving.

She jabs Tomasz until he wakes up.

Ewa: "Listen! There's something in roof. It's not a bird. What can it be?"

The following morning, Saturday, Ewa goes into Pawel's room. She sniffs, wrinkling her nose in distaste. She looks around, frowning at the general disarray. She looks under the bed and pulls out a white plate on which are the stale, half-eaten remains of a pizza. Around the pizza is a scattering of tiny black specks.

She shouts out: "Pawel!"

Pawel comes running up the stairs: "What's wrong?"

Ewa points at the plate, the dust balls, the piles of dirty socks: "How many times I tell you keep your room clean?"

Pawel looks guilty: "Sorry, Mum, I forgot."

Ewa points at the black specks: "How many times I tell you, you must not leave food in bedroom?"

Pawel hangs his head: "Sorry."

Ewa thrusts the plate at him: "You clean. You go shop, get mousetrap."

Sunday morning, Pauline's bedroom. She and her great useless lump of a son cling to each other, looking on in horror at the bloodied little scrap of grey fur caught in the trap on the dressing table. Ewa tuts at their squeamishness and scowls in disapproval at the chocolate wrappers, as Tomasz deals with the dead mouse.

Ewa: "You can't blame the mice. If you leave food in bedroom, of course mice will come, you stupid woman."

Pauline flinches at the gibe but makes no reply.

Sunday night. Tomasz stretches luxuriously in bed. Beside him, Ewa breathes gently in her sleep. Through the wall comes the sound of Tony's TV, the recognisable theme music to Rambo III. Tomasz sighs wearily but it isn't long before Tony switches off his TV and a blessed silence ensues. Tomasz drifts off to sleep, lulled by the distant hum of the motorway. He hears no more unusual noises.

He put his hand to the door handle, turned it and stepped inside.

'You wanted to see me, M?'

'Ah, there you are, 007. I trust that now Blofeld is out of the way, you will be free to spend a little more time on matters of National Security?'

'I hope so, sir,' said Bond, standing in front of M, facing him across the expansive desktop. 'What exactly do you have in mind?'

'A double agent of ours has been working in Moscow for the last three years. But now she has been betrayed and wishes to be rescued.'

'A lady, sir?'

'Her name is Olga. Naturally, we thought of you.'

'Of course.'

'You are to collect her from the Novaya Zyemlya bar in the centre of Moscow at ten o'clock local time tonight.'

'Tonight? That doesn't give me much time.'

'Then you'd better get on with it. See Moneypenny for your flight and visa documents.'

As soon as he was out of the office, Bond made his way down to the workshop.

'Oh, there you are, 007.'

'Good morning, Q.'

'I'm surprised you've got the nerve to show your face in here, after the mess you made of the Aston Martin, the last time you were out in it.'

'It can sometimes get dangerous out there in the field, Q'

'So it seems. Well, try to keep this machine safe.'

'It looks like a typewriter. What exactly is it?'

'It's officially called a Digitalising Optical Ordering and Disordering Lattice Enumerating Regulator.'

'DOODLER for short?'

'Exactly.'

'And what does it do?'

'It's a development based on the latest 3-D printer technology. It will take any 3-D object and transform it into a 2-D image on a sheet of paper.'

'Like any camera,' said Bond, with a hint of sarcasm.

'Not exactly.' Q switched on the machine. 'Watch and learn, 007. Watch what happens when I place this mug of coffee directly in line with the machine's eye and press the enter button.'

The machine hummed, the mug of coffee disappeared from view and a sheet of paper emerged from the rear of the Doodler machine with an image of the mug printed on it.

'Interesting,' said Bond. 'Can it do the same in reverse?'

'Naturally.' Q pressed the enter button again and the paper disappeared into the machine. A moment later, the mug of coffee reappeared on the table directly in front of it. Q picked it up, sniffed it and pulled a face. 'Of course, this is only the prototype model.'

Bond wandered into the lounge area and returned with a glossy magazine. Having searched through the pages, he selected one and, before Q could stop him, fed it into the machine and pressed the button.

Within seconds, the 2-D picture had turned into a 3-D model. A five-foot-four young woman, with plenty of flesh, wearing a polka dot bikini which just about covered all it needed to.

Q scowled at Bond. 'Will you never grow up, 007?'

'Of course not. There wouldn't be any fun in that.' He turned to the girl. 'My name is Bond. James Bond. Who are you?'

The girl shrugged.

'We'll have to call you Doodle.'

'You're not taking her with you on assignment, are you?' snapped Q.

'I don't see why not. I'll get Moneypenny to buy her some clothes and arrange travel documents for the two of us.'

Bond picked up the Doodler machine and headed towards the

door. Q called after him, 'Remember it's only a prototype. It isn't perfected yet. And especially don't forget, after twenty-four hours, your new lady friend will return to the state she was in before.'

With an attractive young woman in the seat beside him, James Bond relaxed on the flight to Moscow. Once there, he checked them both into their pre-booked hotel in central Moscow.

It was still early, so Bond took Doodle to visit a casino he knew down a side street. There he sat at the roulette wheel and forgot about his companion. After several minutes, the owner of the casino approached. 'Excuse me, sir, but is this young woman with you?'

Bond looked up at the man, and then at Doodle standing beside him. 'Yes, but what's she done?'

'She has played every game in the room and won more than we are able to pay.'

'Well done, Doodle.'

'We would be obliged if you would remove her from the premises.'

James Bond changed both his chips and hers and they headed out into the evening air.

It was nearly time to meet Olga at the Novaya Zyemlya bar. But there was a problem. Three men in black suits had followed them from the casino. Bond knew he had to be careful or they would all be arrested and thrown into an interrogation room before they could successfully extract the spy they had come to rescue.

Carrying the Doodler machine and a leather attaché case, Bond took Doodle to the bar in time for the scheduled meeting. Beside a table at the far side of the room sat a woman who was a few years older than Doodle. She looked terrified.

'Are you Olga?' he asked the woman. She nodded. 'I've come to take you out of here.'

'But how? This place is crawling with Russian security men.'

Turning his back on the rest of the bar, Bond placed the Doodler machine on the adjacent table and opened it up. 'Stand in front of this machine,' he told her. 'But finish your drink first. You've got a long journey ahead of you.'

When Olga had taken up her position, Bond switched on the machine and pressed the enter button. Olga disappeared from view and a sheet of paper hummed from the back of the machine. Bond took a quick look at the image. Yes, it was her. Then he slipped it into the attaché case.

Bond now had a few hours to kill before his return flight to London the following morning. Back at the hotel, Bond and his companion relaxed in the bedroom.

'Come along, Doodle. Help me finish off this bottle of champagne.'

'But what about Olga?'

'She's safe enough where she is. Nobody will think of looking for her in the attaché case, so we'll have no trouble getting her out through airport security. Given the time differences, you should be back in London within the twenty-four hours Q gave us.'

'And until then?'

'We have the rest of the night,' said Bond, with a broad grin. 'And one bed.'

Doodle gave Bond a sick smile. 'You remember what Q told you about that machine. He said it was only a prototype and it wasn't perfected yet.'

'Yes. I remember.'

'Well, the prototype machine can only reproduce what it sees. Nothing less, but nothing more.'

'You mean...'

'Yes, James. I am all the woman you can see, but nothing that you can't see.'

Bond sat back, stunned and dismayed. 'So much for Q and his big ideas.'

'It's your big ideas that are the problem, James.'

Bond turned off the bedside lamp. 'We've got an early start in the morning,' he told her.

She leaned over and kissed him gently on the cheek. 'In that case, good night, James Bond. And better luck next time.'

I Came, I Saw
Sara Kingdon
Copyright © 2018 Sara Kingdon
A work of fiction

"I came, I saw, I conquered."
"Been there, done that, got the T-shirt."
"Seize the day!"

Who comes up with these sayings? I wonder, as I look out of the dirty bus window. Who decided sliced bread was so good? What did they go back to before drawing boards were invented?

It's another gloomy British day in March. Spring hasn't quite sprung yet and it's raining; the really fine rain, the kind which gets everyone and everything wet. I'm on my way to work, the number 71 to Richmond.

"Smile, *it's Tuesday."* Yet another useless saying. As if, just because Monday is over it's going to be a good day. Tuesdays are still nothing to smile about. I'm on my way to work, where's the fun in that? If I could give my 16-year-old self some advice, it wouldn't be what you think. I wouldn't tell my younger self to 'study harder' or 'stick in more', it would be plain and simple: Don't work in an office. A dead end nine-to-five job where you stare at a computer screen all day.

As a child I wanted to be a hotel manager, move to Canada and open a small inn in the mountains. Well, that's a world away now. *"Ding'* goes the bell, snapping me out of my daydream of what might have been. This is where Mr Brown Trench Coat gets off. I always wonder about him, What does he do for a living? Does he have a load of fake Rolex watches pinned to the inside of his coat?

We're off again. As we leave Darlington in the rear-view mirror and head on to the motorway, I continue to look out of the window, watching the world go by. My mind wanders again. To think, if I live to be seventy, I'll have been through ten years' worth of Mondays. Talk about Groundhog Day.

'*Tick-tock, tick-tock,*' goes the bus's indicator. We're pulling off the motorway to take the country road to Richmond. I like this part of the journey; the view is nice from here. The countryside always looks peaceful, even on dull days like today. Maybe I should abandon my responsibilities and move to the countryside and become a farmer. Ha! That would be a picture. I don't like mud, never mind having to clean up poo, too. Scratch that idea.

'*Ding*' goes the bell again. Here the young blonde gets off to walk to the dog rescue centre along the lane. I know she works there because every time she walks past, you catch a lingering smell of wet dog. That she wears the uniform is another clue. Maybe I could do a job like hers? Looking after dogs, surely it has to be fun? Getting to play and stroke dogs all day long? Hmm... then again, I'd still have to clean up poo. Cross that off the list, as well.

The bus continues on its never-ending journey; more hills, more farmland. If I could do any job in the world, what would it be? I ponder. I don't really fancy the hotel manager thing now, and I'm probably never even going to get out of Darlington, never mind the UK. Think, think, think, what could I do? I'm not really arty, so I couldn't paint or anything. Can't cook, not sporty in any way and I don't really like kids. I think that rules out pretty much most jobs. Great.

'*Ding*' goes the bell again. We're in Richmond now, my turn to get off. I stand, picking up my bag and putting on my purple raincoat to shield me from the damp weather. I glance around and wonder if anyone is trying to guess what I do for a living. Probably not. I walk down the bank and stand outside the office building. It's painted an off-white colour with grey window frames. Most of the paint has flaked off round the door frame and the entranceway usually smells of wee. I'm sure it's a pit stop for people after a few too many drinks at the weekend. I sigh at the thought of another eight hours in this place, staring at a computer screen; tap, tap, tapping on my keyboard. Heaving another deep sigh, I walk in.

Once I reach my desk, I sit down, looking around me. Most of the others have already arrived and are working away. '*Click, click, click,*' is all you can hear. Heaven forbid there is any talking.

Sitting there in my coat, staring at the log-in screen in front of me, I glance around again. Shaking my head, I stand up, grab my bag and leave, finally with a smile on my face.

Today I came, I saw - and I quit.

Halloween
Derek Shelmerdine
Copyright © 2018 Derek Shelmerdine
A work of fiction

"Come on, in here, the old fool'll never catch us." The three boys pushed open the door to the fancy dress shop and set off the eerie chimes which announced the arrival of a new customer. "You two distract him and I'll find something to nick for tomorrow night's adventures."

Once inside the shop they could see it was decked out for the Halloween celebrations. There were really scary masks, witches' outfits, broomsticks, skeleton suits and, what was that in the corner? A French maid's outfit, covered in blood, and very realistic blood it was too. It was not just the costumes which looked realistic, but the mannequins, too. They looked almost alive. As Tom looked around for something to steal he noticed all the mannequins were models of children, in fact, all the costumes were for children.

"Right you two, get over there, like I said, and distract him." Dutifully, Dick and Harry headed in the direction of the rather wizened proprietor. As they approached their target, Dick pushed Harry into one of the displays and they began to fight. Seeing his chance, Tom grabbed three hideous masks and bolted for the door. Once his cohorts had seen him make it safely out to the street they stopped fighting, swore loudly at the old man and beat a hasty retreat.

The following night, the three musketeers donned their masks and headed to the other side of town. An area they didn't know and where no one knew them. It was quite dark when they stumbled upon a large old house, set back from the road in splendid isolation. By this time, they had already made several house calls and mostly pelted the front doors with rotten eggs.

The three boys walked down the overgrown footpath to the

old, solid oak front door. They rang the bell and waited. When the door opened, they chorused, "Trick or treat, mister."

"Bugger off, you little sods," snarled the householder. He slammed the front door, which was met with a hail of rotten eggs.

Just as the boys were all set to run away, he opened the door again.

"Look, I'm sorry boys," he said. "I was young once upon a time, a very, very long time ago. I have a real treat for you. Come inside boys and you'll love it."

They followed the old man into his house and through to the kitchen. He gave them some of his delicious - his word - home-made toffee and lemonade. Busy looking around for something to steal, the boys had not recognised this was the old man from the fancy dress shop. But he had recognised them. In fact, he knew they were coming. The stolen masks had a magical quality which enabled him to influence the wearers' every thought.

As the sweets and lemonade did their work the boys became more and more obedient. He led them through a door at the end of the kitchen, down the stairs and into the basement. This Pasteboard-like room was full of children quietly going about the business of making masks and other Halloween goodies. The blood was real, the skeleton suits were just that, real human bones woven into macabre onesies. Not all the children were *lucky* enough to work on the production lines. It was like a scene out of *Metropolis*. Human robots, without hopes, fears or emotions.

"These three will make great mannequins for my shop," he muttered to himself. "I love Halloween, roll on next year."

The Migrant
Antony Waller
Copyright © 2018 Antony Waller
A work of fiction

I look into his eyes. And see nothing. No flicker of emotion. No spark of humanity. Just cold and hard, matter-of-fact. He thrusts a life jacket into my shaking hands and shoves me along after the others, a bedraggled snaking line of thirty people. We clamber down the last few slippery rain-soaked steps cut into the cliff, to reach the isolated shingle beach below. Barely visible in the early morning gloom beyond the line of breaking waves, I see the outline of a fishing boat moored alongside a short stone jetty built in the lee of the rocks. This boat is taking me to a new life.

I sink ankle deep into the wet shingle and my feet crunch across the beach. The wind drops, the squally shower ceases and the steely grey light is now tinged with threads of gold. There is a sense of urgency and several figures dressed in dark clothing gesticulate towards the jetty and the boat, pushing us along.

I reach the jetty and await my turn, suddenly racked with doubt. Raised voices; an argument breaks out. An older couple lugging a heavy suitcase and another man in black with dead eyes.

"No baggage, no possessions. Space is for people. People pay. Unless you want to pay more?"

The woman screams and the suitcase is abandoned. It's not the only one.

I take my place on a bench near the wheelhouse. The boat stinks. Reeking of diesel fumes and fish, infused with stale sweat, urine and vomit. It doesn't take any imagination to work out which catch is the most profitable these days. We are shoe-horned aboard, ropes are untied and cast off and the engine coughs and stutters into life to begin the short journey around the point.

I had been desperate to get out for ages. I'd lost my job, was unable to find another, my savings were disappearing and I could see no future in staying. Then I met this man in a pub who knew someone who could offer me a job and a fresh start. An opportunity too good to miss and soon everything was agreed. I just had to make the necessary arrangements, say goodbye to my old life and leave everything and everyone I had ever known behind me. It wasn't easy, the country had changed and these days you had to be careful. Normal channels and procedures were difficult and took time and I realised the only way was a 'moonlight flit'. Phone calls were made, I spoke to faceless people, money changed hands, instructions were received and my journey began.

Now it is nearing an end. The stench of the boat is fading and I trudge across the firm sand searching for the boardwalk between the dunes and the spiky marram grass to lead me to a rendezvous with a man in a white van on a narrow coastal road.

I find my way. A Transit van glints in the early morning sunshine, the driver leans against the side smoking a cigarette and checking his watch. I pass an old millstone at the side of the road and read the now faded lettering.

'Failte gu Alba', it says, 'Welcome to Scotland'.

I turn my back and walk away.

The End
Cathy Lane
Copyright © 2018 Cathy Lane
A work of fiction

He supposed under the circumstances it was quite natural to be nervous. After all, he had never done anything quite like this before, so he wanted to get it right first time.

The timing of course was all important. Timing and preparation, experience had taught him, were the key to most things. He glanced up at the loudly ticking clock on the kitchen wall and then checked the time against the dial of his Rolex. Five minutes to five. He still had some time. She was a creature of habit and, barring the unforeseen, it would be five forty-five before she walked up the driveway. After that he would make his presence known.

It had become apparent she had been seeing someone else for some time, before he had finally found out. She had made a right fool of him in that time. She had been so furtive and clever, playing on the fact he had been devoted to her. Blinded by her apparent love for him, it had never occurred to him that she was just a tramp, dressed up to lure the likes of him with her warm seductiveness.

He had changed quite a lot since his rather unplanned departure, thanks to her bad driving and his inebriated condition after having discovered her affair. Accidental of course. He was rather faded and jaded, a mere shadow of his former self. Certainly not the man he had been. Nonetheless, he had developed certain skills, which he was about to put to good use.

Now he was in her domain he needed to put things to the test. He looked around the kitchen. He rifled through the drawers and strewed the contents around a bit just to disturb her. He tipped the flowers out of the pot so the water dripped on to the floor by the sink. Nice and wet. He poured cooking oil by the doorway, nice and slippery. Time meant nothing to him now but his ability to see and sense and feel had not diminished, it was just different.   Her time was drawing nigh.

He heard the key in the lock, dead on time, and there she was waltzing in as if he had never existed, well he had once, and although he had left her world he was still in his.

She opened the door and turned, not seeing him of course but registering the mess by the sink and the drawers tipped out, the expression on her face worth all the tea in China, and then the loss of balance as she teetered on those stilt-like shoes, skating on the puddled cooking oil and landing unceremoniously on the floor. The noise of the fatal thudding bang on her head like music to his ears. After which he silently left the house.

Ghosts don't leave fingerprints.

The Heavens Weep
Diane Leake
Copyright © 2018 Diane Leake
A work of fiction

At last I am warm. Though I'm aware the biting wind continues to scream and tear at me like an old hag with talons of steel, it is of no concern. Even the frozen furrows which bite through my flesh with teeth of glass have taken pity on me to become as soft as a feather bed. And all around my guides illuminate the landscape with their hidden knowledge: a knowledge divulged to only a few of us. Those of us who have befriended them. Those of us who have given up the way of mortal man.

My name is Erri Flatts. Yes, I know. A strange name from a far land. How, you ask, does a Seanachai, instructed in the Celtic and Druid way, possess a name bestowed by the Norse Gods? And why does a man of peace keep the name decreed by a warrior race? That's a question I would often ask my mammy. Along with why I wasn't called Seamus like my best friend but she was always evasive. However, she did tell me Erri means having a brisk, stout appearance. And as a child this was most fitting, although I realise it is hard for you to determine as much from my present appearance. Later I discovered it also referred to a brisk, bold poet, which I thought fitting to my life-path. Like most things it was predestined. And, of course, Flatts refers to low lying ground, the place of my childhood. With hindsight, I see it must have been difficult for my mammy to answer me truthfully, for I would surely have questioned my siring. No doubt a Sassenach was involved. But the man I knew as father was a father in every way.

Sorry? How old am I? Very old. Many, many moons old. Old enough to remember listening to the whispering of the aspens' secrets, running free on acres of emerald carpet and having a belly full of tatties and meat, or the odd fish, caught by Old Donal in his currach.

Thinking of food awakens me to the knives piercing this earthly body. I must strive to remove my mind from the physical and concentrate on my guiding lights. Yet it seems to me that even they are crying and no knives can compete with the pain infusing my soul. For I know they cry for the blackened earth which lies diseased beneath its glacial covering. But mostly they weep for the cruel inhumanity of man. Yes, they weep for the hopelessness of the starving, the indignity of the dying, but mostly they weep for the souls of the perpetrators, those lost souls whose greed for the material denies their fellow man's existence.

Now I have rested long enough. I must get up. I have to pass on the word. It is my duty to keep our stories and language alive, to bring hope and solace to the oh-so-many needy. And tonight especially, I have to pass on the word. Men will die if I don't. Seamus needs to be warned that the English know about the plot to storm the overstocked grain warehouses. And he will need to find and deal with the informant.

This thought forces a reedy breath from my lungs in a silvery mist and leads me to question my own integrity. Does my part in this deception make me as one with the man who carries a rifle? Am I as callous as the man who throws starving women and babies off his land because they can no longer afford to pay their rent? Is this why the stars are crying? Do I disappoint them? Do they think I have betrayed the knowledge? Do they view me as any other greedy and vengeful man? Yet for this moment I am, for I love this land which is my heritage, Celt and Druid entwined. So, I tell my guides, all I want is the return of a woman's solace as she watches her full-bellied child run barefoot and free. I want men to roar with laughter, their hands employed and their dignity restored. But most of all I want this beautiful land which has been bastardised by avarice and negligence to have the disease excised from its soul, to breathe its purity again. Now, do you still think me selfish and greedy? Perhaps...

Dragging my thoughts into my present reality I try to move, but the furrow has me pinned. Five minutes, I tell myself, pulling the potato sack tighter, a gift from Padraic O'Flaherty. Five minutes and I will have the strength to stand. Five minutes and I will be on my way. As I turn my head to my guides one winks at me.

Two nights later a barefoot scarecrow of a man stumbles over something and curses loudly. The last thing he needs is to be slowed in his escape. He holds his breath to listen in the blackness for the sound of the Garda's dogs. Thankfully all is quiet. Then out of the blackness one star appears to lighten the cause of his offensive downfall and his face falls. Now he knows why there'd been no warning. Crossing himself, he sends a few words to the Virgin. If he ever meets up with the others again, which he hopes he won't as they've all been arrested, he'll let them know the Seanachai was not to blame, so they can stop their cursing.

Pulling the newly acquired potato sack around his thin shoulders he looks to the sky. A jolt of shock or fear runs through him. 'Holy Mother of God, but that star looks to be crying.'

Edie looked down at her knitting and sighed. She couldn't finish it now. The bell-ringers were almost at the end of the Grandsire Triple, so Joanna would be home in the next twenty minutes. She never joined the others for a drink at The Bell Inn afterwards. Maud was very strict about that. 'No daughter of mine will ever set foot inside that establishment. Is that quite clear, Joanna?' Always the tyrant, my sister, thought Edie.

Edie had never married. That was Maud's doing too. She had discouraged every young man who had come to the house to see Edie, either by sheer intimidation or by making Edie out to be soft in the head. Edie had always believed that Maud hadn't known about Harry: dear Harry whose ship had gone down in the battle of the Atlantic. She'd believed it until this morning, when Maud, spry as ever, had caught her reading Harry's last letter.

'Edie! Joanna's rung the breakfast bell. Are you deaf as well as daft? Give me that,' and she'd snatched the letter from Edie's hand. 'You're pathetic, Edie. Harry Forster died sixty-three years ago - which resolved matters nicely, I might add.'

'He was going to marry me. Look, he calls me "his own sweet Edie" and says the bells are going to chime as soon as he comes home.'

'Oh, yes, the bells would have chimed all right, but they would have chimed for me, not for you.'

'What do you mean?'

'Why do I always have to explain everything to you twice? I mean, dear sister, they would have chimed for Harry and me.'

'But he couldn't abide being in the same room as you!'

'The stupid man was embarrassed.'

'I don't understand.'

'No, Edie, you never did. Harry would have married me because I was expecting his child. Joanna is his.'

'But . . . but you married George because you said you loved each other too much to wait for the wedding night. You threatened me. You said if I ever told a soul, you'd have me put away.'

'It worked, didn't it?'

Edie had been silent a moment. 'George never knew?'

'Why would he suspect? As soon as I read about Harry's ship, I went to George and told him I wanted him. He wasn't about to refuse an offer like that.'

Edie's voice had grown smaller. 'Did you love Harry, then?'

'Numbskull Harry? Of course I didn't, but it was great fun seducing him. It would have been even more fun marrying him to spite you, but no fun living with him. He wasn't a patch on George, and George had his limits, so he had to go.'

'George died of a seizure!'

'Yes, he did, didn't he?' Maud had smiled, then slowly and deliberately torn Harry's letter into tiny pieces.

Maud had ignored Edie for the rest of the day, venting her usual spleen on Joanna instead. She'd continued to find fault even after Joanna had gone to bell practice.

'Listen to that. How many years has my stupid daughter been ringing, and she still can't get it right. I shall speak to the vicar. It's an antiquated practice anyway.'

'You wouldn't stop the bells?'

'Why not? I'm not the only one in the village driven to distraction. Besides, it takes up far too much of Joanna's time.'

'But she enjoys it!'

'You wouldn't think so, listening to her efforts tonight. She'd be far better off at home, doing something useful.'

'You treat her like a servant. You always have. I don't think you even like her very much.'

Maud was poking at the fire angrily. 'Since you mention it, no, I don't. No spunk, as we always called it. Like father, like daughter, which is probably the only reason you and she seem to get on. Still, it's far easier to control those you despise.' Then she'd stood, shrugged, and turned to the sideboard to pour her evening sherry.

The hall clock chimed nine. Joanna would be home any

minute. Edie looked down at her knitting again. It was ruined. Maud's blood had soaked into the wool still firmly cast on to the needles which protruded from her neck.

The Most Valuable Thing in the World
Robert Stapleton
Copyright © 2018 Robert Stapleton
A work of fiction

What is the most valuable thing in the world?

Pyrianos was a Greek philosopher who lived and taught in the sixth century BC. He lived on a mountain top a few miles outside the Greek city of Athens and taught the pupils who came to visit him every day. Some of these pupils went on to be great men in Athenian society.

Very few of his stories have come down to us from those ancient times, but the one we do have might well have been delivered in this way:

The great man sits in his usual seat, surrounded by his pupils. And begins:

There was once a merchant who travelled the world, buying and selling objects of great worth. He grew exceedingly rich by his efforts, yet still felt the need to keep trading and to become even richer.

One day, he was crossing the desert of Arabia, seated high upon his camel. He wrapped his cloak around him and looked out ahead across the empty desert. For many miles, he could see nothing but sand.

Then he heard a voice. 'What is the most valuable thing in the world?'

The merchant looked around. Nobody was in sight. He thought he must have been imaging the voice, perhaps he had spent too long in the sun. He continued on his journey.

A little farther on, he heard the voice again: 'What is the most valuable thing in the world?'

Again, the merchant looked around. Seeing no one, he

concluded it must have been his camel who had spoken to him.

'I suppose,' said the merchant in answer to the question. 'It must be a large and perfectly formed diamond, like the one I saw in the market at Baghdad. Surely that must be the most valuable thing in the world.'

The camel and rider continued across the desert, moving slowly and steadily onwards.

A little farther on, the camel again asked the question. 'What is the most valuable thing in the world?'

With nothing better to do, the merchant began to think again, recalling his many buying expeditions.

'I once saw a pearl at the market in Damascus. It was beautiful and of great size. Surely, that must be the most valuable thing in the world.'

The camel continued its plodding journey. The merchant kept looking forward, his head swathed in his cloak, keeping him from the worst of the midday sun.

The camel asked again. 'What is the most valuable thing in the world?'

The merchant was becoming tired of this game. 'Why all these questions?'

The camel said nothing.

'Very well, let me think. Once, in far off Persia, I came across an opal. Rare and lovely. Surely, that must be the most valuable thing in the world.'

A little farther on, the camel stopped and kneeled down in the sand. The merchant climbed down and began to beat the poor creature.

'Come along, you lazy animal. I've been answering your stupid questions all morning, now you're stopping me going about my business. Now get up.'

The camel remained kneeling. Now, a silent camel which you know can talk is far more infuriating than a silent camel which cannot talk at all.

After a couple of hours in the blazing sun, the merchant began to feel very hot. And his thirst grew into a raging fire.

The camel merely turned its head towards him. 'What is the most valuable thing in the world?'

The merchant burned with anger, 'At the moment, my life is the most valuable thing in the world.'

'And to preserve your life, what is the most valuable thing in the world?'

'Water.'

'And in order to find water, what is the most valuable thing in the world?'

'A well.'

'And when you find the well, what then is the most valuable thing in the world?'

'A bucket.'

'And to find this bucket and well and water, what is the most valuable thing in the world?'

'The oasis at Al Baramba, which is only another two hours journey away from here.'

'And in order to reach the oasis at Al Baramba, what is the most valuable thing in the world?'

Pyrianos looked around at his pupils, whose eyes were all riveted upon him. 'What would you say in answer to the camel's question?'

One boy put up his hand. 'The most valuable thing in the world was his camel, Master.'

'You have answered wisely,' said the philosopher.

Another hand went up. 'Surely the most valuable thing in the world is a talking camel, Master.'

Everyone laughed.

'Now,' continued the philosopher. 'Before you came up here to my home this morning, what was the most valuable thing in the world to you?'

One obsequious boy answered, 'To hear your teaching, Master.'

'You have answered wisely. Now, after spending six hours up here in the heat of the day, what is the most valuable thing in the world?'

Another boy answered, 'Supper, Master.'

'You too have answered wisely,' said the philosopher. 'Now, go home, and come back refreshed and well fed tomorrow.'

As his pupils began to gather their things together, he held up his hand for attention.

'So, you see the moral of this story,' he said. 'Quite simply, the most valuable thing in the whole world is not always the thing you might imagine. It depends upon what we may need at any given moment, and it may be different for each one of us.'

The Calling of Two Mighty Yorkshire Peaks
Jackie Walton
Copyright © 2018 Jackie Walton
A true story

Whernside and Ingleborough
15 miles – 17 June 2018

After checking the Met Office weather forecast for the umpteenth time and pressing snooze on my seductively smooth and relaxing wake-up music (I must change this) I finally get myself up and prepare for the day's adventure.

Pretty much everything is ready, except me, as I like to prepare the evening before.

The drive over to Ribblehead viaduct is absolutely beautiful, in any weather. This is the start and finish point for the walk. I pass through towns and villages, watching human life waking up, dog walkers, people mowing their lawns and patches of grass in front of their houses, early morning joggers and cyclists galore. It's a treat to see and hear bird life as it is so frantic at this time of year.

After leaving Hawes and turning off left into the Dales, things begin to change. No more quaint little villages, just rolling roads and hills, stone walls and no phone reception.

I am here!

I arrive along with fellow walkers. The first thing I like to do is to get out of my car, breathe in the fresh air and become acquainted with my surroundings. It's a beautiful morning; overcast, a little misty. Perfect walking conditions.

There's a buzz in the air. More and more people keep arriving, ready to set off on various routes. Our group gathers and we set off at a brisk pace. I know for the first ten minutes or so I will feel a bit out of breath, until I get into the stride. I seriously don't know if I'll be able to keep up, especially as we begin with an ascent. I almost have to break into a slow jog!

Then the mist descends. It feels a bit disorientating but I realise it really helps me to focus, as I don't have any distractions. It becomes like walking in a mist tunnel. We can only see a little way ahead. I realise I have absolutely no idea where I am. This becomes evident when the group all catch up for a mini stop and someone points out that if I go through the gap in the wall, I'll find the Trig point. I question this. I don't realise we are actually on the summit of Whernside. It feels surreal. I locate the Trig point and tag it. I don't know why, but I always do this. It's become a kind of ritual when I reach the summit of a hill, to make it feel complete.

We walk further along the path. Most of us are pretty drenched by now. Layers are definitely the right option for clothing when hiking in the British climate. Slowly, we emerge from the misty tunnel and it's a steady descent down the other side, except, by now, due to the rain, it has become pretty muddy, greasy and treacherous underfoot, interspersed with large rocks. Some choose to run down, some pick their way down in zig-zags. Some, myself included, become a little too confident and slip and fall. I always feel you have become a true walker when you've fallen. It's an interesting assortment of styles. After my fall, I lose confidence in my boots and slow to a gingerly pace. The gap between me and the rest of the group seems to increase significantly during my slippery descent.

Eventually, I reach the gate at the bottom, I pull the large metal hoop to one side to open the gate and slip through, pulling it behind me with a satisfying clatter. The path is flatter now, on large paving slabs. I manage to break into my strange half walk, half run stride. I feel as though I'm really striding out, but I just can't see the group. That's when a whole multitude of emotions push their way up. I'm feeling a bit abandoned, not quite good enough, comparing my ability to the others. Then I change my thoughts to a kind of meditation, breathing in strength and letting go of anything which doesn't help. I remind myself, they'll wait somewhere for me. I see two figures ahead and really push to catch up. Except, it's not my group. I overtake them, impressed at my pace and finally see our walk leader waiting for me. We continue together. The pace is fast. How can they have got so far ahead?

We hit the tarmac of the road and I have to say, usually I'm not a fan of walking on hard tarmac but this is a most welcome break. We could be entered for a three-legged race with this monumental effort. There ahead, nestled in a row, sitting along a stone wall, are several hungry, munching walkers. It's a luxury to find flushing toilets and a real (or polystyrene) cup of tea along the route.

After what seems like the speediest lunch stop ever, we're off again. This time towards Ingleborough, without mist. It has such a distinct shape, standing there proudly. This feels more like a pilgrimage. The different sound and feel of walking on boardwalks is welcoming and saves us from soggy feet. Halfway along the boardwalk I spot a rather large, hairy caterpillar crawling along. I point it out to some oncoming walkers as I think they'll be delighted to see it and also, I don't want it being flattened. Then it's on to the beautiful paving slabs, which apparently came from cotton and woollen factories in Lancashire and Yorkshire. I like this part as it feels sociable, with families, older people, younger people all coming towards us. Nearing Ingleborough the slabs turn into rocks which need careful navigation. Not for the faint-hearted.

Towards the top it becomes more of a scramble, my favourite part. The views are absolutely incredible, but you really have to concentrate on your footing here. Finally, we reach the plateau of Ingleborough. It's vast and moon-like. The Trig point is way over to the right, which feels like a bit of an effort after all that climbing but I don't want to feel cheated. I need to tag it. What a feeling and this was just two peaks. Turning round to walk back the way we'd come, I pass a very scruffy-looking sheep and its lamb. I think I've read about this sheep. It doesn't seem the kind of place a sheep would hang out up here on this barren land. I think this is the famous sheep who shares walkers' sandwiches and packed lunches.

Thankfully, we don't have to go back down the same way we came up, but take a different route, with views of Pen-y-Ghent and Whernside in the distance. We stride out and make good time, chatting happily on the occasions when we aren't climbing. Then in the distance we can see the viaduct again and our tiny-looking cars. This spurs me on, knowing my half of Guinness will soon be in my clutches.

Somewhere during my descent down the long, steep grassy bank from Ingleborough, I find myself split from the group again. I pick out muddy steps to follow, I zig-zag and attempt to run but slow and steady is my best way. As I start to flag a little, I hear the distinct call of a cuckoo in the distance. I stop and listen. There is always an advantage to being away from the crowd.

The last part of the walk is through a disused quarry, which has been made into a nature reserve. It's full of tiny pink and yellow flowers, adding colour to the grey background.

My energy levels are pretty well exhausted at this stage. My thighs feel like steel, my feet feel slightly abused, my shoulders are a little achy. But the pub is in sight. We sit, wonderful, on the picnic benches outside and I wrap my hands gleefully around my half a pint of Guinness and slowly sip, savouring its velvety taste.

My day is complete.

Halifax Rain
James H Jones
Copyright © 2018 James H Jones
A work of fiction

Chapter One of the forthcoming novel
'Hudson's Personal Services'

It was raining when Steve Hudson drove into Halifax. Typical. It was how he had always remembered it. Wet and miserable. He'd left his home town of Thirsk bathed in warm early morning sunshine, and now here he was driving through a torrential downpour, the windscreen wipers barely able to cope.

This was serious rain. Bouncing-off-the-tarmac, cats-and-dogs-style rain. As if Halifax wasn't a depressing enough place to be on a Tuesday morning, anyway. It suited him fine, though. It meant people were too busy keeping their heads down and scurrying for shelter, to bother paying any attention to an anonymous dark blue Saab 9,5 rolling past.

The town hadn't changed much since his last visit, back in 2003. Back when brother-in-law Vinnie and his wife Julie had lived here, before they moved to Oakwood. It was pretty much the same old, same old: oppressive, grey, run-down streets, now with a liberal sprinkling of bookmakers and charity shops. The same old smell, as well, an unpleasant blend of the local brewery and the carpet mill, with undertones of urban decay, held down by the all-pervading dampness of the atmosphere. The kind of smell you can taste in the back of your throat for hours afterwards.

One thing which gave him a wry chuckle as he drove through the town centre, was the message emblazoned on a succession of banners strung across the streets, announcing the forthcoming 'Halifax Festival of Culture'.

"Yeah, right," he said out loud, to no one at all. "Halifax? Culture? Oxymoron, or what?"

First things first, he thought. *Locate the target house, recce the area, then think about getting some breakfast.*

While he waited at some traffic lights, he pulled on his plain navy-blue baseball cap and donned a pair of low-mag black-framed reading glasses, bought in Boots for the princely sum of £18.00. It paid to be extra careful, in this age of the omnipresent surveillance camera. He wasn't worried about the Saab; Terry had worked late in the workshop last night, making and fitting false plates, so the car was ready for him first thing this morning. The registration it was wearing for this trip matched an identical Saab, registered to some guy in Huddersfield, so there'd be no problems with any police ANPR cameras.

Tomorrow morning it would be back on the forecourt at Hudson Executive Cars in Thirsk, wearing its own plates and a fresh set of sale stickers. He reminded himself to pay Terry a decent bonus for a job well done.

Fifteen minutes later, he was parked in a quiet, tree-lined avenue in the Savile Park area, about a hundred metres or so from the house in question, studying a detailed street map while appearing to be heavily absorbed in a phone call. He realised it wasn't far from where Vinnie used to live. The houses in this street were much the same style of imposing stone-built Victorian mansions, which probably began life as homes to rich mill-owners and textile merchants.

He couldn't help wondering what this Martin Perry bloke had done to incur Vinnie's wrath. He hadn't asked. It wasn't his business. And even with the 'family discount' he had given his brother-in-law, it was still a great little earner. There was definitely a long weekend in Paris coming up for him and his darling Cindy.

Not to mention the added bonus of the help Vinnie had promised to give him later in the week, dealing with his own little family problem. Not direct personal help, as such. Old Vinnie never got his hands dirty. But he'd promised to let Terry help with the heavy lifting, which was all Steve needed, really. Good old Terry would do whatever was required and could be relied upon to keep his mouth shut. No matter what. A Vinnie Wyte man, through and through.

Which conjured up an image of Vinnie and Julie, no doubt reclining right then by their pool on the Costa del Sol, sipping cocktails and soaking up the sun. A careful man, Vinnie Wyte.

Always sure to have a rock-solid alibi.

It looked like the job should be a piece of cake. Come nightfall, what few streetlamps there were would be rendered pretty much useless by the trees. He'd already eyeballed a suitable place to park, just around the next corner, from where he could quickly walk to the victim's door, virtually unnoticed. Especially if it was still raining.

But never assume anything, as another old pal was fond of saying. Check and double check, then check again.

For the third time, he drove slowly past the house. He'd already spotted some security lighting but, thankfully, there was no sign of any CCTV. Which had to be something of an oversight, if this Martin Perry was the kind of bigshot Vinnie had made him out to be. Perhaps he thought he was untouchable, tucked away in his Victorian mansion here in quiet Savile Park, Halifax, far from his field of operations in Leeds.

Which was where Vinnie operated.

Which, come to think of it, was probably more than enough explanation for this little trip. When it came to matters of business, Vinnie Wyte had never cared much for anyone foolish enough to try encroaching on his territory.

It was time to move on, before he attracted the unwanted attention of any local residents. He drove out of Savile Park, then left Halifax behind for the time being, heading for the M62.

Late breakfast for Steve was an all-day at the motorway services, where everyone could see him but no one would remember, and where the Saab was just another unexceptional businessman's car, one among hundreds in the rain-drenched car park.

After breakfast, with bags of time to kill, he took the opportunity to head west, over the tops into Lancashire, somewhere else he hadn't been for a while. There was a place in Salford he needed to check out. One of Vinnie's business associates had a little job lined up there for Hudson's Personal Services. And there'd be no 'family discount' this time. It would earn him the means to buy in some more cars and have enough left over to take Cindy on a trip to Lake Garda.

He headed back for Halifax in the late afternoon, taking his time, a kind of nostalgia trip, following the old A58 through Bolton, Bury, Rochdale and up over the moors again to

Ripponden and Sowerby Bridge, where he'd served his time as a policeman back in the nineties, and where he'd first come to know Vinnie Wyte. The dirty old town was another depressing shithole which hadn't changed much over the years. He thought briefly about the TV drama, Happy Valley, which had been filmed mainly in and around Sowerby Bridge and which he had liked for its gritty reality. Not to mention the sterling performance of its star, Sarah Lancashire.

He climbed up into Halifax via Pye Nest just as darkness was falling. The rain was still coming down in buckets.

He pulled into a car park in King Cross, retrieved his black nylon rucksack from the passenger footwell and made short work of the sandwiches and ginger beer he'd bought at the services that morning. After placing the empty wrappings and the glass bottle in a plastic bag and cleaning his hands thoroughly with a wet-wipe, he fished out the Glock and screwed on its suppressor. Oh, how he loved the smell of gun oil.

When he drove past the Perry house, the lights were on, and there was a bloody awful gangster-wannabe black Chrysler 300C parked in the drive, alongside a pearlescent purple Jeep Grand Cherokee. Appallingly bad taste. Not the sort of motors you would ever see on the forecourt of Hudson Executive Cars but good news for Steve, nonetheless. Their presence meant the Perrys were home, possibly enjoying what they couldn't know was to be their last supper.

Briefly, he wondered if there'd be any young children in the house. Vinnie had said not, but you never knew. In any case, he was committed to leaving no witnesses, and Vinnie had insisted on a complete wipeout. A clear message had to be left for anyone else foolhardy enough to consider stepping on Vinnie Wyte's toes.

He parked in the next street, in his previously chosen spot and shrugged into his dark blue gaberdine raincoat, the one with the extra-deep pockets; plenty of room for the Glock, even with its suppressor fitted.

It was still belting it down. The rain hadn't eased all day, which could only mean the gods were on his side. He turned his collar up, tugged the baseball cap lower over his eyes and stepped out of the car. As he had foreseen, the combination of rain and trees meant the streetlamps were throwing more shadow than light.

With any luck, he would be back in Thirsk by nine-thirty, at the latest, in plenty of time to park the Saab in the workshop, stash his stuff away in his hidey-hole and switch to the Subaru Legacy he'd been using for a while. He could be home by ten. By ten-thirty he could be snug in his bed and deep in his darling Cindy. Job jobbed.

He walked past the cars in the driveway, climbed the two stone steps up to the double front door, rang the bell and waited.

The door was answered by a tall brassy-blonde woman, dressed in slutty tight clothing and displaying an inordinate amount of patchily powdered cleavage.

Steve smiled at her pleasantly. "Lara Perry?" he said and when she replied, "Yes," he shot her right between her voluminous breasts. She crumpled silently on to the deep pile of the hall carpet.

He stepped past her fallen body, closing the doors behind him, and stood in the hallway. A male voice called out from the room on the right.

"Who is it, honey-bun? If it's those flaming Jehovah's Witnesses again, tell 'em to piss off and stick their bloody Watchtowers where the sun don't shine."

Those were to be the last words of the bigshot gangster Martin Perry.

Steve entered the room, gun raised.

"Hello, Martin," he said. "I have a message for you from Vinnie Wyte."

In the event, to Steve's great relief, there were no children in the house, just Martin and Lara Perry. She died in the hallway. He died at the dinner table, struggling desperately to rise from his seat. The subsonic 9mm round from the Glock 17 punched a neat hole through the front of his serviette, which he was wearing tucked into the top of his shirt, Italian-style. Their last supper had been tagliatelle carbonara.

Steve turned and left, using his coat sleeve to pull the front door closed behind him.

"Thank you, Halifax rain," he said to himself quietly, as he unscrewed the suppressor from the Glock and walked back to his car. "You've been good to me today, but I hope I never have to pass this way again."

The Rose
Helen Johnson
Felicity and Sam Part One
Copyright © 2018 Helen Johnson
A work of fiction

Hubert Bennett permitted himself a moment of satisfaction as he promenaded around his garden, his daughter on his arm. His house and gardens were impeccable, prepared for the guests who were due to arrive tomorrow.

And impeccable too was his daughter, newly returned from boarding school, transformed into a Young Lady.

Amongst his guests were three Prospects for Felicity, each one of them Eminently Suitable.

Felicity was all loveliness, in billows of green-sprigged white muslin. Slippered feet stepped on close-cropped turf; soft fingers held the parasol protecting her face. Surely the young men would find her irresistible?

Beside them, flowers from across the Empire shimmered in the heat. Brilliant orange, luminous yellow, radiant purple: the Long Border showcased the skill of Hubert's gardeners.

Felicity knew she must believe her Father had her best interests at heart. She struggled to listen as he spoke of people whom she did not know. Sons of Lord this and Baronet that: all that Felicity comprehended was, one of them must become her husband.

She had been sent to boarding school to learn to be a Lady. Being a Lady, Felicity discovered, was all about what one must not do. Do not run. Do not laugh. Neither wear stout footwear to walk freely, nor go barefoot to dabble toes in sparkling streams. Do not speak of anything that matters, nor of anything interesting. To be a Lady, one must extinguish oneself.

Behind the Michaelmas daisies, Sam inserted a trowel and hooked out a small dandelion.

Unlike other boys of his Station in Life, Sam was well-grown. As a countrywoman, his mother had never lacked a rabbit for pie, or vegetables for soup. And while Hubert fondly believed his family received the best fruits from the Estate, Sam knew differently. As a boy ranging the kitchen gardens, he knew every fruit, every berry, and instinct led him to each at its prime.

Now, his healthy body revelled in its strength, in the warm sunshine, in the perfume of the flowers, as he bent to extract a tiny thistle.

The African War had not been unkind to him, reflected Hubert. Need of his factory's gun-carriages had enabled him to assist a baronet suffering financial embarrassment in his African ventures. Consequently, Hubert became a landowner. Occupying the Baronet's land, however, proved not to admit him into the Baronet's circle of acquaintance.

Sam considered yesterday's newspaper. How could there be war, when the Kaiser was the King's cousin?

Beside him, the nest in the hedge was empty, the chicks fledged. But, perched higher up, the blackbird watched him. Sam eyed the bird. They had an understanding.

Every year, Sam had watched the nest. Would the birds continue to raise chicks if he wasn't there? Would the garden stay the same if he wasn't there to care for it?

He observed Felicity walking with her father. She stepped sedately but her fingers twisted at the parasol.

He recalled the girl who ran, hair streaming behind her, to race to their hidey-hole in the hollow ash tree. Now her hair was piled precariously upon her head, her body constrained by stays.

Sam wondered what the Army was like. Here, there was always someone to give him orders. Maybe the Army wouldn't be so different.

He straightened up. Yesterday, Mr Bennett had spoken about a new shrubbery. Perhaps he had more to say?

"Afternoon Sir, Afternoon, Miss," said Sam, muddy finger tapping his cap. His teeth flashed in the sun.

Not for the first time, Hubert regretted he had not sooner discovered how the Governess allowed his children to play with the servants' children. She claimed it provided healthful exercise. But the habit was detrimental. The Governess was dismissed; the children sent to school. Hubert nodded at Sam and steered his daughter away. Felicity was to marry a high-born man; she must not converse with gardeners.

Sam watched Felicity's retreating back. It was stiff and straight under the stays, but her neck and hips, escaping the stays, trembled - a tremble imperceptible to anyone except Sam. He took in the tense neck muscles, bracing her head, that her hair might not come tumbling down.

He turned to the rose bush behind him. Surveyed it carefully. He knew perfection was impossible to catch. The fleeting, transient moment between unfurling and overblown, when the petals fall. Sam plucked a rose: palest pink, petals opened, perfume heavy and sharp; poised between bloom and decay.

He strode up the lawn, long, muscular legs closing quickly upon the delicately stepping master and daughter.

Sam stood square in front of Felicity. She studied him. Muddied boots. Grass-stained britches. Rolled sleeves exposing bare, muscular arms. Blue collarless shirt. Pulse throbbing at the base of his neck.

Sam offered the rose.

Leaves hung heavy and silent in the heat.

Felicity reached out and took the rose. The bright, liquid eye of the bird on the wall watched.

Felicity smiled.

Sam inclined his head a fraction. A bee, heavy with pollen, lurched from flower to flower.

Felicity's heart banged painfully against her stays. Her lips parted slightly. She did not pant – a Lady does not pant - but her breath came fast and forced.

Hubert glowered at Sam.

Sam's eyes rested on Felicity. "The bird's nest is still there," he said.

She remembered how, when she was little, Sam had first shown her the nest. Three yawning yellow beaks, three grey little bodies; their soft cheeping sounds. The feel of his cheek, smooth and dry as he'd leaned close to whisper: "Don't move, or the mother will abandon them."

"How many chicks?"

"Three."

"All fledged?"

"Yes."

She smiled.

A drop of blood on Sam's finger dripped on to Felicity's dress: a dark stain on white muslin.

Hubert harrumphed. Nobody heard him.

Felicity lifted Sam's finger and kissed it. His blood was warm and salty.

She fingered the rose in her hand. Raised a thorn-pricked finger. Touched it to Sam's bloodied finger.

The bird flew down to feast in the ground Sam had disturbed.

They had an understanding.

Sam slumped in the corner of the train compartment. He'd searched for an empty one; now he sat, head against the cool, moisture-laden glass, eyes unfocused, rain blurring cranes and ships and trains and sea. Lines of marching men, great guns dragged by teams of horses. Condensation from the window soaked into his Red Cross armband. His khaki jacket collar itched his neck and smelled of wet wool.

As the train began to move, the door flew open and a dishevelled bundle flew into Sam's compartment. It subsided on to the seat and became a woman. Grey woollen coat. Hair swept under a white cap marked with a red cross. Cheeks flushed, chest heaving. "Sorry," she gasped. "I thought I would miss the train."

Sam grunted, nodded, shifted his gaze back out of the window. Raindrops streamed diagonally across it, swept by the movement of the train.

The woman spoke again. "Sam?" She sounded puzzled. "Is it you?"

He jerked. Looked more closely. "Felicity!" The pulse in his temple pounded against the window. "Whatever are you doing here?"

She indicated her cap. "I'm a nurse. I'm doing my bit."

"But why here?" demanded Sam. "They made a hospital at Duncombe Park. You could do your bit there."

Felicity hung her head. "I wanted to get away."

"Get away?" Sam recalled home: birds building nests in the sanctuary of the walled garden. The town of honey-stone houses clustered under red tiled roofs. Velvety fields of tender green.

Trees growing strong and free, flowers blooming in peace, all under the shelter of purple table-top moors. "Why ever would you want to get away?"

Felicity leaned forward. Gently, she laid a finger on the back of Sam's hand. "Oh, Sam." The train jolted, and her hand slipped on to his thigh. Sam pulled away, his skin tingling. Felicity withdrew her hand. "You're a stretcher-bearer, aren't you?"

Sam kept his eyes lowered and nodded.

"I've nursed more stretcher bearers than soldiers."

Sam looked out of the window. The rain had stopped. The sun dropped below the clouds and shot a spear of light through a clump of trees. Sam watched the trees draw nearer. The trees drew level, then passed behind him, out of sight.

Felicity took a shuddering breath. She stood up. A shaft of sunlight illuminated her white cotton cap. The edges were frayed, battered by too much laundry. She crossed the carriage and sat down beside him.

Swiftly, he glanced at her. Her throat throbbed. Her cheeks were pink. Her breath was short, fast, delicate. He was sure she could hear his blood, thundering, pounding in his ears, throbbing in his thighs. Quickly, he turned his gaze out of the window again.

"Sam." Felicity's voice was just a breath. She put her hand into his. Her hand was small, the bones delicate. It trembled. It felt just like the chick Sam had rescued when it fell from the nest, light and shaking, as he cradled it in his hands and returned it to the nest.

Gently, Sam withdrew his hand.

Felicity withered before his eyes, caving in upon herself. Her right eye, the one he could see, slowly watered, glistening in the sunset. Her skin turned greyer than the wounded he had carried from no-man's-land. How could he cause so much injury to such a fragile creature? Sam felt like a monster. He took her hand back in his.

"Every day," Felicity's voice was barely a whisper. "Every day, I pay for not having the courage to defy Father."

One hand cradled Felicity's hand. Sam put his other hand into his pocket and grasped his pledge card. The sun sank below the horizon, extinguishing the light on Felicity. His heart pounded so strongly, he did not notice the jerk as the train stopped. The train convulsed again as their carriage began to move backwards.

"Where are we going?" asked Felicity.

"They're dividing the train. Front half to Amiens, rear half to the Front."

"Are we going the right way?"

"We're going to the Front." Sam's voice was flat, that of a doomed man.

The train bumped again as it began to crawl away. Felicity slipped on her seat. The varnish on the slats was peeling, revealing patches of bare wood, worn grey and stained.

Her lips were soft, moist, the colour of the rose Sam had given her that day, the day when she came home from school a lady, and Sam knew he was hers. Hers forever.

Gently, Sam withdrew his hand. "Felicity." He gripped his pledge card tight. "Tha's married."

The bird-like hand in his shook. "I'm there for a purpose, that's all. For serving dinners to his friends and," she shuddered again, "Begetting heirs."

A silver streak on her cheek glimmered in the twilight. Sam stared at a single star which shone in a pale green sky.

"I'm so lonely, Sam." She turned to him. "He talks more to his dog than he does to me."

Sam stared at the ruins of a forest. Broken stumps of once-noble trees clawed at a land drained of colour. The train gathered speed, plunging into the growing dark.

"Lonely?" Sam's voice was a croak. "Lonely isn't silence. Lonely is when you're the only man in a frenzy of war who remembers it's a sin to kill. Lonely is a Chapel where everyone's silence proclaims you a coward. Lonely is to be bombarded with feathers wherever you go."

The mutilated forest passed by, replaced by grey fields that stretched into unseen distance. Felicity ran a slender finger over the red cross on his armband.

"Stretcher-bearer." She wrapped her hands around his arm. "That's my Sam, you always save things. Remember when the chick fell out of the nest and you rescued it from the cat?" Dumbly, Sam nodded. He was as helpless now as the chick back then. "Bernard couldn't wait to kill Germans. He counted them like shooting grouse."

Unbidden, Sam saw the men he'd bandaged, desperately trying to staunch the red gush as their life ebbed away. He shuddered.

"We're going to die, Sam." Felicity gripped his arm. Sam shook his head. "Certainly, you're going to die."

She turned her face to him. Lifted herself higher. Her lips, so soft, brushed his, gentle as a warm breeze, sweet as summer fruit. Sam's heart thundered. His pledge card, signed after he drank the pub dry, was a crumpled ruin in his right hand. His left hand, crushed against Felicity's arm, trembled.

He flinched. "No!"

She fell from him, crushed as the egg the crow stole from the nest and dropped on to the stone path.

Sam looked out into the depths of the Flanders night. "I could never stop. I want you forever. Always have. Always will."

Regina Del Mare
Robert Stapleton
Copyright © 2018 Robert Stapleton
A work of fiction

Life in the small seaside town had never been happy for Erin. Ever since her parents had split up, she had been living alone in a small flat. Working at a boring factory, trying to avoid boring people who claimed to be her friends, Erin found life pointless. Aimless. Depression, self-harm, suicidal thoughts had all plagued her life in recent years. Whenever her Black Dog depression hung over her, Erin would wander down to the sea and stroll along the sand. With tears trickling down her face, she would look wistfully out at the sea. Perhaps out there she might find the solution to her despair. She longed to walk into the waves and end her sad life. But a spark of hope, or perhaps cowardice, always held her back.

One morning, as she was preparing to leave for work, Erin heard a letter land on her doormat.

She opened it, curious to know who had bothered to write to her. She couldn't imagine who it might be. Even when she opened it, she still couldn't make any sense of it.

The paper smelt of the sea. The writing, in an immature feminine hand, looked unfamiliar. The name at the bottom was unknown to her: Ayesha.

The letter invited Erin to meet Ayesha on the Chinese Steps at high tide on the following Saturday morning.

The Chinese Steps were a place where local people met. Lovers had their trysts. Smokers held conversations and coughed in harmony. The name came from a row of wrought iron decorations welded to the handrails. They'd been there for years.

Intrigued, Erin kept the appointment. As promised, a young woman was waiting there. She was dressed in a flowing robe which billowed out around her in the breeze.

'Hello, Erin.'

'Hi. You must be Ayesha.'

Ayesha had a slim, elfin figure. But her smile seemed to light up the gloom of that dull morning. 'I'm glad you could come.'

'How do you know me?'

'I've seen you every time you've come down here to weep.'

'You've seen me? But where were you?'

'No matter now,' said Ayesha. 'Erin, I would like you to be my bridesmaid.'

Erin's face lit up. 'You're getting married? How wonderful! But why me?'

'Because we are very much alike, you and I.'

'Are we?'

'Sure we are. What do you say?'

'It's a bit sudden. Okay, great. But when?'

'Now.'

'This very moment?'

'Say yes, Erin, and I'll take you to see my people.'

'Your people?'

Without a hint of embarrassment, Ayesha explained, 'I am what many of your people might call a mermaid.'

Erin laughed. 'I can't believe you're a mermaid. Where's your tail?'

'Tails are optional, just as legs are.'

'I'd be delighted to come with you.'

'It means going into the sea.'

'Oh.'

Ayesha took Erin by the hand and led her down the steps and into the water. Ayesha dived into the sea. Erin followed. The water felt cold.

'I can't' go any further,' moaned Erin. 'I'll drown.'

'No, you won't. Not with me here. Just breathe as normal.'

Erin dived below the surface and swam beside her new friend. It was now that she noticed Ayesha's legs had turned into a beautiful tail.

Swimming as well as she could and helped along by her friend's strong tail strokes, Erin descended into the depths of the sea. Even down there, the seabed was brilliant with undersea light. She saw people, sitting together in groups or moving around, busy with various tasks. Some had legs but others had tails like those of a dolphin.

And. Yes. Erin found she could both breathe and talk under water.

'Who are these people?'

'They are my people. Sea people. And they are here to celebrate my wedding.'

Ayesha led Erin to a large rock, on which was sitting a large merman with a splendid tail.

'This is Melchior,' said Ayesha. 'He'll take care of you while I get myself ready.'

Erin and Melchior fixed their eyes on each other. Melchior smiled. 'A human, I see.'

Erin nodded. She sat down when her insides melted and her knees felt wobbly. 'I'm Erin.'

'Hello, Erin,' he said. 'Tell me about yourself.'

'Nothing much to tell. I'm local but my life turned stale a long time ago.' When she had told him all of her story she felt she could, she looked up at him. 'Tell me about yourself, Melchior. I see you have a ring on your finger. Are you married?'

He laughed and shook his head.

'What's the design?'

'It's a trident. A three-pronged spear.'

'It's lovely. But what does it mean?'

'You really don't know?'

'Of course not. I'm new here.'

'It's a ring of authority. The signet ring of the King of the Oceans.'

'Wow! Are you the King?'

'Oh, no. Not me. That's my father.'

'You're a Prince, then.'

Erin felt her insides now swell with pride and joy as she relished the presence of this man of the oceans.

A more elderly merman took his place on another huge rock and called for everyone's attention.

'Come along, Erin,' said Ayesha. 'This is your big moment.'

Erin stood beside her friend and alongside another merman, Ayesha's betrothed. He looked handsome. A fitting complement to Ayesha.

Even before the ceremony had ended, shadows began to move slowly, moving between them and the daylight filtering down from above. The sea people cowered away and hid themselves in crevices in the coral and rock.

'It's the shark-boys,' said Ayesha. 'It's just like them to come along and spoil the celebrations.'

'Shark-boys? Are they dangerous?'

'Not really. Just a pain in the tail. But the real trouble is never far behind.'

Erin looked back at Melchior. Of all the mermen, he was the only one to show no fear. He stood upright and still, as if awaiting the arrival of some momentous event.

A huge dark object emerged from the murky depths. The cry went up, 'It's the Kraken!'

A creature with a huge body, powerful tentacles, enormous saucer-like eyes and an evil beak, pushed its way into the gathering, sweeping aside any who threatened to stand in its way.

'What does it want?' asked Erin.

'It wants to hurt and kill our people.'

'And me?'

'Yes, if it can get hold of you.'

It was now, as the Kraken's huge body smothered the wedding site, that Melchior stepped forward. 'Your business is with me, Kraken,' he cried, his voice booming.

'We have been enemies for a long time, Melchior,' growled the Kraken. 'Now I have the chance to finish you off, then I shall be the one to rule the seas.'

As Melchior stepped forward, without any form of protection, the Kraken reached out one of its powerful tentacles and wrapped it around the merman. Erin watched in horror as the monster squeezed the life out of the Prince and allowed his lifeless body to slump to the seabed.

Erin hurried over to the dead merman, knelt over him and wept. Here was a man she had fallen in love with at very first sight. Now her only chance of happiness had been snuffed out. The King of the Oceans would not be the only one to mourn his son. She kissed him on the mouth.

Then Erin turned to face the huge Kraken. 'Kill me, you evil monster,' she cried as she approached its cruel beak. 'I've nothing to live for now.'

The same tentacle that had killed Melchior now twisted

around her body.

As she took one final glance into the creature's evil eye, she recognised fear there. The animal's hold on Erin loosened and the Kraken backed away.

Erin looked round, and saw, standing on the wedding rock, the figure of Melchior himself. Alive. Fit. And now more powerful than ever. Holding a gigantic three-pronged trident.

'By the authority of the King of the Oceans, I command you to go back to your hole, you evil beast,' yelled Melchior.

In an instant, the Kraken and the shark-boys were gone.

Erin hurried to Melchior's side. 'I thought you were dead.'

'I was. But the Kraken was never going to win. Love is more powerful than death. Your love, Erin.'

Melchior wrapped his arm around her. 'Will you come with me and share my life beneath the seas?'

'I'd like that more than anything else in the world.'

'But first, you need a new body.'

'With a tail?'

'Whatever you choose, whenever you choose.'

Together, they swam away, to face their new life together.

'And don't forget to invite me to your wedding,' called out Ayesha.

Two days later, the body of a young woman was washed up on the seashore. The coroner suspected suicide whilst the balance of her mind was disturbed - but declared it misadventure.

Whatever you may make of this story, if ever you find yourself drinking coffee at a particular café displaying the mermaid logo, remember to raise your cup in silent salute to Erin, the Princess of the Oceans.

La Mauvaise Fenêtre
Antony Waller
Copyright © 2018 Antony Waller
A work of fiction

The small terrace of linen-workers' cottages on Rue D'Albert had seen better times. No longer were front steps scrubbed daily and kept clean. Louvred shutters, once so colourful in their vivid bright hues were now dull and listless, hanging precariously or missing altogether from many of the upstairs windows.

Where before, brightly painted front doors had stood open, sounds and smells from within drifting out on to the street, now they remained tightly shut, faded and peeling like a row of upended coffins leaning against a wall. Once a street of friendly neighbours, chattering housewives and playing children, the inhabitants now only spoke in hushed tones and minded their own business.

Each evening the menfolk employed in the local linen factory trudged homewards, heads down, their eyes focused on the dank pavement and grey cobbles of the street, anxious to reach the relative obscurity of home. Rarely did anyone linger over a glass of wine or pastis at the café at the top of the street.

Not since the arrival of the Germans.

Jean Martin clung to the shadows as dusk fell, waiting and watching whilst lights were lit and curtains drawn. It was the third time this week and his was an unfamiliar face on this street. He did not want to be stopped and questioned. He looked at his watch and then across at the empty window. No vase of flowers. He would give it five more minutes.

At number twenty-two, Francine Dubois was excited. She loved freesias, the bright colours, delicate petals and the heady and scented bouquets which would soon fill her room. They reminded her of times past, those idyllic Sundays when Alphonse would call for her at her parents' house, when she would open the door and see him standing there, looking awkward in his best clothes, one hand behind his back hiding a bunch of flowers, a bouquet of freshly picked freesias tied with a ribbon. Her mother would take them to arrange in a vase before giving the flowers pride of place in the centre of the table by the window in the front parlour.

She and Alphonse would go for a stroll through the apple orchards and afterwards would return for afternoon tea and cakes to a room filled with the fragrance of the fields. She hugged Alphonse, kissed him on the cheek and marvelled at how he had acquired a bunch of her favourite flowers. She snipped and shortened the stems, arranging them in her mother's vase before placing the vase in the window of their front room.

The man across the street smiled with satisfaction when he saw Francine Dubois place the flowers in the window. He stepped out from the shadows and into a dim pool of light cast by a rusting streetlamp. Dressed in a long dark leather coat and a wide-brimmed black fedora he raised one hand to his lips to blow shrilly on a whistle. In his other hand, down by his side, he held a pistol. The rhythmic tramp of jackboots on cobbles reverberated along the narrow street as a squad of soldiers came around the corner from one end of the street. From the other end an army truck skidded to a halt in front of the small terraced cottage.

Boots and rifle butts splintered the front door. There were shouts followed by screams, the crash of smashed crockery, a female voice crying out, sobbing, and the sound of breaking furniture. Then Alphonse and Francine Dubois were dragged through the broken doorway out on to the pavement, kicked and beaten where they lay before being unceremoniously dumped into the back of the truck. The soldiers climbed in after them and the truck lumbered off into the night, leaving the man in the leather coat alone on the pavement He picked his way through the shards of the door frame and entered the house. A minute later he reappeared, pushing the stem of a red freesia into his buttonhole. He sniffed at it, smiled and walked away.

Further up the street, Jean Martin had seen enough. He shrank further back into the shadows and closed his eyes. An eerie silence returned to Rue D'Albert and he left.

The following morning in the busy town square, people were going about their daily lives, trying to pretend it was business as usual. In the Café Centrale Jean Martin sat at a table toying with a teaspoon and an untouched espresso. He glanced up as a shadow flicked across the red and white checked tablecloth and a man clutching a corduroy cap slid into the vacant chair opposite.

"What happened last night, Jean?"

"The Gestapo were waiting. It was a trap, a set up; they were watching. Someone tipped them off but they made a mistake. The signal was a vase in the window containing daffodils, not freesias; daffodils. The Germans raided number 22, where Francine Dubois had placed a bunch of freesias in her window. The wrong flowers in the wrong window on the wrong day. Is that fate or just sheer bad luck? "

"Or our good fortune. Life can be so cruel sometimes, Jean."

Jean Martin bit his lip and said nothing.

The Listening Mouse
Cathy Lane
Copyright © 2018 Cathy Lane
A work of fiction

I am a mouse in moulded-metal ornamental form only. A black mouse.

I am not real. I am solid not soft to feel. I am not cuddly. I am cold but once held I warm up, as I do when I am in the hands of the someone who finds solace in the hushed stillness of the early hours, when there is no one else to hear or feel private thoughts. These thoughts are only shared with me. I am this person's confidante and because I am not real, I will never reveal all that is passed to me.

I am quiet, I have no voice, I cannot squeak, I just listen. My large ears are tuned to hear silent private whispers. My poise is that of one who waits and serves, my little paws held before me as if waiting to receive something private, and my tail is coiled for balance, and I wait and listen.

I was given as a gift by someone who is loved by the person who received me and is a token of that person's love in return. I am precious. I cannot be broken and I will never die. I will not run away. I am just here...I am near.

I have a place. I sit on the table beside the bed. Like a shadow just there. I am dark in the dark. I blend in but I can be found by a warm searching hand which clasps me, wrapping fingers around my body, and its warmth warms me and I listen. I have no heartbeat of my own but I can sense another's pulse beating and I listen. The words are not spoken out loud but are *thought* words, hopeful words, or words of anger and frustration, wishes and lamentations. I am the keeper of those thoughts. I am the silent receiver. I am held for as long as it takes until the fingers uncurl, rested, and the mind is filled with calmness.

Sometimes I am placed under the pillow, or sometimes back

in my dutiful place on the table but I am never far away. In the dark hours I am there.

A listening mouse called 'Shadow'.

Ghost
Diane Leake
Copyright © 2018 Diane Leake

Please leave
Let me mourn
My unrequited love
With chocolates and 'what ifs'.

Please go
No more your voice
To echo my failure
It's timbre ringing in my ears

Please! Please!
Release me
From the ghost in the mist
Who steals my thoughts
Day and night

Team Players
Jackie Fallows
Copyright © 2018 Jackie Fallows
A work of fiction

Marty's girlfriend Jade reflects with her best mate Becks on a recent important work meeting.

'Honestly Becks, I don't care what Sasha said at the big team briefing about us all pulling together. That's just a load of bollocks, and we all know it.'

'Except her.'

'Well, duh, of course all except her.'

'She thinks the sun shines out of the big boss's you-know-what.'

'She would, though, wouldn't she? She's sleeping with him.'

'She's never!'

'Saw her sneaking out of his room at half-past five this morning, didn't I? And she didn't have her clipboard.'

'What were you doing on the top floor corridor at that hour?'

'Wouldn't you like to know? Anyway, I've been thinking. There is a way we can make this place work properly.'

'Oh yeah? You been at the booze already?'

'No, I have not. Cheeky cow. Look, listen up. What if we workers get our own team together to get rid of Sasha?'

'Cool. How?'

'She's got that presentation to the Board next week, right? Well, I sneaked a peek at her notes for it, and I reckon I can get Marty to sabotage it. He's really good with computer stuff. What if I get him to substitute madam's presentation with one we all put together? Show the Board what it's like on the front line, as it were? You know, dealing with the freaks, the losers and the downright weird. Everyday stuff.'

'You mean like Donna and Mr Preston?'

'Exactly like Donna and Mr Preston.'

'That was good as the diplomatic corpse, if you ask me. Worth a banker's bonus, that was.'

'Good job I filmed it, then.'

'You never! What, on that new phone? Go on, let's see.'

'You can see it on our presentation, when Marty's got it sorted.'

'Cool. But I don't see how that's going to get rid of Sasha.'

'Ah, see, now we come to the clever bit. I've been doing a David Attenborough, filming animal behaviour.'

'I thought he just did the nattering.'

'Woteva. Anyway, on my phone, I've got some classic Sasha. You know, the alpha female thing? When she's being all Batwoman, and totally it's-a-good-job-I'm-always-here-to-save-you-from-yourselves-and-how-would-you-ever-manage-without-me?'

'Like when she was having a go at Katya for using the trouser press to flatten that air-bed when the bung got stuck? She was mega-mean that day. I thought Katya did really well. She had to do something with that stupid air-bed before the big boss saw it.'

'Exactly like her having a go at Katya. That was the best bit I filmed.'

'And she didn't see you?'

'Why would she? She was so up herself with super-smugness, she wouldn't have seen if the big boss had been stripping off in front of her.'

'Right, so you've got all this video on your phone. Now what?'

'We get Marty to edit it so the Board see Sasha having a go at Mr Preston instead of Katya. Right at the point where she's going on about customer satisfaction, and how professional we should always be.'

'Cool. Isn't it a bit short though?'

'Well, duh, that's not all of it, is it?'

'So how would I know? Go on, tell us. What else've you got?'

'That's where our team thing comes in.'

'Like, how?'

'Like, we act all flustered with the customers whenever Sasha's about.'

'We can't do that! She'd sack us on the spot!'

'So, we film ourselves acting it up in the staff-room, and

then ...'

'But ...'

'And then, we get Marty to make it look like that's what's happening.'

'Oh, right. So he cuts in bits of Sasha being her normal charming self as well?'

'Exactly. Then we finish up with the piece of resistance.'

'What, you mean we stand up to her?'

'No, Dumbo. The piece of resistance. You know, the grand finale. Donna's diplomatic corpse, but obviously with a different scumbag, not Mr Preston, and - wait for it - with Sasha clearly nowhere in sight. The clincher. Well, that and the film I took of her this morning coming out of the big boss's room in her silk kimono and matching slippers.'

The wintry sunset cast an eerie light over the little Norman church and the handful of mourners standing on the bleak hillside by the open grave

"We therefore commit her body to the ground...earth to earth...ashes to ashes...dust to dust..." the priest droned. He glanced across at the girl and was instantly touched by the rawness and beauty of her grief-stricken face. Her hair was black as a raven's wing, caught loosely in a ribbon of black lace at the nape of her neck; her sapphire-blue eyes brimming with unshed tears as they followed the coffin.

Florence Grainger shuddered as her mother's coffin was lowered into the dark earth. Her father roughly yanked her hand and deposited a cold clod of wet soil into it. She looked into his face for a trace of comfort - it afforded none. She crushed the cold sticky earth between her fingers before throwing it into the gaping hole. It landed with a heavy thud on the coffin lid concealing the brass lettering: *Esme Granger 1884 - 1922.*

Florence's mother, Esme Grainger, had celebrated her thirty-eighth birthday barely a month ago whilst attending Yarm Gypsy Fair. They were travelling north intending to camp within striking distance of Appleby in Westmorland for the ensuing winter months. And it was then Esme fell ill, dying quite unexpectedly in the rear of the bow-top wagon just prior to reaching the nearby village of Stoneygill, in whose graveyard she now lay buried.

Blood poisoning, the doctor said: septicaemia, due to a small cut on her hand that had become infected. Esme had developed a temperature and a high fever. Her daughter and husband suggested she rest in the back of the wagon for a few hours. But when they halted their journey to rest and water the horses, Florence had looked inside the back of the wagon only to discover her mother had died.

I'm so sorry Mother, Florence mouthed silently now, leaving you here... in this strange and lonely place. But I'll come back... and visit you... I promise, she vowed, gazing up to the heavens.

She felt the touch of a hand on her shoulder and turned to find the priest standing close behind her.

"What will you do now, my dear?" he enquired. His voice was soft and full of concern; the warmth in his eyes gave her a measure of welcome comfort.

"I...I'm not sure what I'll do," Florence replied hesitantly.

"Will you come back to the parsonage and have a bite to eat, please? My wife will be glad to - "

"Thank yer kindly for givin' my missus a decent burial - and for your invitation," Benny Grainger interrupted. He handed a thin roll of notes to the priest. "Me and my daughter have a fair way to go and it'll be dark soon. C'mon, let's away Florence," he said sharply.

The priest stood watching until the bow-top wagon disappeared down the road and out of view. There was something about the girl he couldn't quite put his finger on; something that had stirred an exaggerated concern in him. But it's too late now - they've left. And there was no way her father was going to hang around. The priest tried to shake off the uncomfortable feeling the man had imposed on him; and shivering, headed back to the warm cosiness of the parsonage as the first snow of winter settled on the footpath.

And, unbeknownst to Florence, she would be included in his prayers that night.

"Look sharp an' take them over to t'barn!" Benny Grainger growled impatiently. "I'll go and see if it's all right for us to stay here the night."

Florence jumped down from the wagon and led the horse into the barn and waited for her father's return. They had arrived only just in time for the snow was coming down thick and fast and blowing across the moor, causing deep drifts; the road they'd driven along was no longer visible.

Florence placed her hands on the warm chest of the horse

and buried her head in his neck. "It's all right, Ginger Dick, I'll soon have you fed and watered, lad," she said, hugging him.

"What d'yer think you're doing?" her father bawled, "I thought I told you to get that bloody horse seen to! Are you bloody deaf?"

She hadn't heard his approach and the flat of his hand struck her sharply across the back of her head, causing her to stumble. The pain was blinding, but she swiftly regained her balance and spun round to face him.

"Your mother's not around now to protect you. Yer an idle git an' you'll do as yer told from now on; an' I don't give me orders twice! D'you understand?"

His cold eyes blazed down into hers, and Florence, too stunned to reply, started work on Ginger Dick immediately. She relieved him of the heavy wet harness and quickly making a straw wisp she proceeded to rub him down briskly. Father's never liked me, she thought, tears flooding her eyes. What on earth will I do without mother here? He'll be hell to live with. Well, he's not going to beat me, she resolved in that moment. I'll leave first. I'm a good worker, 'specially with the horses. And since the war things have changed... maybe not so much in the travelling community... but women are doing men's work on farms and suchlike.

Florence finished grooming Ginger Dick then took the empty water-jack to fill at the pump in the farm yard. It was five in the evening and it had stopped snowing. The sky had cleared, allowing a full moon to emerge lighting up a snow-covered landscape. She turned up the collar of her worn tweed coat against the cold and trudged through the deep snow to where the pump was located. She looked up when the door of the farmhouse was flung open and a woman carrying a pail scurried over to the pump.

Florence took the empty pail and filled it for her.

"Thank yer kindly, girl," the woman said, pulling an ex-army great-coat tightly round her. "Come away in for have a cuppa an' get thissen warm lass - I've a grand fire goin' in the kitchen."

Florence hesitated for a moment, but the thought of a warm fire and a cup of tea were too much to resist. "Thank you, that'd be most welcome," she said. Then setting down the water-jack, she picked up the other woman's pail of water and carried it back to the house.

A blazing fire crackled in the grate of a shiny black-leaded range. The woman gestured to one of the spindle back chairs at the fireside before disappearing into the scullery. The woman returned with a plate of buttered tea loaf and poured tea from a teapot resting on the range before sitting down.

A log shifted in the grate producing a shower of sparks.

"Thank you, missus, it tastes lovely," Florence said, biting into the moist sweet loaf plastered with butter, "an' thanks for letting us take shelter in your barn."

"Oh, that's no bother to us. Now, tell me lass, how on earth do you manage to get through these harsh winters?" The woman frowned, shaking her head. "It's hard enough here for me and my husband - and that's with a solid roof over our 'eads!"

"Aw, you get used it, Missus," replied Florence, "'specially when folks are kindly - like yourselves."

"And yer mother? I couldn't help notice there was only you... and er, yer dad is it?"

"My mother died ...the other day. W... we buried her... this morning, at... Stoneygill." Florence's voice was thick with emotion and tears began to well in her eyes and clog in her throat.

Mary Dalby set her cup aside and reaching out took Florence's hand in her own. "Ah, I'm sorry lass, here." She handed her a clean white handkerchief from her pinafore pocket. "What's yer name? I can't keep calling you lass."

"Florence Grainger," Florence snuffled, wiping her eyes and blowing her nose.

"And I'm Mary Dalby, an' you can call me Mary, an' me 'usband's name's Arthur. He's just feeding up he shouldn't be too long. Stay and have a bit o' tea with us, love, eh? You'd be more than welcome."

"No, no I can't. My dad will be wondering where I've got to an'... an' sometimes he gets a bit angry."

Aye, I bet he does, thought Mary. She'd already concluded he was a mean looking man; and had she not seen Florence at the side of him when they drove into the yard, looking pale and tired, she'd have told him to keep moving. She and Arthur hadn't been blessed with children, but she couldn't complain, they'd been reasonably happy the last twenty years. Glancing across at Florence now, Mary wondered how that man had managed to sire such a pretty daughter; and assumed the girl's mother must have been a good-looking woman.

"Here, take the rest of this loaf with you I've more in the larder," Mary said, wrapping the remainder up in greaseproof paper.

"You're very kind, Mrs, thank you again."

"Think nowt of it lass, I mean, Florence. My, but it's a pretty name, Florence, it suits you." Mary smiled at her. "Now there's no need to be rushing off in this bad weather, love. Tell yer dad, I said it'll be all right for you to stay on a while, if you want to that is."

"Oh, thank you, I'd like that very much!" Florence beamed with delight at the prospect of staying on for a few days. "And in return I can help you if you like. I can turn me hand to most things; cooking, cleaning, washing..."

"You just come over in the morning," Mary interrupted, gently patting her arm, "an' I'll find summat for you to do. Be nice to have a bit of female company about the place; it can get lonely in these parts, particularly during these long hard winters we get up here.... Aye, I'll see you in the morning, Florence. Fetch that handkerchief back with you and I'll have a clean 'un for you."

Florence's heart soared as she made her way back to the barn. She liked Mary Dalby and it would be nice to spend a few hours in that nice warm house every day, away from *him!*

Benny Grainger eyed Florence suspiciously when she entered the wagon.

"Took yer bloody long enough to get some water!" he snapped, "an' what's that yer've got there?" He snatched the tea loaf out of her hands. "Ah, good... so you've got friendly with the farmer's wife, eh? Now that could be useful. What's she say? Does she want us gone in the mornin'?"

"No, Dad. She said we could stay, a...an' I can help her in the house in return for us stopping here."

"Not gonna pay yer anything for working? Bah, bloody cheek of some folk! Typical bloody gorgios taking advantage of us gypsies... thinking we 'ave to be grateful for any crumb they toss our way..."

"Well, at least we've got somewhere to stay through this bad weather and I don't mind helping out in the house - honest I don't. Please... please can we stay, it'll be Christmas soon!"

"Get summat cooked for me tea, never mind harpin' on about bloody Christmas!" he snarled, "I decide how long we stay 'ere for."

"What's the matter with you, Dad? What's wrong?" Florence was fed up of his shouting and bullying her; he'd changed. The coolness he'd displayed towards her in the past, had, these last few days, deteriorated into downright cruelty. "You've been nasty to me ever since Mother passed away - it's not my fault she's dead!"

"Well, now she's gone I don't have to pretend to like yer any more, do I?" His voice was low and menacing. "Cos I don't like you... I never have - it's all been a bloody sham; and when the time comes to leave here I'll be leaving on my own."

Florence gasped aloud, unable to believe her ears.

"Aye, that's shocked yer hasn't it?" A grim smile creased the corners of his mouth.

"W-what about me... Dad, d...don't you care?" Her voice held a tremor as she struggled to take in what he was saying. He didn't want her with him... Her own father didn't want her!

"Dad? Hah, that's a bloody joke. You can quit calling me Dad now your mother's dead, cos' *I'm* not yer father. Yer mother was carryin' you in her belly when I married her, an' that's why she married me; cos no bugger else would 'ave her. Soiled goods. 'Ad a fling with some gorgio she did, at Topcliffe Fair."

Benny Grainger raised his head; as his eyes examined her carefully he relished the pain in her face. "Yer ill-gotten - whatever yer breeding – an' it's no bloody concern of mine."

"What?" Florence felt physically winded and her hand shot up to her mouth to stem the sharp pain shooting through her. Her eyes were wide with horror as she stared in disbelief at the cruel man before her - a chill began to steel over her. What a nasty, ugly man, she thought, staring at the pinched features; his nose and cheeks reddened by a network of fine broken veins. It was as though she was seeing him for the very first time. And when a sudden unexpected realisation of this truth washed over her, she thanked God it wasn't his blood coursing through *her* veins. And then lowering her hand from her mouth, Florence started to laugh; quietly at first, and it wasn't long before her whole body began to shake with laughter.

"You think it's funny, do yer, your mother being nowt but a

whore?"

Florence stopped laughing. She glared into the face of the vile being standing before her. A man whom she now loathed and detested; a man with whom she wanted no connection with ever again as long as she breathed the breath of life.

Yes, he would be easy to forget. The sooner he was gone the better.

Garrett Ferrensby looked out of the drawing room window to the snow-whitened moorland - illuminated by a full moon in a darkening sky. A log shifted in the grate disturbing the Great Dane who'd been sleeping peacefully on the rug by the hearth. The dog jerked his head and glanced at his master. Garrett picked up a long iron poker and pushed the log back into the flames.

There was a tap on the door and a young girl entered.

"Mrs Baxter says I've to see if yer want the fire buildin' up an' the lamp lighting, sir," she said.

The girl's thick Yorkshire accent belied her delicate features. For there was nothing delicate about the folk born and raised on Hamer Moor; they were as tough as the sheep that roamed it and able to withstand whatever hardships life threw their way.

"No, *I do not* want the fire building up and I'm quite capable of lighting a lamp. Now you can go back and tell Mrs Baxter I am not completely useless!"

The girl, no longer taken aback at her master's rudeness, nodded, turned, and hurried from the room. The dog opened his eyes at the sound of his master's harsh tone; then seeing it was not directed at him, discharged a contented groan before closing his eyes again.

Garrett struggled to his feet with the aid of a walking stick and prodded the dog. "Move, move Bruno!" he griped. Bruno clambered to his feet and stretched before retreating to a safer distance to the other side of the fireplace. Garrett hobbled across the room with difficulty and lit the oil lamp. Then grimacing, made his way back and crumpled wearily into the chair.

The door opened with a simultaneous knock. Ivy Baxter blustered into the room. She stood before him, arms akimbo. Garrett stiffened and waited. His housekeeper was not only beginning to get on his nerves – but also getting out of hand and forgetting her station since his return from the war.

"Are you wanting rid of *all* my staff?" she demanded, "Because if you are you're going the right way about it!"

"Don't you talk to me in that manner! How dare you?"

Ivy Baxter ignored his counter blast. "I'll tell you how I dare, *sir*, 'cause no buggers going to come and work up here in the middle of nowhere if you keep shouting and biting their heads off. Now," Ivy added, her tone softening, "your dinner will be served in the dining room in fifteen minutes," she concluded before leaving the room.

Garrett stared blankly at the closed door. He'd taken his meals in the drawing room since he came back from the war.

What's got into the blasted woman? Damn her!

Garrett ran his hand down his thigh, allowing it to rest upon the damaged limb. Had it not been for that brilliant young surgeon, I'd have lost it, he thought, gently massaging his leg. He recalled the Belgian doctor, who thankfully, ignored his superior's advice to amputate the leg and saved it.

Most of Garrett's regiment had been killed; blown to smithereens that day at Passchendaele in October, 1917. Five years ago, now. Still, the graphic nightmares continued, and he would wake up sweating and crying in the middle of the night. In the recurring nightmare Garrett would be fighting his way through heavy, stinking sludge, where thirty days of heavy rain had converted the soil to mud so deep that men and horses drowned in it; nothing less than a grinding swampy slaughter.

He glanced at the clock on the mantelshelf, which read seven o'clock.

"Looks like Mrs Ivy Baxter means what she says, Bruno." At the mention of his name, the dog rose from the hearthrug.

"There you go now, sir, I'll put your stick where you can reach it." Ivy said. Her tone was gentle, like that of a mother speaking to her child. She smiled broadly at her employer as he made his way to the dining table.

"Grouse," she said, "shot on the moor last week; and poached pears for dessert. Enjoy yer meal, sir." Ivy quickly scanned the table ensuring everything was within easy reach before leaving.

"Ahem!" Garrett coughed, and Ivy stopped at the door. "Just a moment, please, Ivy."

"Yes, sir?"

"Thank you for... for all of this," he said, waving his fork over the table, "and, er, the young girl... tell her from me please... she's doing a grand job."

"Aye, I'll tell her. It's good to have you back in the dining room, sir."

Garrett looked around the huge room. He sat at the head of the table which seated twelve, twenty with the extensions inserted. At each end of the table stood silver candelabras, separated by a large ornate silver fruit dish in the centre. Dark, heavy Victorian furniture graced the sides of the room, and a strong smell of beeswax filled the air. He recalled the laughter that used to ring out in this room, years ago, before his parents had died ...and before the bloody God-awful war. His older brother, Robin, was married and living in London with his wife, Felicity. He rarely visited nowadays. But when he did, he would come to stay for a few days during the grouse shooting season; often accompanied by two or three colleagues longing to get away from London and its unremitting smog.

Robin had returned from the war physically and mentally well, seemingly unscathed by its horrors, unlike himself. And having taken up politics he was fast becoming a big noise at Westminster.

The next morning Garrett woke up feeling rested. It was the first night since arriving home from the war he'd managed to sleep through - undisturbed by the hideous nightmares. His leg felt stiff and sore as he hobbled without the aid of his stick to the bedroom window and drew back the heavy curtains.

Dawn was breaking.

The sun's weak ascent cast a watery glow across a landscape of vast barren moorland; moorland formed thousands of years ago when the ice sheet melted; and which rambled all the way to the east coast, gradually losing height along the way.

High Agra had been in the Ferrensby family for four generations. The estate, some twenty thousand acres in total, boasted one of the best grouse shoots in Yorkshire. The land was tenanted out to sheep farmers who lived in the tiny cottages dotted about the moors, scraping a meagre living from the harsh land as their ancestors had done before them. Many of the farmers were old; deprived of sons to carry on farming after them. The sons whose bodies lay buried in French soil, with the thousands of other young men who'd lost their lives; a loss echoed throughout Britain – nobody could avoid the impact of war.

All at once, his eyes hardened. They settled on a fold in the moor beyond the long drive and the main gates to where a tumble-down hovel, Hamer Bridge, crouched in the depression, interrupting his panoramic view.

Old Tom Pickles had owned the property. He had died more than six months ago and, as yet, there was no indication of a *for sale* sign. Only last week Garrett had paid a visit to his solicitor in Ryeburn, instructing them to make enquiries regarding the property but had not heard anything back from them. He craved ownership of the property, and who other but himself was the obvious buyer?

And after I've bought it, I'll damn well demolish it... it's a bloody eyesore! What the hell was father doing selling off land and a cottage - ripping the very heart out of High Agra? And to bloody old man Pickles? I can only assume father must have been a bit strapped for brass at the time...

Garrett straightened his back, bringing his attention back to the present moment. Looks like a fine day, he thought, scanning the clear blue sky.

"Come on, Bruno!" The dog jumped to attention, his tail beating madly. "It's about time I was back in the saddle, my friend, and *you* can accompany me. We'll ride into Ryeburn together, that should please Ivy Baxter – getting me out from under her feet."

Friday in Ryeburn was market day. People travelled from the neighbouring villages, assembling in the open square to sell their wares. Their voices rang out from beneath canvas-covered stalls crammed with home-made chutneys, jams, cheeses, butter, rabbit skins; anything they could barter with - or exchange for a few pence.

Garrett made his way to the Three Feathers Hotel where he liveried his horse. He then weaved his way through the busy market square to his solicitor.

"Mister Ferrensby, what a pleasant surprise. I didn't know you had an appointment? Is Mr Hatch expecting you?"

"No, Miss Brown, he's not. But, I happened to be in Ryeburn and hoped he would give me a few minutes of his valuable time. Ah, here's Clive now," Garrett glanced to where a tall, thin, cadaverous looking man emerged from the office.

Clive Hatch extended a bony white hand which Garrett shook. "Do you have five minutes, Clive, please? As you've probably already guessed I don't have an appointment."

The solicitor took out his pocket watch.

"Ah, it's almost lunch time, Miss Brown," Clive said to the middle-aged spinster who'd been with the firm for as long as Garrett could remember. Her pursed lips softened a little when the solicitor leaned towards her, affectionately resting his hand on her elbow. "I'll be back in an hour or so. Come, Garrett."

Clive Hatch wiped his mouth and dropped the napkin on the table. "I can't find out a damned thing about Hamer Bridge, Garrett, I'm afraid," he said, with a puzzled expression. "I've made enquiries for miles around: Thirsk, Northallerton, Malton, every town within thirty miles of here - and nothing! God only knows who's dealing with the man's estate. I take it that no sign has been put up at the property then?"

"No," replied Garrett, shaking his head, "and nobody's been to view the place either since the old boy died. The workers keep their eyes open for me; any comings or goings – but not a dickie bird. Well, thank you Clive, I'd better be making my way back. No, no, my pleasure," Garrett insisted taking out his wallet.

He paid the bill and pressed a shilling into the hand of the young waitress who'd attended their table. The waitress looked up and rewarded him with a wide smile on seeing the generous tip.

Garrett smiled back; the noisy chatter of the rest of the diners muting into the distance. All he was aware of was the smallness and softness of her hand and how it impacted greatly on his senses; that he didn't want to release his hold; he didn't want to lose the warm glow which spread unwittingly throughout his entire body. Nor did he want to relinquish the stirring sensation in his loins, something he hadn't experienced in a very long while. The girl blushed as he continued to quietly stare at her but

Garrett didn't care.

Most of those taking lunch in the hotel were well aware who Garrett Ferrensby was: his family was well-known and respected for miles around; the Ferrensby's were the local gentry. The townsfolk were also aware that the squire had sustained injuries during the war and that he didn't venture far from High Agra, so today would set their tongues wagging, especially those observing him now smiling down at the pretty young waitress. The room had fallen silent as the diners stopped eating and chattering and turned to look at him.

The solicitor coughed loudly.

"I'd better be getting back to the office," he said, dragging Garrett's attention away from the young waitress. "I'll let you know if I hear anything."

"Yes, do that, Clive." Garrett said, watching the waitress retreat to the safety of the kitchen - the glorious moment gone.

On leaving the hotel, Garrett was mindful of his faltering stride. His leg ached terribly because of the ride into town along with the strained effort of trying to hide his limp. But he didn't mind too much. What mattered most to him then was that he felt alive inside again. The desire to take that young waitress in his arms and crush her to him was proof enough for him.

There was a stiff breeze blowing across the moor as Garrett made his way home with Bruno running alongside his horse. A red-brown flash of a grouse rose from the snow-covered purple heather. It took flight with a deep whir from its strong wings, its plaintive call fading into the lonely distance. The cold wind whipped his face, but Garrett couldn't stop smiling to himself as he recalled the young waitress smiling her thanks at the tip he'd given her and he pondered her warm, soft young body. It had been a long time since he'd made love to a woman – too long.

"Something I must rectify, Bruno," he said to the loping dog. "Come on boy, we're almost home!"

The Machine
Robert Stapleton
Copyright © 2018 Robert Stapleton
A work of fiction

Yesterday I killed a man. If I told the police, they wouldn't believe me. And when I tell you, I can guarantee you won't believe me either.

It began when I met a man in a London pub. Personally, I blame that last pint, because by then he had grown a little too careless about what he told me.

He said his name was Gerald Powfoot and he was celebrating. Celebrating what? A tremendous success. A success unprecedented in the history of the world.

Leaning close to me, he said, 'Mr Daniels, I am an inventor. A genius.'

'Really? Tell me more.'

'I have just finished building a machine that will transport me anywhere I wish.'

'Yes,' I said. 'I know a taxi-driver who will do just that.'

He reached into his coat and took out a small rectangular plastic box. On the top was a red button and, beside it, a blue light which was flashing slowly on and off.

I looked up at him. 'What does that do?'

'It's a vital part of my machine, my invention. Half an hour ago I was sitting in the basement of my rented house. Then I pushed a few buttons and was immediately transported to this place.'

I shrugged. 'I have to admit, I didn't see you arrive.'

'I was transported.'

'So what?'

'Imagine the power such a machine can give to any man or woman who wanted to change the world.'

I couldn't imagine.

'You don't believe me?' said Powfoot. 'Then let me show you.'

Grinning, he handed me a card, giving his name and address.

'Meet me at this address tomorrow, after work, and I will show you.' He then picked up the black box and pressed the red button. Still grinning, he disappeared from view.

After another double scotch to steady my nerves, I considered the situation. I decided to take Powfoot up on his offer.

The following afternoon, yesterday, in fact, I called at the address on the card. I rang the intercom. The door buzzed and clicked open. Inside, I heard the voice I recognised.

'Come on in, Mr Daniels. I'm down in the cellar.'

I followed a flight of steps down into the basement. There I found a glass cubed box, approximately seven feet square, with an opening cut into the side. Powfoot was standing inside the cube.

'What on earth have you got here?' I asked.

'This is my TLS machine. Trans-location in Space.'

'Like the Tardis?'

'No. This is real life, Mr Daniels.'

'What does it do?'

'As you saw yesterday, it transports people from one place to another. Instantly.'

'But how?'

He laughed. 'Now I have your attention, let me show you. Come and join me inside.'

I stepped through the opening and entered the cube.

On the floor at the centre of the cube was a square of blue glass and, on the far side, a device like a musical keyboard.

'This is the Q-box,' said Powfoot, indicating the keyboard. 'As you can see, it has an LED screen, three knobs, a switch, a red button and a blue light.'

'I can see all that,' I told him.

'And yesterday you saw what it can do. It made me appear and disappear at will.'

'But you had another box with you.'

'That's right. My remote-control device.' He reached into a drawer on the side of the Q-box and took out the same device I had seen the previous evening.

'But how does it work?'

'Watch the LED screen.' He flicked on the switch and the screen glowed into life, displaying a detailed map of London. As he turned two of the knobs, I saw two lines move from the edges of the screen, until they intersected.

'There,' he told me. 'The moment I press the red button, whoever is standing on the blue square will be transported instantly to the position indicated on the screen.'

'Fascinating. And the other knob?'

'That determines the height above or depth below the surface.'

'I still don't believe it.'

'Then allow me to demonstrate.' He pointed towards the blue square. 'Please stand there, Mr Daniels.'

I did as I was told.

'Now, where would you like to go?'

'Why not the Ritz hotel?'

'Not very adventurous. But just as you wish.' He adjusted the two lines until they quite clearly intersected at a position indicating the Ritz.

'Now, take a firm hold of the remote-control, and when you want to return, simply press the red button.'

I took the remote-control and, clutching it tightly, watched Powfoot reach for the Q-box button. 'Ready?'

I nodded.

'Good luck.'

I saw him press the button, watched the blue lights on both the Q-box and the remote-control flash on and off.

The room vanished, and I found myself standing inside the foyer of the Ritz hotel.

I was amazed. I checked I still had the remote control in my hand and looked around. I was attracting disapproving glances. I was obviously not dressed for the occasion.

I decided to take something back with me, to prove I really had made the trip. I wandered around, picked up a menu and returned to the foyer. I held out the remote control and pressed the red button.

To the amazement of a member of staff standing close by, I disappeared and, to my own amazement, returned to the basement where Powfoot was waiting for me.

'Well?'

'Fascinating,' I told him. 'But what practical use can it be put to?'

'The possibilities are limited only by the imagination. It could transport an army behind enemy lines. It could even allow me to enter the vaults of the Tower of London and steal the Crown jewels. An assassin could infiltrate a building guarded by the most sensitive alarm system.'

'But you wouldn't do that.'

'Wouldn't I?'

A wild look entered Powfoot's eyes. I looked at the Q-box, and saw that he had already reset the coordinates - to the Palace of Westminster.

'Since I unwisely invited you here,' said Powfoot. 'You might as well be useful. Until now I have had to press the button myself and try to step quickly on to the blue square in time to leave, which hasn't always worked. Now I have you to press the button for me.'

'And if I refuse?'

He grinned at me and produced a small gun from beneath his jacket. 'Then I shall kill you. This machine has other settings. Some you can hardly imagine.'

'When will you go?'

'This instant.'

Powfoot took the remote-control and stepped on to to the blue square. 'Press the button, Mr Daniels.'

My mind raced with thoughts of what he might do, and how I might stop him.

'Press the button, Mr Daniels,' he repeated. 'If you value your life.'

I stepped to the Q-box and reached slowly for the button. With my other hand, in the instant before my finger pushed the button, I frantically twisted the coordinating knobs.

Powfoot disappeared.

I kept my eyes on the blue flashing light. A moment later, the Q-box exploded, showering the room with glass and metal debris, and starting a fire.

Half an hour later, the Fire Service had filled the basement with foam and buried whatever remained of the TLS machine.

But what had happed to Powfoot? I had altered the coordinates at random, so where had he ended up, and how would he take out his revenge upon me?

This morning, my newspaper carried a report of a man knocked down and killed by an underground train, on the tracks beneath Liverpool Street. The description fitted Powfoot. Dead. Together with an undischarged gun and a mysterious black box. I wondered if the powers-that-be would ever know how close they came to having an armed maniac running loose inside the Houses of Parliament.

And the blue flashing light? I've seen it. And it is still flashing.

Dragunov SVU
James H Jones
Copyright © 2018 James H Jones
A work of fiction

The lift doors opened at the seventh floor and there was Big Sam, as usual, on guard outside his boss's door. Time, and a bad diet, had not been kind to him. His little piggy eyes were lost in pale folds of flab. His shirt buttons were stretched to their absolute limits and he was badly in need of a new, much larger suit; preferably in a colour which didn't show the dandruff.

He struggled to his feet and blocked my way.

"Got any weapons on ya?" he said, stone-faced as ever. "Ya know the rules."

I placed my SIG Sauer on the small table at the side of the door, pushing aside a Coke can and a half-eaten Ginsters to make room.

"That all ya got?" he grunted. I nodded. "Go on in, he's expecting ya."

I pushed the door open. Freddie Stoker sat behind his enormous desk, swinging back and forth in his Mastermind chair. I swear, the little scrag-end chose his office furniture to compensate for his lack of inches. From the open picture window behind him came the sound of traffic seven storeys below.

"Ya blew it, kid," he said. "Ya shot the wrong guy."

"You what?" I was flabbergasted. "It was a clean shot. Straight through the driver's side window. And it definitely *was* the right guy. I saw him plain as day through the sights. Good as took his head off."

"Yeah, great shot from a thousand metres, I'll give you that," he said, waving a big fat stinking cigar at me. "And a nice touch, leaving the Russian rifle behind, the Drag-something. And how do I know all this? Because it's been on the news already, that's how. Which is how I also know ya shot his twin brother. Yer target was in the back seat."

"You never said anything about a twin brother," I said quietly, looking him square in the eye. "You told me the guy always drives himself, you said he never lets anyone else behind the wheel of his precious Cayenne. You never said anything about him being driven around by his own brother."

The snivelling little creep set me up, I thought, *he obviously knew about all this, all along*.

"Whatever," he said, still waving his stinking cigar. "Like I said, ya blew it, so if you want yer money, yer'd best get back out there and put it right."

"Oh, I'll put it right, all right," I said. I vaulted the desk and picked him up by his scrawny turkey neck, carried him, kicking and squirming, over to the big open window and chucked him through it.

When Big Sam came bursting through the door I shot him straight between the eyes with my silenced Glock 17. It was his own fault. He shouldn't have been so sloppy. He should have searched me properly.

"I sure as hell got the right window this time," I muttered to myself as I picked up the SIG and headed for the stairwell.

So, no money this time. Better that, though, than having those two goofballs shooting their mouths off and besmirching my hard-won reputation.

Ad hoc News
Antony Waller
Copyright © 2018 Antony Waller
A work of fiction

"Our special guest today is a Roman general and statesman, so a warm salutation and *'Salve'* to Julius Gaius Caesar. So, Julius Gaius, if I can make so bold, welcome home from your latest campaign in Asia Minor and please tell us all about it. Where did you go, what did you see and what did you get up to over those long months away?"

"*Veni, vidi, vici.*"

"Ha ha, very *'ad rem',* to the point. Seriously Julius, there must be a little more to your campaign. I'm sure your audience is dying to know."

"Well, no, that's about it really. One campaign is much like another. *'Audere est facere'*, to dare is to do, as we say in the military. You set off with the lads from Legio Decem; a few forced marches; a little sightseeing, getting to know the lie of the land; mingle with the natives; negotiate with their rulers, which on this occasion culminated in a bit of slash and bash and a battle at Zela. Then we split a few amphora of wine, had an impromptu bacchanalia, before a triumphant return home to the adulation of the plebs."

"Oh *'mea culpa'*, such modesty, Jules. There must have been one or two hairy moments, a few escapades and incidents you can share with us. You know, anecdotes from the edge of the world. You must have kept a diary or despatched the odd wax tablet or papyrus to Rome you can let us in on? Just between us, *'bona fide'*, it'll go no further."

"No. As I've already said. *'Ceteris paribus'*, all things being equal, it was all in a day's campaigning."

"Oh. Well you must have been showered with tributes, must have looted and taken treasures from conquered tribes, brought back captured chieftains in chains and cartloads of slaves for the glory of Rome?"

"Er ... *'ars gratia artis'*, art for art's sake, the usual trinkets, some gold for my own coffers, a couple of good horses. That's about it. The lads in the Legion laid waste to the odd settlement or two, got smashed and raised merry hell, as I said earlier, and generally subdued the populace leaving our *'Roma invicta'* stamp on society. Like I said, all in a day's campaigning."

"So, no new discoveries then. No exotic creatures, wild animals, foods and spices, drinks, customs, wonders of the world?"

"No, *'nihil novi'*, nothing new."

"Oh. So what's next for our glorious commander-in-chief? A Gallic charm offensive? Silencing the Germanic hordes? *'Pax Brittanica'?* Or something closer to home? Anything you'd like to tell your audience today, Jules?"

"No, I don't think so."

"So, back to work then, Roman nose to the grindstone, ha ha. No time in your schedule for a few weeks off; perhaps a well earned trip south to the Bay of Naples, a spot of R and R, chillaxing in Pompeii or Baia?"

"Well if you must know. I'm looking to further my political ambitions. *'Lacta est alea'*, the die is cast, as you might say, I'm crossing the Rubicon. As for you; you are the stench of a low-life latrine with the brains of a sleeping two-year-old. *'Vade retro me, Satana'*, get thee behind me, Satan. No, sod it. Here, you deserve this. Suck my gladius, *'Valete'*."

The Scream
Cathy Lane
Copyright © 2018 Cathy Lane
A work of fiction

The scream was inside her, squashed inside her chest like an alien wanting to get out. She wanted it out, she was desperate to release it. But she couldn't, not here in the flat where other people would hear it. Not at work where it would cause havoc and startled reactions. Not in the street where it would alarm people who would think she was mad...not anywhere she could think of.

It had lain there embedded, growing like a mould from all the built-up tension of the years, the episodes in her life where she had said nothing and hidden it away. An invisible pain, paracetamol-resistant, alcohol-resistant – well, maybe for a bit.

"Try talking it over," they say or "Get it off your chest," but none of these paths had resolved anything, not for her anyway. It was like waking up every morning with indigestion.

She imagined opening her mouth and letting it out so it could be free, so she could be free but she needed to be somewhere else, not here, not anywhere public. It had to be done in a place of solitude, no listening ears, no exclamations, no judgemental gestures. Not on a bridge, like in that painting in the gallery by some artist called Munch. No, not on a bridge with people watching, but that picture, that picture so simple, had visually expressed for her exactly how she felt, all scrunched up and wavy with the character's mouth open like a venting valve. She had bought a postcard of it and stuck it by her bed. She needed to do what that person was doing...just open her mouth and let it have its freedom so she could have hers.

It would have to be a very special place. It might be better at night - or dawn so she could be unburdened to face a new day. There must be somewhere. Her head searched, her heart searched...she pored over maps and places she remembered. Where had she been? Where had she felt comfortable? The ocean...the cove with the projected headland with its craggy rocks, its isolation...now she remembered. She had been there as a child on a family holiday, in a caravan. Devon. It was Devon, near Hartland Point.

It was time to go. She took two days off sick. Well she was sort of sick and this was a much-needed way to feel better.

It had taken a lot of planning and a lot of courage to come this far. But this was it. It was more remote than she remembered. Their caravan must have been parked somewhere else. A difficult track, very exposed. But definitely this was where she wanted to be.

Dawn was breaking, fragile, quiet, a strange place for a woman to be, on her own in a car waiting to expel her scream but it was just right. Quite alone...quite alone.

As the dawn's rays cast their mellow light she got out of the car and stood facing the sea, legs braced, chest out. She inhaled a deep, deep breath and opened her mouth like a trapdoor and SCREAMED. She didn't know she could be so loud. It disturbed the resting sea-birds and they, too, screamed as if in unison but they didn't reach her pitch, it was so high. The wind whisked her scream away like cream and left it cavorting amongst the waves who ate it up and tossed it around, swallowing it whole. It was gone, at last it was gone. She had emptied herself of her burden and her lungs collapsed like punctured balloons. Salvation, unburdened, revived. Life goes on.

It's a new day, it's a new day and she 'whooped' as she drove away.

Nobody Ever Notices the Servants
Robert Stapleton
Copyright © 2018 Robert Stapleton
A work of fiction

New Providence in the West Indies was a lawless place in the eighteenth century. A place where pirates and thieves mixed and conspired to steal from the wealthy, especially to plunder the rich ships that passed through the waters of the region.

One of these pirates was a man known as John Tewkesbury. He was captain of a ship called the *Hell-hound*.

After returning from a particularly successful series of raids, Tewkesbury called a meeting of like-minded seafarers, at the tavern called the *Blue Mermaid*, near the waterfront.

The gathering was to be select. The small assembly would take over the rear room of the inn, where they would be provided with food and as much wine as they could drink. The proprietor of the inn agreed and called in extra staff to help.

Becketty offered her services and was taken on to help serve these rough characters.

The men gathered early in the evening and, as usual, enjoyed more food and drink than was good for them. Or anyone, come to that. It was Becketty's job to make sure the men had as much wine as they wanted. And so, when every other servant had been excluded, she alone was left standing in one corner of the room, holding a large pitcher of wine, stepping forward whenever the mugs looked to be running dry.

Nobody ever notices the servants, she thought to herself.

Tewkesbury pushed aside his platter, wiped his mouth on the sleeve of his coat and looked around at his companions. All pirate captains, each one a leader of his own bloodthirsty crew.

'I bet you're wondering why I called you here tonight,' said Tewkesbury.

'Aye,' they replied in unison, nodding their heads.

'The truth is, I need your help in finding something special. Buried treasure.'

The others turned to each other with excited expressions.

'Together, we are some of the most determined men in the Caribbean,' said Tewkesbury. 'Black Jack Bengal here is the captain of the *Admiral Salisbury*. He and his crew are feared across the islands.'

Black Jack gave a broad grin, showing a few stumps of rotted teeth.

'Then we have Shanghai Pete, who has contacts amongst the honest traders of the West Indies. And makes good use of his knowledge to intercept their ships.'

'And long may they rot at the bottom of the ocean,' muttered Pete.

All drank deeply of their wine, and Becketty stepped forward to refill the mugs.

'That makes three of us in charge. The rest of you can rot in hell.'

Laughter filled the small room.

'But we got our problems, too.'

'Aye,' they called out.

'Willy McMasters.'

Boos erupted from the men.

'Aye, Willy is my enemy, and has been for many a year. And if you join me, he'll be your enemy as well.'

'He already is,' muttered Black Jack.

Tewkesbury leaned forwards across the table and drew the others into conspiratorial closeness. 'And rumour has it he's hanging around here somewhere.'

'So I've heard,' said Shanghai Pete. 'Together with that whore of his. She's bound to be close by, as well.'

Aye, closer than you think, thought Becketty.

'Now, listen here,' said Tewkesbury, taking a sheet of parchment from his pocket. 'I've got this here treasure map. Captured it from a trading ship we sank a few weeks back. But I needs your help to lift the treasure.'

Wide with wonder, all eyes stared at the parchment as Tewkesbury spread it out across the table top. It showed the map of an island.

'See, 'tis the island of New Dover. This here mark shows the place where the treasure is buried.' He looked around. 'Are you with me?'

'Aye,' they chorused. 'We're with you.'

'Then, to each of our captains, I will give a portion of the map.' He took out his knife and carefully sliced the map into three sections. 'Each one of these is essential to finding the treasure. So 'tis in your own interests to keep faith.'

All agreed to keep the faith, in the hope of sharing the hidden riches.

Becketty watched on as Tewkesbury handed a piece of the map to both Black Jack Bengal and Shanghai Pete.

'I will be in touch with each of you when we're ready to move.'

The pirates cheered, and drank each other's health.

Becketty stepped forward and refilled the mugs. As she tipped the wine into Tewkesbury's mug, she also tipped the contents of a small glass vial. Everyone was too drunk to notice.

As time passed, heads began to nod.

The first head to hit the table was Tewkesbury's.

Only Shanghai Pete stood up and staggered outside.

Becketty had to act quickly now. When the others also rested their heads on the table, she stepped up behind Tewkesbury, checked he was dead, removed his portion of the treasure map, and hid it in her clothing. Then she stepped up behind Black Jack's unconscious body, slipped the empty vial into the man's inside pocket, and removed his portion of the map. That was two of them. Just one more.

Moving quickly but quietly, Becketty followed Shanghai Pete outside into the sultry night air. Where had he gone?

Then she saw him, staggering along the quayside.

In the darkness, she crept up behind him. 'Shanghai Pete,' she whispered.

He looked round. 'Huh?'

'Tewkesbury wants to make sure you have your portion of the map.'

The pirate captain pushed his hand into his pocket and drew out his piece of the parchment. 'Of course I have,' he slurred.

'Perfect,' said Becketty, as she slid the blade of her knife between his ribs, plucked the map from his dying hand and allowed his body to tumble into the water of the harbour.

'Have you got them all?' came a voice from the darkness.

She turned. 'Aye. Every one of them.'

Willy McMasters emerged from the shadows and took her into his arms. 'And nobody can make any connection with us, my love?'

'Tewkesbury is dead. Black Jack will be found guilty of poisoning him. And Pete's body is now floating in the harbour.'

'And the treasure is ours for the taking.'

'Just goes to show,' she told him. 'Nobody ever notices the servants.'

DC McUseless
James H Jones
Copyright © 2018 James H Jones
A work of fiction

I bumped into David McDonald in the centre of Brighouse, one bright sunny morning in July 1977. I hadn't seen him for ten years, not since I'd left the police force in '67, leaving the salubrious Sowerby Bridge behind me forever.

He hadn't changed much. Still the same scrawny, underfed appearance. The same beaky nose. The same lank, mousey hair, maybe a little thinner on top. Still the same Glaswegian accent, although perhaps no longer requiring subtitles to follow the gist.

I can't say it was a pleasure to see him. I had never liked the obnoxious little prick, a view which, I remembered, was shared by all my colleagues, back in the day.

"Hey, Jack," he said. "Long time no see. What you up to these days? Where are you staying?"

"I'm an operations manager for Texaco," I said. "I scout around for possible new sites for filling stations." Puzzled at first, I remembered how, to a Scotsman, *staying* meant *living*, so I told him a little white lie. "And I live in Headingley."

"Wow! Texaco, eh? I bet that's lucrative," he said. "I expect they give you a decent car, as well, eh?

"Good enough," I said, recalling his savagely materialistic outlook on life. "A V6 Cortina. Texaco being an American company, it has to be either a Ford or a Vauxhall. So, what are you doing these days? You must be at least a Detective Inspector by now."

"No, no, I'm retired," he said, swelling, rather strangely I thought, with pride. "Did my twenty-five years and bailed out. I was a Detective Sergeant, so I came out with a decent enough pension. You should've stayed on, you know. You could be retiring as well, a few years from now."

"To do what, exactly?" I said. "Settle for some crap security job? Sorry, that was rude of me. I should ask, what are you doing now? Please don't tell me you're working for some security firm."

"Nothing," he said, beaming with self-satisfaction. "Like I told you, I'm retired."

That figures, I thought, *he was always an Olympic champion at doing absolutely nothing.*

"And how's your wife doing? Ella, right?" I asked, changing the subject.

"I've no idea," he said. "And I don't bloody care. She left me in 1970 and I haven't seen her since. The divorce came through in seventy-five. Good bloody riddance and good luck to her, wherever she may be."

We parted company and I strolled on, looking for a shop which would sell me a decent street map. I couldn't do my job without one. In 1977, Google Earth was not even a pipe-dream.

My mind drifted back to the sixties. I could still see McDonald, tearing through the main office like a tornado, causing a draught as he passed and leaving dust mites spiralling in his slipstream. He would invariably have a manila file tucked under his arm. Someone would say hello and he'd barely give them a glance, muttering things like, "Can't stop."

Nobby Clarke would say, "Prick."

Sergeant Briggs would shake his head, muttering, "Arsehole."

WPC Chambers would say, "Language, please!"

Inspector Wilson would express his opinion by loudly breaking wind in front of the fireplace.

"One of these days," my mate Roy would whisper, "One of his farts'll catch fire and blow straight back up his arse."

Then McDonald's colleague would roll up. The real detective, Tony Sanderson. Unshaven, hair long and unwashed. Dirty, ragged jacket and scruffy denim jeans. Shoes which had never seen polish. He was the one who got the work done. He'd spend his days in pubs and snooker halls, where no one knew he was a policeman and he would get to know what was really happening on the patch.

And he would always take the trouble to sit down with us uniforms and pass the time of day, have a cup of tea, dish out the cigarettes, share information. While upstairs, Toerag

McUseless would be feverishly busy doing absolutely nothing. Sweet Fanny Adams.

I remembered the evening David and Ella McDonald threw a party. I can't recall what the occasion might have been but I know most of us went. Not for him, of course, but for her. She was well-liked by all us lads. She was kind, quiet-spoken with a lovely lilting Edinburgh burr. None of us could figure out what the hell she was doing with David McShitbag.

Halfway through the evening, Ella and I met head-on in the doorway to the living room.

"Ah, just the man I wanted to see," she said and, reaching over my shoulder, she hit the light switch, plunging the room into darkness, and took me into her arms and kissed me.

It wasn't the longest kiss I'd ever experienced but it was certainly one of the most memorable, and not just because of the lipstick which I discovered later, smeared all over my collar.

After a few seconds – which seemed like forever to me – she flicked the light back on, managing to look as surprised and bemused as everyone else.

"Oh!" she exclaimed, a picture of innocence. "Must've been some sort of power surge or something."

Pushing the memories to the back of my mind, I finally managed to find the much-needed street map. I set off to do a decent day's work, driving round Brighouse and its surrounding areas, finding nothing suitable. In the end I decided I would have to come back the next day and dig a little deeper.

I arrived home in Harrogate about six o'clock. I was met by a loving wife, a bouncing cocker spaniel and a beautiful aroma of roast lamb.

"You'll never guess who I bumped into today," I said, when she'd finally let go of me.

"You're right, I won't, so tell me," she said.

"Your ex-husband," I said.

The Presence
Cathy Lane
Copyright © 2018 Cathy Lane
A work of fiction

There were lots of pre-wedding nerves about, all jingling and jangling together. She was nervous - well it was a big step to take. This day. A bit scary. All the fuss and bother.

Maria had been waiting in the wings, as it were, for them to make a decision. And now they had and she was going to a wedding - but not as the bride. Too late now, she had lost him to her sister. Sarah. Sarah the bright one, sparkly, fanciable. Her sister would never know how she, Maria, had been close to Malcolm. Extremely close. Malcolm the flirt, always eyeing up the girls. Not just flirting, a darn sight more than that. And Sarah, pretty, vivacious Sarah, in her arrogance so totally in denial of his philandering ways and oblivious to her own sister's jealousy.

Maria became aware of all the chitter-chatter going on all around her. She wasn't comfortable in herself. She felt so jealous, so cheated. Missing out. She wore a sort of floaty dress, terribly uncomfortable. It had been chosen for her, not by her. Just chosen. The dress made a sort of draught as she moved.

Now the time approached. People were assembling downstairs, spilling into the hallway, waiting for the cars. She had to go now. The bride was the centrepiece, not little miss invisible. Sarah wore her typically smug expression as she glided out to the waiting car. Their father with her to give her away. He limped badly since the accident and his left arm hung uselessly by his side, They'd said he'd been lucky to have survived.

Maria joined her mother in the second car, along with Auntie Carol. She felt subdued. Her mother, rather solemn-faced, did her best to ignore Auntie Carol's constant nattering.

"You must be so relieved, Paula, now this day has come, so pleased."

But her mother had one of her faces on and wiped her left eye with her hand.

"Weddings are very emotive, Paula, for mothers. Yours aren't off your hands yet. You'll see. I have only one now."

Auntie Paula went silent. It was a quiet drive to the church. We assembled, waiting to go in, but naturally I had to wait for *The Bloomin' Bride*.

There she came at last. Malcolm was already inside of course. I trailed in behind her. She was smiling that cocky smile of hers but not at me, she looked right through me. She glided down the aisle and I drifted behind her, like a servant. Halfway down the aisle I reached forward and pulled at her hair. Her pretty pleated strands fell apart. She jerked, losing her decorum and people gasped. Then somehow her veil just fell away - it was only pinned on - and the buttons on the back of her bodice un-popped, exposing her white lace bra with those little half-cups. Which lifted her boobs, making them look like great big bulging, quivering pink blancmanges.

She stood stock still. The music stopped and Malcolm turned around. The look on his face was amazing, and the vicar went white as a sheet, as if he'd seen a ghost.

You see, there are *some* advantages in the spirit world.

Revenge!

Woman in Red
J Severn
Copyright © 2018 J Severn
J Severn is a pen name of James H Jones

"Are you ready to order?" the waiter said,
To the plug-ugly man and the woman in red.
"Yes, my good man, I'm ready and able,"
Said the smug-faced fatso at the table.
"For starters, spaghetti with garlic bread,
No, wait, I'll have the paté instead,

"Then sirloin steak, nice and bloody and lean,
And tell the chef he's not to be mean
When he's dishing out the old French fries,
And make sure the mushrooms are a decent size,
And I'll have two portions of refried beans."
The woman in red sat still and serene.

"And bring some dips, mayonnaise and chilli
For dipping m'chips in, and don't be silly
By bringing 'em in those tiny pots,
Bring 'em in bowls - and bring me lots,
And I'll 'ave a big dish of piccalilli.
And you can cancel the paté, I'll 'ave the fusilli."

The waiter turned to the woman in red,
"And what would Madam like?" he said,
"She'll 'ave same as me," the man interjected,
"She can't disagree with what I've selected.
And don't go forgetting my garlic bread."
The woman in red quietly hung her head.

"Have you chosen a wine, Sir?" the waiter said,
"Yes," said the man, "I'll have the house red."
"And for Madam?" said the waiter, tongue in cheek,
But again, she wasn't allowed to speak.
"She'll 'ave same as me, lad, just like I said.
Best make it three bottles of red."

"Enough!" cried the woman. "I've something to say,
You've clearly forgotten it's Valentine's Day,
And you know I never eat meat, you swine,
You can stick your red wine where the sun don't shine.
I'm sick and tired of your bullying ways,
I'll choose my own food - and I'll drink the rosé."

To Lay with You Again
Diane Leake
Copyright © 2018 Diane Leake
A work of fiction

I knew it was you. That gait. The slight dip to your right, courtesy of a car that sent you flying from your bike like a bird. The biker's jacket may have morphed into a leather carcoat and the faded second-skin Levis into straight-leg jeans, but your pale blond mane still shimmered like precious metals, though it no longer caressed your shoulders. At least your fear of going bald had not been realised.

How I longed to walk up to you, tap you on the shoulder and smile into your disbelieving green eyes.

Instead I wait...

And I question. Has the time come? Have the years slipped away? Dare I let you see the person I've become? The old woman with lines where once peachy plumpness existed, the slow walk where once there was purpose and enthusiasm. I want – no, I need – to see those beautiful emeralds burn with desire again. No pity. No disgust.

So, I wait...

Every Monday morning at eleven-thirty I stand in the same place, hidden behind the foliage at the entrance to the river walk.

Selfish it may be, but I'm hoping you're single. Not that I want you to have suffered the pain of loss. I want you to be free to want me again. Are you? Could you? Will you? My heart pounds and my guts churn. After forty-three years desire still runs strong.

I want to lie sated with you, legs entwined, my head on your chest to listen to the silence of our love, same as I used to. I want to feel again the ecstasy of love's freedom, security, rawness and gentility.

So I wait...

From the back I can't see your expression, but some days I

notice a slight slump to your shoulders. Are you unhappy? In pain? Are you thinking of me? Do you miss me? When sleep hides from you do you remember our love, our laughter, our lust? Or do you focus on the pain we caused each other?

And it was pain. At least for me. Though I'm sure you must have felt that deep searing, as though your guts were ripping apart to join your throat.

We were wrong, both of us. We were wrong. Yet, maybe it was Lady Fate intervening, hand raised, halting us. All I know is that I thought I'd go mad. I did go mad, saluting oblivion with Guinness and whisky. Oh God, how I loved you.

I should have told you the men I paraded before you were merely cloaks to hide my love. Things to be worn and cast off. A bitch? Yes. But I was desperate. But not desperate enough to pour my soul into your hands. I couldn't be certain you wouldn't let it slip through your fingers.

So I wait...

Your shoulders are low today, as though empathising with the grey morning. And though my heart beats like a traction engine in my ears, I know I have to do it. I have to know.

Keeping my head down and my hand in my bag as though searching for something, while praying my voice and eyes won't betray me, I limp at top speed and nudge you in the back. As you turn I look up.

'Jamie?'

'Paula?'

The emeralds glow. I am home.

A Thearsby Story
Thearsby is a fictional North Yorkshire market town, subject of
an ongoing group project to write a serial drama or 'soap'

Mid-morning, Jane tugs on her mauve jacket, sets off across town and calls in at the local Costa Coffee. Tilly is sitting in the window, gazing aimlessly out at the morning market scene. Jane collects a cup of coffee from the counter and sits down beside her: 'Hello, Tilly.'

Tilly looks up: 'Oh, hi there, Jane. What are you doing this morning?'

Jane shrugs: 'Not much. How about you?'

Tilly: 'Daydreaming. Wondering what I would do with the money if I won the lottery.'

Jane: 'Which lottery are you thinking of? There are so many nowadays.'

Tilly: 'The latest one, of course. The Thearsby Community Lottery.'

Jane: 'Oh, that thing. It's in aid of the town recreation budget, isn't it?'

Tilly: 'Yeah. And also in aid of whoever wins it.'

Jane: 'But it's a lottery. Nothing but pure luck.'

Tilly: 'Well, not quite. You see, Jane, you have to pick a series of six numbers and write them on the card they give you.' She takes a card from her bag and waves it at Jane.

Jane: 'Is that one of these new tickets, then?'

Tilly: 'Oh, yes. Worth a bomb to the winner.'

Jane: 'I told you. It's pure luck.'

Tilly: 'But not with a little help from your friends.'

Jane: 'What help? What friends?'

Tilly leans forward, conspiratorially: 'My goldfish is psychic.'

Jane laughs: 'Your goldfish?'

Tilly: 'Sure. It predicted the winner of the Grand National last year.'

Jane: 'Shortly before the poor fish died.'

Tilly: 'Doesn't matter. Psychic is psychic, even from beyond the grave. Anyway, I've got a new fish now.'

Jane: 'That's nuts.'

Tilly: 'Is it?'

Jane: 'Prove it.'

Tilly: 'Okay, I will. Finish your drink and come with me.'

The two girls make their way across the square, towards the flat where Tilly lives with Jacob.

Tilly: 'It's okay. He's out. It's market day.'

As they come inside, Jane stands with her arms akimbo: 'Well, where is this miraculous psychic goldfish of yours?'

Tilly is already standing in front of the small tank, gazing at the goldfish swimming lazily around inside its glass home. Jane joins her, and they both look in at the fish.

Tilly: 'We sometimes try it on the football results. It got the Liverpool and Newcastle games right last weekend.'

Jane: 'Wow. And you think it can do the same with this lottery thing?'

Tilly: 'Only one way to prove me wrong.' She takes the lottery card out of her bag again, picks up a stubby pencil and turns to the fish-bowl.

Jane looks at Tilly, her mouth as open as that of the fish.

Tilly: 'So, we need six numbers.'

Jane: 'Is that all?'

Tilly: 'Go on, start counting.'

Jane begins to count. 'One, two three ...' The fish gives a wiggle of its tail and darts away to the far side of the tank.

Tilly: 'That's our first number, then. Three.'

As they continue, Jane becomes quickly drawn into the excitement as the fish chooses another five numbers.

Jane: 'Fascinating. And you really think it'll work? That you'll win?'

Tilly: 'Bound to. Go halves with me on the cost of the ticket, and we'll both double our money, at least.'

Vernon
Cathy Lane
Copyright © 2018 Cathy Lane
A work of fiction

Vernon wasn't popular, well vermin never are
And he knew he wasn't welcome at the farm where he resided
Down the end of Back End Bar.
Vernon roamed there quite freely, stealthy and quick
And the cat they employed to catch him was, quite frankly, thick.
So Vernon was free-range like the chickens in the yard
And there was plenty of grub about so living wasn't hard.
Well actually he had had a few close shaves
When the farmer nearly caught him underneath the bales of hay
But Vernon had shot out quickly and safely got away.
And though the farmer had a shotgun he was getting on a bit
So actually 'aiming' it he appeared to have lost the knack
So Vernon wasn't worried about the threat of that.
He'd had some near misses in the cow pen foraging about
Cos a cow nearly got him with its foot and gave him quite a clout.
But never mind all that, living here was swell,
There was lots of grub about and female rats as well.
In fact he had a family of seventeen – His own ratty-type
'hareem'.
Now Vernon was becoming a little over-confident, so the day was
bound to come
When he was tempted by a tasty morsel just inside the old barn
door.
It was something different and had not been there before.
Vernon was always listening wherever he might be for any danger
that may be evident
But his nasal senses were attracted by this rather sumptuous
element.

He twitched his nose and whiskers just to test the air and then he thought he'd take a little bite.

Well it tasted really good so he gorged upon this unexpected treat with great foolish delight.

You see he didn't know about rat poison it didn't shoot or bite,

It didn't have claws that could trap you it was as silent as the night –

So poor Vernon had lost his stealth and poise

Because through his misdemeanour he hadn't heard any unusual noise

.

Friendly Warning (Oxymoron)
James H Jones
Copyright © 2014 James H Jones
A work of fiction

When I began writing this, the time/date in the bottom corner of my laptop screen read 08:08 AM 17-Nov-13. It was Sunday morning.

I write every Sunday, working on my latest novel, or on a short story for my writing group, Little Bretton Writers, but this was exceptionally early for me. Especially considering how just a few hours prior, any thought of writing this particular story was far from my mind.

But after having lain awake for the entire night, watching the hands of the clock creep round, churning things over in my mind, finally, about five a.m., I came to a decision. And made a resolution.

I decided I would write the story, no matter how personally distressing it might be.

I resolved that come Monday morning, I would lodge an official complaint against two heavy-handed and incompetent police officers.

Let me be clear. This story is true. No names have been changed to protect the innocent. I am the 'innocent' in this story, after all.

If you think me foolhardy, remember this. It isn't slander or libel if you are telling the truth. Perhaps it may serve you best if you regard this not so much as a short story but rather as a clinical record of events. Like a witness statement, perhaps.

To paint the picture properly, we need to go back to February 2013, when Samantha and I first moved to our new home in the quaint old market town of Little Bretton. A small town. The clue, as they say, is in the name.

A lovely, spacious, well-appointed house, on a nice, quiet

residential estate. A short walk into town and, the main reason for the move, our daughter and her family just around the corner, so now they had readymade babysitters, a minute's walk away. Ideal. Great neighbours, too. Paradise. Ideal for two writers.

We familiarised ourselves with the town. We joined the local writing group, Little Bretton Writers. I began work on my third novel, an adult ghost story.

I established a morning routine. Buy our papers from Millers newsagents in the market place. Occasionally, if anything was needed at home, nip to Asda.

So you get the picture: Millers every morning, Asda some mornings.

Sometimes - I say again, *sometimes* – I would see a woman from further up our estate, who rode a bike into town. *Sometimes* I'd see her as I was going to my car, *sometimes* near Millers, *sometimes* at Asda, and would say 'good morning', like you do.

She stood out, this woman. The bike was far too big for her, and she was a bit unsteady. Not to be unkind, but she was a good age, and I thought she looked unsafe. And, forgive me, bloody comical.

One morning, not long after our move, she was outside Millers and I said something like, "Lady on a bicycle." Which elicited a laugh.

She told me her name, Janet. She knew we had moved into 'Gena's old house'. I also learned she had undergone a hip replacement. Not something I needed to know, particularly, but it explained the dodgy cycling.

A few days later, we bumped into each other in Asda, where she proudly told me that she made jam – or was it lemon curd? - and promised to give me a jar out of her next batch. I responded politely, secretly hoping she would forget all about the jam/lemon curd offer.

Those were the only two chats of any length I can recall, and they happened back in the February, or early March. From then on we exchanged nothing more than the usual meaningless stuff whenever we passed. Like, 'how ya doing?', or 'nice to see you', or 'good morning'. Always pleasant, trivial two-way exchanges. And never more than twice in any one week.

The last occasion before I had cause to begin writing this story was Friday morning, 15 November, 2013. It was bucketing down. Absolute cats and dogs. As our paths crossed, me on my way out of Asda, her on her way in, looking like a drowned rat, I made some inane remark about it not being good weather for cycling. Yes, I know, such finely-honed wit.

Neither of us was stopping. She, in fact, kept her head down and muttered something unintelligible as we passed. A bit rude, I thought, but dismissed it. Life's too short, and all that. And it was chucking it down.

So, Saturday, 16 November. Sam and I did our weekly Aldi and Asda run, as usual. Later, we had the granddaughters for a few hours. I sat at my laptop, trying to decide between working on my novel, or writing my next story for Little Bretton Writers. We meet every fortnight and set ourselves homework, to write a story on a given theme, which we read out at the next meeting.

Now here's the really weird part. The theme we had decided upon on the Tuesday evening was 'stalker'. I sat there, early Saturday afternoon thinking, *this is a tricky one.* I was having trouble, you see, coming up with a suitable storyline. I was well out of my comfort zone with this one. Then, lo and behold, the story was dropped right into my lap. Not one that I would ever have chosen, mind.

There came a knock at the door. Sam answered it and the next I knew she was telling me there were two police officers wanting to talk to me.

"What do they want you for?" she asked, naturally enough.

"I have no idea," I replied. But I soon found out.

Two of them. A man and a woman. Young, of course – aren't they all? Full uniforms, his somewhat scruffy, his boots badly in need of a polish. A Ford Transit police van was parked halfway on the pavement, right in front of my house. You could almost hear the neighbours' net curtains twitching.

"Do you know a woman named Janet Godfrey?" asked the man, after first establishing that I was actually Michael Forrest.

"I know *a* Janet," I replied. "Rides a bike, lives further up the estate. Is she all right? Has she had an accident?"

"She has complained that you are stalking her," he announced, which stunned me. Understatement. Flabbergasted would be a better word. Gobsmacked, even.

Apparently, she alleged I was 'always there', wherever she

went. I assumed 'there' meant Millers and Asda, as I didn't go anywhere else much in town and certainly never came across her elsewhere. I also had to assume that, in her twisted mind, once or twice a week had somehow become 'always', and exchanging banal neighbourly courtesies amounted to stalking.

Bloody silly. Like I said, it's a small town. You see the same people almost every day and, being in Yorkshire, most people say 'good morning' in passing.

She'd told them she was convinced I was trying to get to know her better, whatever the bloody hell that's supposed to mean. Dear God, you should have seen this woman. At least seventy, and a face like a bag of spanners. Inappropriately dyed black hair. Not to mention the burgeoning bald patch. So I won't.

What I will mention is the stunning raven-haired beauty who had answered the door to these two clods. Surely the sight of my gorgeous Samantha should have set alarm bells ringing, even in their dull brains. I mean, what would any man want with a wizened old bat like Janet Godfrey when he had such a beautiful, talented wife at home?

My protestations were cut short.

"It's just a friendly warning at this stage, Sir," said the male officer. "Just to tell you not to speak to her, to keep your distance."

Well, that got my hackles up, let me tell you. I told them I would not accept their so-called *friendly warning*, because I had done absolutely nothing to warrant being given any warning, of any kind, friendly or otherwise.

I was told, by both of them, that they were just doing their job. They repeated the 'friendly warning' crap. It was blatantly obvious, they had only one, firmly-fixed agenda in mind. That *doing their job* entailed no more than giving the 'stalker' a *friendly warning.*

They made no attempt whatsoever to establish if the silly woman's claims had any substance, or were simply imagined, frivolous, or even, maybe, downright malicious.

So I suggested, politely but firmly, they should simply go away. They were talking absolutely unsubstantiated nonsense and I had nothing further to say to them.

"We've told you, Sir," said the male officer, in a deliberately measured, eyeball-to-eyeball manner. "It's a friendly warning. We could quite easily be taking statements and arresting you. If you've done nothing wrong, why are you being so defensive?"

Did you get that? Priceless. *If I'm innocent, why am I protesting my innocence?* The lad should be in politics. He certainly shouldn't be administering the law. Their whole demeanour was intimidating, the arrest comment was delivered in a manner which I found threatening and deeply offensive. I was, quite clearly, 'Guilty Until Proven Innocent', and said as much. Never a moment's thought for my side of the story.

The Ice-Maiden fixed me with a beady stare and repeated the nonsense about them *just doing their job*, and it being a *friendly warning*. I'm no mind-reader, but I could read hers, loud and clear. Friendly was not a word I would have chosen. Contemptuous, on the other hand, would have been right on the button.

The young man repeated his threat of arrest, then asked for my date of birth, which I thought irrelevant, but they weren't about to leave without this crucial information. For the record, 29 November 1961.

I found the entire incident intimidating and threatening. As for their oft-repeated claim to be *only doing their job*, let me tell you, they had only done half of it.

They had taken as gospel the fevered imaginings of a deluded old woman, without question. They had completely failed to hear the other side of the story, choosing rather to brand me as a stalker without any further enquiries.

I was so shaken, I didn't even think to take their details. But I did get them the following day: He was PC Andrews, she PC Martin.

The entire conversation took place outside my door. Like I said, our granddaughters were in the house.

There was a fleeting moment when I thought I might be dreaming, that I had nodded off in the middle of trying to think up a 'stalker' story. But no, this was disturbingly real.

Fortunately, Sam saw the whole affair as nothing short of ridiculous. She knows me better, you see. Thirty years is long enough to get to know anyone thoroughly. And she knew the woman concerned. Well, was aware of her, at least. It would be ungentlemanly to record her opinion of the woman here, because she expressed it in terms much stronger than mine. I leave it to your imagination. Suffice it to say, she was furious.

We discussed it. She thought it best not to react and, initially, I agreed. But then she began to worry about what damage this silly woman might be doing, if she was spreading her malice around the estate. So I decided to sleep on it. If only.

So, on Sunday morning I wrote the story so far, while it was still fresh, knowing there would be more to follow. I determined to use real names. Like I said, when you're telling the truth, it isn't slander or libel.

As for Ms Godfrey. I never would have spoken to her at all, if I had known how being neighbourly was, in her tiny mind, an offence.

It isn't of course, but what *is* an offence, is wasting police time.

The next morning, Monday, 18 November, 2013, I lodged an official complaint against the two officers, with the duty sergeant at Northallerton, John Simons. A satisfying interview. He believed me. Why wouldn't he?

Subsequently, the two officers were disciplined. Ms Godfrey received a *friendly warning*, from the good sergeant himself, for wasting police time, and was cautioned not to spread any of her slander around the neighbourhood. Although, it was probably too late.

I never again so much as glanced at Janet Godfrey.

Eight months later, 15 July, 2014, Ms Godfrey was killed in a hit-and-run accident, both her body and her bicycle left broken and mangled on the road into town. We heard about it when we got back from our two-weeks holiday with our son and his family in Torquay.

Tragic. They never did catch the culprit.

We were questioned by the police, extensively, but were of no help to them, having been away at the time. They were clearly suspicious, though, and made a point of checking our alibi thoroughly.

Somehow, you see, they had made the connection between Samantha Forrest, best-selling writer of gritty northern crime thrillers, and her father, my father-in-law, who just happens to be Eddie 'Chainsaw' McLeod, notorious Manchester crime overlord.

They dropped the enquiry soon enough. If I was a betting man, I'd lay odds their Manchester colleagues will have advised them not to rattle Eddie McLeod's cage. A few of their officers had mysteriously disappeared over the years. Those who had mistakenly failed to realise just how untouchable our Eddie was. And how he always wreaked swift revenge upon his enemies, crooks and police officers alike.

Getting on a bit, now, is our Eddie, but you still wouldn't want to cross him. He's very much what they call a 'connected man'. And extremely protective of his family. Especially his beloved daughter. And her husband, naturally, who also knows better than to ever do anything to upset him.

The Seals
Robert Stapleton
Copyright © 2018 Robert Stapleton
A work of fiction

It had been a hard year for Andrew. His work in London had been demanding, stressful and lacking the buzz it once gave him. He needed a break and decided to visit his aunt in Orkney. The journey north took several hours. Train to Edinburgh. A flight to Kirkwall. And a short boat trip, through rain and cloud, bringing him finally to the island where his aunt's whitewashed house stood, overlooking the cold, grey ocean.

'We take each day as it comes,' Aunt Meg told him. 'But it's autumn now, so we have to put up with whatever nature sends us, here in the Orkney Islands.'

The first morning he woke up in his aunt's house, Andrew found the sky had cleared. From the window of the guest room, he looked out across the island's typically short springy grass, towards the now blue ocean beyond. A place of beauty, serenity and perhaps even magic. He wanted to explore.

'You'll have to watch out for the seals,' said Aunt Meg. 'Treat them kindly, mind, or they'll remember and bring their revenge upon you.'

Andrew smiled. He had met his aunt only a few times in his life and she always talked the same way. Of ancient folklore, superstitions and tales of the supernatural. He decided to wander down to the beach, to see the ocean, to feel the gentle breeze and to savour the sea air.

He found the beach easily enough and wandered slowly along the foreshore. Before long, he came across the seals. A colony of grey seals, many basking lazily on the hard, grey rocks or on the soft white sand. Then he heard a strange, unearthly sound. Arising from the seal colony itself.

'They're in good voice today.'

He turned around and found himself looking at a strange but

beautiful young woman.

'Who?'

'Why, the seals, of course. They're singing. Can't you hear them?'

'Is that what it is?'

'They often sing like this. But today is special. The autumnal equinox, you know.'

'Is that special?'

'Sure, it is. It's a magical time for seals.' She chuckled. 'Come and meet them, Andrew.'

'You know my name?'

'Of course.'

'My aunt told you.'

'No need.'

'And your name?'

'I'm Rona.'

As Rona led the way, Andrew noticed she wore a robe of thin spider's web fabric, which blew about her in the gentle breeze. The seals relaxed when they saw Rona approaching. In her presence, some of the seals even allowed Andrew to stroke their dog-like heads.

Andrew looked up at his new friend. 'Do you live around here?'

'Oh, yes. Right here.'

'How do you mean?'

She cocked her head and smiled. 'Would you like to come for a swim, Andrew?'

'I've nothing to wear.'

'Don't worry. The seals are a broadminded bunch.'

Rona swam like a fish, leaving Andrew to struggle in her wake. They laughed. They had fun. They enjoyed each other's company. Back on land, Andrew dried himself with his shirt and was surprised but rather pleased, when she kissed him on the mouth. Her skin smelt of the sea. Her kiss tasted of fish.

'The tide's turned,' she said abruptly. 'It's time for us to go our different ways.'

He watched as she rounded the headland of the bay, turned to wave, and then she was gone.

'You've been with the seals, then,' said Aunt Meg.

'Well, yes.'

'I can tell.'

'And I met the girl who lives somewhere down there.'

Aunt Meg stopped preparing the meal and looked at him. 'Girl?'

'Yes. Rona.'

She nodded, sagely. 'I thought so. It'll be one of the Selkie Folk. It's autumn, so there's bound to be one of them about here somewhere.'

'Selkies? Who are they?'

'People say they are the souls of men and women lost at sea. They spend their time living as seals, but once in a while they come up on land, cast their skins and become like human folk.'

'You're joking.'

'I most certainly am not.'

'Nothing but folktales.'

'And what's wrong with folktales? You've heard of mermaids, haven't you?'

'Of course.'

'Well, this is something similar. You'll likely never see her again, so don't go looking for her.'

During the next few days, the weather grew colder, and low cloud and rain again covered the island. Andrew busied himself reading some of his aunt's extensive collection of books. So, it was nearly three weeks later when Andrew again heard the seals. It was at night. He was lying in his bed, watching the moon rise across the ocean. At first, he thought it was the wind. But the night air was still. Then he remembered. The seals. They were singing.

He climbed out of bed, got dressed and went to stand outside.

Something seemed to be drawing him towards the water's edge. In the cool light of the moon, he saw a figure dancing on the moonlit shore.

He recognised her at once.

'Rona.'

She stopped dancing and looked up. 'Hello, Andrew. Have you come to join me?'

He sat down. 'No. Just to watch.'

She laughed and continued to cavort along the silvery strand.

The colony of seals watched as well, as though they wanted to join her.

Andrew soon felt an overwhelming urge to join in the dancing.

They danced until he collapsed, exhausted. She laughed, and joined him as he lay on the sand, gasping for air. They laughed together.

'I have to go,' she said.

'So soon?'

'It's time.' She picked something up from the sand. Perhaps the empty skin of a grey seal.

Intrigued, he watched her pull off the cloak, step into the skin, and pull it around her.

'One day I'll get one of these for you, Andrew,' she said, before slipping into the water and disappearing into the darkness of the sea.

He struggled to take in what he'd just seen and heard.

'Aye, you've been with the seals again,' said Aunt Meg the following day. 'Perhaps it's just as well you'll be going home again soon. You don't want to get too involved with those seal-folk. The Selkies are not always what they appear.'

'Perhaps not. But she seems harmless enough.'

It was the end of the month and Andrew was due to leave for home the very next day. The islands were enjoying another break in the weather, and the full moon shone brightly from a clear night sky. And Andrew again lay in bed, listening to the seals singing.

He climbed out of bed and looked out across the green island, towards the dark sea. He was not surprised when he saw a figure standing on the edge of the land. Even from that distance, he recognised her. He felt his heart leap. He wanted to say a last goodbye to this strange young woman. Even if she was half woman and half seal, he had grown very fond of her during his short time in Orkney. He hated the idea of never seeing her again.

He made his way out into the night air, and felt a light breeze blowing in from the sea.

The two figures met on the edge of the land. For several minutes, they gazed into each other's eyes. Then, hand in hand, they turned and walked towards the sea.

Aunt Meg watched them from the house and nodded. Perhaps, after all, two hearts had become one. And who was she to stand in their way?

Although Andrew and his shape-shifting friend were never seen again, a legend says anyone visiting Orkney on a clear night in early autumn, might just catch a glimpse of a couple of figures dancing on the sand, beneath the glow of the bright and mystical moon.

The Road to Somewhere
Cathy Lane
Copyright © 2018 Cathy Lane
A work of fiction

Her past hadn't been good, at least that's what she was told. She had asked the Guardians of her past if she could have the key but it had been denied her. She wasn't allowed to go back, that door was well and truly locked and bolted.

For her own good, they'd said.

Steer your own path, they'd said, when she was old enough to do so.

So, she had tried and her present was now. Not the best, not what she had dreamed of but how are you supposed to know how to deal with the present when your past is hidden behind a firmly shut door and you don't know who the hell you are or what happened? It's like losing a chapter in a book. How can you follow the plot if you've lost the beginning?

Anyhow, here she was - and she had the key to her future. They had given it to her. They'd said she had to go over the horizon to find her future. It felt strange. Scary. Give them their due, the Guardians had guided as best they could. They'd said that now she was her own person she must find her own way. She had the map and she must follow the instructions explicitly, they'd said.

"Choose carefully when you get to the signpost. It is your decision."

She had swallowed hard but the lump in her throat stuck between hope and fear. "My, my," she said, She wanted to cry but crying wouldn't do any good, she would drown herself. "Back straight, chin up," she told herself and soldiered on. She was for the time being still in her present but now it was like a box. Not open and airy but getting claustrophobic.

Her legs dragged her in the direction she had been given. She came to the door and the key in her hand became hot. She was shaking as she inserted it into the keyhole and -.and turned it. She heard the mechanism clicking - and then it opened - and the key fell to the ground and melted into the soil. Slowly, the door closed behind her as she stepped into her future.

Before her was a beautiful landscape, a cloudless blue sky, green, green fields and the scent of blossom. Ahead of her at a crossroads was a signpost. She approached it and looked up. There were three directions to choose from. It was decision time. In one direction the sign said, 'To Nowhere'. The second said, 'To Anywhere' and the third said, 'To Somewhere'. Oh! She sighed to herself and the words in her head said, 'I don't know, I just don't know,' and a single tear ran down her cheek.

Then a new voice came into her head, a soft voice, a kind, guiding voice. 'Think, think of where you have been.' And she thought, well, she had always been 'Nowhere' in particular, and she didn't want to go just 'Anywhere' but when she studied the signpost her inner thoughts drew her to 'Somewhere'.

Yes, 'Somewhere' would be nice. It really sounded like a positive, real place. Somewhere where she could be someone, somewhere where she could make her mark, somewhere where no one would know of her past, even if she didn't know it herself. So, she stood firm and with a lightness of heart, ignoring a slight flutter of trepidation, she turned right, right along the road to 'Somewhere', without a key in her pocket, simply driven by golden hope and dogged determination.

After trudging for several wearying miles she came to a bridge arching over a pretty sparkling stream. It was so lovely, this place but she felt she hadn't quite reached her destination yet. She plodded on until, yes, yes there it was. Bright, sunny, with a warm, welcoming feel about it. However, she was extremely nervous and, although there were lovely butterflies all around, they were also fluttering in her stomach.

As she got closer someone approached, smiling pleasantly. An official maybe.

"Hello, my love, I'm glad you have found your way," he said. "I am so pleased to see you. I am your Protector. I have been awaiting your arrival. May I ask, do you have a name?"

She was confused for she had never had a name, only a label, stating, 'no name'.

"Oh," she said. "I don't have a name, I am just called 'no name'."'

"Oh my dear, that is not a true name is it? We must give you one, as you are now in Somewhere and we all have names here, each and every one of us."

"But I don't know any names," she said, a lump in her throat. "I am just me."

"Well, well," said her Protector. "That's just fine because - now let me see." He rubbed his chin. "'Yes, yes," he went on excitedly. "You can be 'Iyame'. Pronounce it, 'I-yam-mee'. Pretty, pretty Iyame from Nowhere. What do you think of that?"

"Oh," she said, breaking out in a big beaming smile. "'I-yam-me'. I like it, I like it, I am me!"

"That's who you want to be, isn't it? Yourself?" And he took her hand and led her into her future.

The Return
Diane Leake
Copyright © 2018 Diane Leake
A work of fiction

I don't know why I'm here. I swore I wouldn't come, but it seems my feet outvoted me. So here I am - waiting. Why? Surely, if I wanted to flail myself with castigations I could do it at home, out of this biting north-westerly. Yet here I am – waiting - hating myself for being so weak, so voyeuristic.

Mrs Jones, my nearest neighbour, waves from the front of the crowd, her face as red as a Hunter's Moon. She's been excited about this day for weeks – as if a supermarket has never been opened by a celebrity before. So, though I don't feel like smiling, I feel obliged to lift my chin and spread my lips, all the while wishing the celebratory mood of the crowd could wash away this leaden feeling in my gut.

Perhaps if I left now, went home, I'd feel better. Only that's not true, my head would still be here. Same way my feet are glued to the cobbles.

What's wrong with me? Why can't I just let her go? Let her be the big celebrity. Let her open the supermarket then disappear back into her celluloid world. After all, she's the one who left this place without a word to me. What kind of friend does such a thing? My gut churns with the answer.

Defiantly, I question why anyone in her situation, who's escorted and wooed by famous actors, needs to return to a piddly little village in the middle of nowhere to open a grotty little shop? It can only be to gloat. She knows I won't be able to resist being here. No doubt she wants to rub my nose in it. To show me how she's made something of her life. To show me how suffocatingly insignificant and small my life is by comparison. But why pound our once-shared dreams into dust? Shaking my head, I berate myself yet again for putting myself through this. I should go, only my feet remain glued to the cobbles while the devil in my gut breathes fire.

Mr Blackburn's shout drags me from my turmoil. He's pointing at the black limousine, gliding down the narrow street towards us. As though on command, a communal hush fuses with the electricity of excitement. Then the car draws to the curb and the cheering starts as the crowd presses forward, leaving me an island.

Any minute now, I tell myself. Any minute now.

Mr Blackburn, in his official role as Leader of the Parish Council, is bursting with pomp and ceremony: his freshly-dyed hair shines like oil on wet tarmac, which only serves to accentuate his bloated cabbage-doll features. As he leans into the limousine's darkness and extracts a beringed hand, I question whether he has forgotten how he once called her – and me - a 'sacrilegious thug' for spray-painting Banksy-esque graffiti on the wall of the church hall.

At the sight of a high-heeled, brown suede boot emerging from the car, my stomach settles in my throat. It's all too surreal. I can't breathe. I can't breathe. I'm floating, and the noise of the crowd is coming at me through tin cans. She's moving through the crowd now, stopping here and there to drop a kiss on someone's cheek or to hug another. Unbelievably, she is even more beautiful than as a child, or as a teenager, and no magazine could ever do her justice.

Tears spring to my eyes and the desire to keen is so overwhelming, I'm forced to hug myself tightly. I should go home before I make an exhibition of myself. Suddenly, a kiss is dropped on the top of my head and another pair of arms enfold me.

'Oh sorry, sweetheart didn't mean to make you jump.' Geraint drops another kiss. 'Thought I'd find you here when you weren't at home. Hey, what's up?'

He turns me round to face him and I tell him nothing's up, I'm just cold. Brushing my tears away, he looks into my soul before kissing me firmly on the mouth. And as I turn back to face the crowd I'm grateful for his comforting hold.

Maddie – or, Sapphire as she's now known – has moved through the euphoric crowd. As she reaches the supermarket doors, she looks up and our eyes meet. The smile slips from her lips and she falters. And in that split-second of wall-dropping, when I'm enveloped in her hyacinth gaze, I understand. I see her loneliness and I know she misses me as much as I miss her. I want to go to her. To wrap her in my arms and reassure her, to let her know I'll always be here for her. Though perhaps it is my need more than hers, for her eyes also tell me there will be no telephone calls to look forward to. There'll be no more nights of divulging secrets or laughing at shared gossip. We inhabit different worlds now.

Then her eyes drag from mine to Geraint's and my stomach lurches. I follow her eyes to search Geraint's face for signs. Still, I question. But the light in Geraint's hazel eyes is no different from when he meets anyone else he knows as he mouths a 'hello' at her. And as my eyes return to hers I catch the haunting sadness within, just before her wall rises and she moves out of sight.

Guilt and loss chew at me. I want to run after her. I want it to be like it used to be. I want to tell her how much I still love her. How I wish things could have been different. How I'm sorry for hurting her. How I wish we could have talked, giving me a chance to explain. And how I've devoured every magazine, newspaper or television programme she's been in or appeared on. Of course, I don't. Instead, I grab Geraint's hand and turn my back on the closest friend I've ever had.

The wind continues to suck the life out of everything, forcing trees to bow in contrition as Geraint and I make our way back through the streets to the organic farm we run. As we turn off the High Street, Tracey Smith is coming towards us. Two young children totter on tiptoes grasping either side of the pushchair which Tracey pushes adeptly, while a child cries from within.

'Been to see that Maddie Smith?' For some reason she always shouts.

'Hi, Tracey. Yes.'

She sniffs. 'Huh, calls herself Sapphire Storm these days, eh? Who the hell does she think she is?' She sniffs again and nods in the direction of the supermarket. 'Always did think she was better than the rest of us. Ha, a bloody clothes-horse, that's all she is. Anyway, see you later. Gotta get this lot home and fed.'

As Tracey walks away Geraint gives me his secret smile and pulls me close. We're almost home when he stops and turns to me.

'Maddie looks good.'

'Mmm,' is all I can say, my green monster on red alert.

Geraint leans in close to me. 'Maddie may look good, but I've no regrets. I definitely chose the right girl.'

And the Rain Came
Jackie Walton
Copyright © 2018 Jackie Walton
An essay

And so, after a long, sun-kissed summer - with scorched fields, dried up ponds and rivers, thirsty humans and animals, roofless cars, picnics and barbecues, long mountain hikes, bronzed legs, overheated dogs and children, hats and sunglasses, ice creams and prosecco - the rain came.

It came with an energy akin to too much suppressed emotion. It was dramatic, heavy, hard, ferocious, angry, messy - but extremely necessary.

It was as if a monumental sky-tap had been turned on. The rain came down with such speed, bouncing off the roads, off car bonnets, off windows and tin sheds, off umbrellas and off paving slabs. Within minutes, puddles and floods appeared. Shoes and the denim jacket, held in desperation over the head of the carrier, were soaked. Dogs damp. Horses, cows and sheep stood either under shelter or near the edges of fields. Their ears flat and their coats drenched.

We knew it was coming, yet it still took us by surprise.

The ground needed this heavenly liquid so much, so did the fish. It rained and rained and rained. It was relentless. One creature who relished every second of this delightful on-going downpour was the toad. And his fellow toads. From where they came, we don't quite know. They took up their positions on the country road, looking like miniature Staffordshire bull terriers, all proud and stocky. There they sat, still, strong and yes, they could quite possibly be smiling.

People drove, walked or took the bus to get home; it was too cold and miserable to be out in the street. Walking with sleeves pulled down over hands, collars turned up, umbrellas grasped and puddles avoided. Riding on the bus, sitting pressed up against the window, gazing through the raindrops hammering against the outside. The centre aisle of the bus had a mini stream from the drips of soaked umbrellas.

A car driver, windscreen wipers on full speed, demister set to maximum, drove cautiously through the running torrent of surface water. Once parked, he waited for the rain to soften, to make a mad dash to his front door. Except it didn't soften, it rained even harder. He still made the mad dash. He felt like he was being pebble-dashed all over. Cheeks battered, he reached the front door. The handle had a line of nine bulbous drips suspended, equally spaced, from the underside. When the handle was pushed down, the bulbous drips slid into each other and became one huge drip, which fell on to the driver's foot. What was one more drip in the scheme of things?

Leaves were scattered like giant, scruffy confetti into all the wrong places...in shop doorways, all over newly cut lawns, stuck to shoes, gathering alongside kerbs and in gutters. In gardens, it not only rained rain but also leaves, apples, pine needles, acorns, conkers, sycamore seed-pods and twigs.

Autumn had announced its arrival – 'I'm here! Bring out your scarves, gloves, jumpers, wood burning stoves, hot chocolate and hugs.'

And the rain came...

Small Change
J Severn
Copyright 2017 J Severn

"Can you spare me some change?"
The homeless man cried
As we passed him by on the street
He was dirty, dishevelled
And stank of booze
And had cardboard shoes on his feet

"You're wasting your money,"
My girlfriend cried
As I threw some coins in his hat
"You know he'll just up
And spend it on drink."
I told her of course I knew that

I knew he'd be heading
Straight to the pub
I knew how he spent his days
All that I wanted
Was to make him smile
I knew he'd not change his ways

But still she went on
All the way home
'Til I couldn't take any more
It was time for a change
So I packed her things
And quietly showed her the door

Daddy Longlegs
Robert Stapleton
Copyright © 2018 Robert Stapleton
A work of fiction

Daddy Longlegs was dead. The tragic victim of a misunderstanding between the insect and the sole of the gardener's boot. Never again would his wings fly him above the rich garden or the nearby spreading meadow. Never again would his long legs give him a high standing among the insects of the vegetable patch. The days of the famous insect were over. But at the moment of his funeral, much was to be remembered and celebrated about this venerable crane fly.

The creatures of the garden gathered in the shadow of the compost heap to remember their old friend and to contemplate the shortness of their own lives.

On that overcast morning, the black beetle assumed the role of Master of Ceremonies and invited anyone present to contribute their own offerings to the proceedings.

Speedy the slug told them he remembered Daddy Longlegs with great affection and began to write his obituary with the slime-trail he left across the nearby lawn. He took his time but his little heart was completely committed to his task and he was determined to leave his mark.

Wiggles the earthworm wiggled forward and turned to face the gathering.

'I may only be the lowliest of all creatures in the garden,' he told them, 'but I too have my happy memories of Daddy Longlegs. Sometimes, when the rain had been falling for many hours and the air was muggy and close, I would burrow my way to the surface and exchange a few words of greeting with him. He always had something cheering to tell me. About life beyond the garden wall. About Mrs Higgins hanging out her washing or Mr Johnson washing his vintage car.'

Many of the creatures nodded their agreement at these words and added their own voices to the growing eulogy in honour of their sadly departed companion and mentor.

Dolly the ladybird alighted on to a leaf and folded her wings beneath her colourful wing-case.

'Yes, I remember Daddy Longlegs,' she said in her quiet refined voice. 'He was always a perfect gentleman. My sisters all agree and have sent me along here to express our collected appreciation of him, and our regret at his sad loss.'

Pullman the cabbage-white caterpillar looked up from his munching on a lettuce leaf. His unusual name had been given to him because of his similarity to a railway carriage one of the moths had seen in the nearby railway yard. Long, with lots of moving parts.

'Just like me, Daddy Longlegs had once been a tiny grub,' said Pullman, 'but he developed into the most magnificent crane fly, one we all loved and now remember with great affection. He always encouraged me to look forward to when I grew up, to when I would get my own wings. His advice to me was to keep on eating, which is exactly what I have been doing ever since.'

A silk web hung close by, moisture glistening like pearls in the daylight, and from its centre the figure of the spider glared out at the gathering.

'Daddy Longlegs was nothing special to me,' she said. 'Just another insect who might have become entwined in my net. I'd have taken him into my larder and I would have had a good feast on his skinny body. Just as I will do with any of you who venture too close.'

Sally the snail emerged from her shell and looked around.

'You may all think I'm deaf, lying curled up inside my shell,' she said, 'but I can assure you I have been listening to every word you have been saying. We snails take life slowly, dealing with each day as it comes. One day we might have to shut up shop and stay at home because of the lack of rain. Other days we can come out and explore. Daddy Longlegs was an explorer, too. He kept an eye on us and gave us warning of danger before it arrived. I hope somebody else will now take on that job. I for one feel a great deal safer with somebody keeping an eye on the garden. The gardener is all very well, he does what he can, but he does like to encourage birds to come into the garden.'

At the mention of *birds* the creatures began to wail and moan, whilst some uttered exclamations of defiance.

'Yes,' said the black beetle, 'the birds have always been our enemies. The blackbirds, the starlings and the other birds who love to crunch on a tasty beetle, grub or mollusc.' The groaning grew louder. 'So, I suggest we bring our proceedings rapidly to a close, by singing the hymn dear to all garden creatures: *If I Were a Butterfly*. Then we can consign our dear friend to the compost heap and allow him to rest in peace.'

As the tiny animals of the garden sang, croaked and squeaked their song, a dark shadow flew over their gathering. Wings flapped and a sharp, hungry beak drew closer.

The creatures scattered in all directions, as fast as they could. Some slithered, and others ran for their lives, as a huge thrush landed beside them. The cruel beak snatched up from the ground the only thing that still remained available. The inert body of Daddy Longlegs himself.

With the legs of the crane fly protruding from its beak, the thrush spread its wings and flew away across the garden, heading towards the holly-bush beside the gate, where it had built its nest and now had its hungry youngsters to feed.

By the end of the morning, the only reminder of the funeral which had taken place there was the slime-trail left by Speedy the slug. It read: 'Hurray for... SPLAT.'

'Stupid slugs,' groaned the gardener, wiping his boot.

Found Out
Cathy Lane
Copyright © 2018 Cathy Lane
A work of fiction

When she found out for sure, Sonia was not entirely surprised. She'd had the feeling something was going on. She'd noticed the glances between them when they'd all been out together as two couples, her with her other half, Mike, and the bitch with her husband Don.

She wasn't daft - and she had hoped it wasn't the case - but there were too many 'looks' and too much familiarity between them. Did they think she was blind? Don, bless him was as thick as two planks and so adoringly besotted with his wife, he would never have even thought about it. Soft as he was. She had him wrapped around her little finger. Twiddling him about, playing the good wife. She was one of those women who danced around like a firefly, teasing and testing.

Usual story, she worked at Mike's firm. Mike had always been a bit of a flirt but had never, as far as Sonia knew, had an affair. She would have sussed it, she was sure she would have, but this showed him in a completely different light. He'd obviously taken the bait and swallowed it. Whole. Hook, line and sinker.

As a foursome, they had been out quite a lot but it had just registered with Sonia how there seemed to have been quite a lot of late nights at the office, recently. Late night flings with the bitch, more like.

How thick had she been? Well she wasn't going to stand by and let them get away with it. First time and last time for Mike, because she was going to wipe the floor with him. And pulverize her, the little cow!

Sonia was a judo instructor and a karate expert, at the local gym, which was going to be her trump card. The bitch may be a pretty little witch but she hadn't bargained on Sonia's talent.

She decided to make a nice gesture and invite the bitch round for a coffee when Mike and Don were playing golf. Oh, yes, Mike was happily playing the game and being all friendly with Don. No doubt giving the impression of being a good mate, when all along it was Don's wife he was 'mating'.

The bitch was flattered to be asked and arrived on time, flighty little flirt. Sonia welcomed her in. No doubt she had been intrigued, eager to see Mike's home and keen to get friendly with 'the wife', to keep her sweet. They had coffee and cake while they chatted about nothing in particular. Then Sonia asked if 'flirt' would like a little something alcoholic.

"Ooh yes, please," came the response.

Actually, it was quite a *big* something with a sort of sedative in it and it had quite a punch. The real punch came when Sonia had her pinned against the wall and gave her a karate chop.

"You little bitch," Sonia hissed. "You leave my husband alone."

The little bitch seemed to understand well enough and the bruise wasn't that bad. Sonia ran her home and told Don his wife had had a bit too much to drink and had unfortunately fallen against the sideboard. The bitch didn't blink an eyelid, especially not the one covering the painfully swollen black eye.

Strangely enough, later that day Mike had a similar misfortune and couldn't play golf for several weeks.

Don, bless him, was totally phased by the inexplicable withdrawal of contact with his golfing buddy. Sonia felt quite sorry for the bloke, really. He was quite nice, soft and malleable. She quite liked seeing him when he joined the gym and they enjoyed quite a fling.

Overtime after work.

She Knows Me, She Knows Me Not
J Severn
Copyright © 2018 J Severn
A poem of unrequited love

She knows my name, she knows my age
She knows the house I live in
She even knows where I was born
And the schooling I was given

She knows the places I have lived
She knows my resumé
She knows the ups and all the downs
I've lived through on my way

She knows what foods I like to eat
And the films I like to see
She knows what songs I love to hear
And sings them all for me

She thinks she knows me well enough
She knows the things I favour
But she knows me not - she'll never know
Just how much I crave her

Trespassing Through
Elizabeth Jackson
The first chapter of her forthcoming novel
Copyright © 2018 Elizabeth Jackson
A work of fiction

The grey-haired man admired the skewbald stallion galloping across the paddock, his mighty power thrusting him forward into the sunset as the sky set alight. The restless animal skidded to a halt at the boundary fence. Still teeming with energy, he whinnied loudly, rearing up on his hind legs.

The man smiled to himself; he'd enjoy breaking this fella, he thought. He leant against the fence and tapped his pipe sharply on the heel of his boot before refilling and lighting it. Drawing deeply on the pipe he studied his latest acquisition from Topcliffe Fair. He'd paid a fair price for the young stallion, knowing it would fetch him a handsome profit come Appleby Fair time.

The sun dipped below the horizon and Ambrose Wilson took a last look at the animal cropping at the grass at the far end of the field, then he slung the lead rein over his shoulder and walked back to the house.

As he neared the back door a rapping noise sounded at an upstairs window. He stopped and looked up to where his wife's pallid face smiled down at him. Tears welled behind his eyes as he forced a smile and blew her a kiss.

Twenty minutes later Ambrose carried a tray upstairs. He paused a moment outside the door and took a few deep breaths before entering the bedroom. The bed was positioned by the window, so his wife could watch the daily comings and goings in the yard and the paddock beyond.

"How're yer doing, me darlin'? Look, see what Mrs Hardy's left you - a nice bowl of oxtail soup." Ambrose spoke cheerily while repositioning a stack of pillows which wedged his wife's emaciated body into a sitting position.

He placed the tray on her lap.

Her voice was faint when she spoke and Ambrose leaned in close.

"Sit down, Ambrose," Florence whispered. "There're things I have to discuss with you."

"Later, later. Not now, me darlin'. We'll talk another time when you've eaten up an' you're feeling stronger."

Florence shook her head in frustration, slapping her hand down on the bed beside her. "No, no," she pleaded. "Sit down, Ambrose. Listen to me. Even if you don't choose to talk, I do, so humour me...please. Here, take this away," she said, pushing the tray aside. "I'm not hungry. I'll only be sick again if I eat it."

Ambrose removed the tray and sat on the bed beside her. He sought her hand, lifted it to his mouth and kissed it. She relaxed her frail body, allowing it to sink back into the pillows; her breath came in shallow gasps as she wrestled to regain her composure.

After a few minutes, her breathing calmed. She raised her hand and pointed to a roll-top desk at the far end of the room.

"Open it, please, Ambrose," she said.

Without protest Ambrose walked over to the desk.

"There, do you see? On the left-hand side ... an envelope. It's for Ethan..." Florence's voice grew agitated. "Make sure he gets it after I'm gone... Ambrose! Look at me, please."

Ambrose turned to look at her; her shrunken frame scarcely visible in the large double bed; her skin as white as the sheet which covered her.

"Will you do that for me ... Please?"

Ambrose swallowed hard, his voice choked with emotion. "Yes, I'll mek sure the lad gets it ... I promise."

"Good ... I don't need to say any more on the matter then ... Now, come here... lie down beside me... hold me ..."

Ambrose turned his face from her and closed the desk, wiping the tears from his eyes. Returning to the bed, he lay down beside his wife and gathered her in his arms.

She sighed.

Ambrose felt her delicate breath on his neck when she whispered faintly, "I love you, Ambrose, don't forget that ... will you?"

"No, I'll not forget."

The bedroom was in darkness when Ambrose heard the front door bang shut. He switched on the bedside lamp and looked down at his wife asleep in his arms. She was smiling, her eyes closed. Ambrose touched her face. It was icy cold. He gently released her and dropped a kiss on her forehead, which was still damp from his tears. A few strands of hair had fallen across her face - he tenderly brushed them aside.

"Your suffering's over, Florence. No more pain for you, my love." Then rising from the bed, he straightened the candlewick bedspread and left the room.

"What do yer mean, sell up?" Ethan yelled. "Yer can't sell the place, Dad."

"Oh, yes, I can, lad, and I will," Ambrose said, "Make no mistake on that account. I've no desire to stay here now. I've given it a lot of thought over the last six months since your mam died, an' it's time for change. I'll buy a small cottage with a bit of land outside town somewhere. There'll always be somewhere for us to come back to."

Ethan winced as the pain of betrayal struck again.

After his mother's death, it had come as a huge shock and a betrayal, to discover the true circumstances of his birth. His mother had left him a letter, begging his forgiveness for not telling him sooner that Ambrose wasn't his real father. She told him his real father was a man called Garrett Ferrensby, who resided on the North York moors at a place called High Agra; and who, to this day, remained ignorant of Ethan's existence.

Other than telling him he'd inherited a property called Hamer Bridge, the letter contained few details, leaving Ethan with many unanswered questions.

Ethan now looked at his sister who'd not said a word so far. "And what about our Priscilla, does she have a say in any of this?"

"I want to go with you, Dad." Priscilla rose from her chair and went to stand alongside Ambrose. "It'll be exciting, Ethan, you must come, too. Please."

"No, I'll not be coming." Ethan shook his head and glared at Ambrose. "But if you want to go with him, roaming the countryside in a bloody gypsy wagon - well, that's up to you, Priscilla, I can't stop you. But I'll tell you this, you're making a big mistake. You were born here... in this very house." Ethan threw his arms wide. "All your friends are here. An' truth be known it's not what our mam would've wanted for you either. She'd 'ave wanted you to get on in the world ... better yourself."

Ambrose had heard enough. Boiling with anger, he took a step towards Ethan, who towered head and shoulders above him. But that didn't bother Ambrose. He wasn't a man easily riled as a rule, but Ethan had overstepped the mark. Telling him what his Florence wanted and didn't want had pushed him to his limits. He prodded Ethan in the chest with a finger while looking him squarely in the eye. And when he spoke, the tone of his voice was calm and coolly threatening.

"Don't you speak like that in my house again! I loved my wife more than you can imagine an' would never go against her wishes. Never! Do you hear me?"

Ethan didn't reply.

It was too late, anyway. Because in that moment it wasn't the boy he'd accepted as his own who glowered defiantly back at Ambrose – it was Garrett Ferrensby's son. On hearing she was pregnant by another man, Ambrose had promised Florence he would love Ethan as if he were his own flesh and blood. And not only had he meant it, he had actually believed he'd done just that over the years. Until now. Now he could clearly see he'd been play-acting all those years and it had all been for Florence's sake. Now she'd gone, what was the point of keeping up the pretence?

I'll see the lad right financially, of course, he's owed that, but nowt else, Ambrose reasoned to himself.

"I'm putting the place on the market and once it's sold, I'll buy a little place in one of the villages outside Thirsk," he said. "You can both come and go as you please, stay when you want for as long as yer want. Now, that's me final say on the matter. Tek it or leave it. It's up to the pair o' yer."

Ambrose quietly walked from the room and out of the back door, closing it firmly behind him. Priscilla began crying and Ethan put his arms around her.

"C'mon, it's all right, Sis, don't cry," he said, giving her his handkerchief. "It's about time I flew the nest. And you, you're almost eighteen. Most gypsy lasses are wed and saddled with a bairn at your age."

"Oh, Ethan, why did mam have to go and die and spoil everything?" she sobbed.

Ethan looked down at her mass of black hair as she wept into his shirt. *Spoilt bloody rotten all her life by Father*, he thought, stroking the back of her head. *Whereas Mother, I think, mostly favoured me.*

Priscilla, eight years younger, had been too young for the land army during the war, which Ethan thought a great pity at the time. It would have been good for her to have got away from home and tasted the real world. Consequently, he was away fighting while Priscilla continued having the best of everything: decent clothes, jewellery; no expense spared for his sister.

That was something Ethan had to credit Ambrose with; he'd always been a good provider.

Eventually, Priscilla's tears subsided. Ethan said, "Do you really want to take to the roads with Dad and live in a bow-top wagon, Sis?"

"I do, oh, yes, I—I want to know what it's like to live the kind of life my grandparents and great grandparents lived. I'm curious ... it's our heritage ... our blood. They're our people, Ethan. Aren't you one bit curious?"

"No, not in the least," he assured her. "But, that's probably because I'm nowt but a half-breed." He shrugged his shoulders. Then the corners of his eyes wrinkled and he smiled at her. "But you!" Ethan said, feigning disgust and jokingly pushing her, "You're a full blown, black-haired didicoy!"

They playfully shoved one another, laughing till their sides hurt.

"You're deadly serious about this, aren't you, Sis? I know ... I can see it in your eyes." They'd stopped laughing and Ethan was looking into Priscilla's eyes. It was like looking into his mother's. Only Priscilla's sparkled and danced like his mother's never did. "I'd no idea you felt so passionate about our gypsy side. But just now when you were talking, saying how you're curious to know what it's like to live that way of life—I don't think I've ever seen you look so ... so alive."

Priscilla, overcome with love for her brother, flung her arms around his neck. "Oh, Ethan, come with us," she pleaded. "How on earth will I manage without you there to keep me straight... make me laugh?"

"You'll manage very well indeed, I should imagine. You'll have every gyppo and traveller lad falling at your feet to do your bidding. And, should you change your mind an' want to come home; come and live with me at Hamer Bridge."

"Hamer Bridge? You mean y-you'll actually go and live there?"

"I'm going to give it a try. I have to."

Priscilla's eyes brimmed with tears again and Ethan reached for her hand. "Please try and understand, Sis, this is my blood calling me, like yours is calling you. Can't you see that?"

"Yes, of course I can," she said. "I'm just being selfish." Her face lit up. "I've just had a great idea! Why don't I come and stay with you for the winter, Ethan? Because believe me, no matter how much I enjoy the gypsy way of life - or not, for that matter - when winter arrives, I'm out of it. I will definitely need the comfort of bricks and mortar, electricity and warm running water. How's that sound?"

Ethan spat in his hand and held it out. "Sounds perfect to me, Sis. It's a deal."

"Deal!" Priscilla said, spitting on her palm and grasping her brother's hand firmly.

Peak Dark Pete
Cathy Lane
Copyright © 2018 Cathy Lane
A work of fiction

Billy and Tommy were in the pub bar.

'Bloody 'ell, Billy, it's fuckin' packed in 'ere, 'ardly room ta move.'

'Well, it's t' only pub in town and it's Sat'day night. What d'ya expect, Tommy? Anyway, gives it atmosphere. What's t' point in comin' to an empty pub, with no atmosphere?'

'Well, that's as maybe, Billy boy, but I can 'ardly lift me glass to me lips.'

'Stop yer moanin' an' get swiggin', the night's young yet.'

Tommy peers over his shoulder and spies an empty table in the darkened recess by the bar.

'Eh up, Billy, there's a free table in t' corner, let's grab it.'

With difficulty, he turns towards it but Billy grabs his arm.

'Nah, Tommy, it's not free, it's tekken'.'

'Are ya 'allucinatin' or summat, mate? It's empty. Can't ya see there's no one there?'

Billy keeps hold of him.

'it is tekken', Tommy, it's reserved. It's bad luck t' sit there.'

Tommy stares at him.

'Are ya bloody bonkers, Billy? Ya needs yer eyes testin'.'

'Okay, Tommy, let me explain, before Peak Dark Pete meks 'is presence felt.'

'Who the fuckin' 'ell is Peak Dark Pete, when 'e's at 'ome? Go on then, tell me. But let me get anuvver drink. I might need to control me nerves - *I don't think!* I'll get you anuvver as well, 'cos seems like ye're already pissed anyway, and ye've only 'ad one!'

Tommy fights his way to the bar and returns with two fresh pints.

'Cheers, mate. Get on wit' t' story, then. I'm all ears.'

'Well, Peak Dark Pete is the son of the man whose table that is - or was. Peak Dark Pete's dad died in suspicious circumstances out on t' moor. 'is son found 'im – 'eadless. Peak Dark Pete 'as never spoken since but that table is permanently reserved. Later this evening Pete Dark Pete will come in, get 'is usual two pints - one for 'issel' and one for 'is dad - and 'e'll tek 'em to that table to sit with 'is back to t' room, supposedly facin' 'is dad, jus' like what they used ter.'

'Bloody 'ell, what an ol' cock 'n' bull story, Billy. Surely you don't believe it? What a load o' ol' bollocks!'

'You wait then, Tommy lad, jus' wait. You'll see.' He clinked his glass against Doubting Tommy's. 'Cheers mate. Wait and see.'

As darkness fell, the door opened and in walked a swarthy, bearded man. A hush fell over the room and all eyes followed him as he worked his way to the bar. Without a word being spoken, he was served two pints. The crowd parted for him as he walked to the table in the recess. He sat with his back to the room and picked up his glass. At the same moment the other glass rose up and the two chinked together in mid-air.

The room was silent except for Doubting Thomas.

'*Fuckin' ell, Billy, fuckin' 'ell!*' he yelled, choking on his beer.

The Lady Wore Red Boots
Antony Waller
Copyright © Antony Waller
A work of fiction

It was late in the afternoon on one of those damp and gloomy, cold early winter days. Mist had been hanging in the air all day and was now creeping earthwards, muffling familiar landmarks.

The light from the streetlamps was being pinched and squeezed by darker shadows reaching out along either side of the street. An eerie quietness was spreading like a cloak, suffocating sound and choking the last of the day.

And that is when the nightmare began for Eddie at number three Railway Cottages, jolting him from his cosy armchair next to a crackling log fire. At first, a quiet tap-tap-tapping on the window pane, then the sound of shuffling feet and a loud persistent knocking.

With a deep sigh Eddie put the book down on the arm of the chair and got up to answer the door. He was not expecting anyone and certainly not on an afternoon like this.

He drew back the bolt, turned the key in the lock and opened the door a fraction. A narrow shaft of light spilled across the doorstep, illuminating a pair of red boots with three-inch heels, below an ankle-length skirt.

As the door opened wider, more light revealed a figure wearing a jacket over a high-collared blouse, with an umbrella over one arm and a well-worn Gladstone bag at her feet. A hat with a cockade of feathers was perched upon her head and from beneath the brim could be seen a pair of twinkling blue eyes and an ever-widening smile.

"Hello, Edward, I do hope I'm in time for tea."

Eddie just stared back. She was not a young woman, but not exactly old either and perhaps she did seem vaguely familiar. Before he had the chance to reply or ponder further, she picked up her bag, pushed past him and dropped into the armchair by the fireside.

"A pot of tea would be nice. There's a darling. Then I think you and I need to have a little talk. And could you warm and butter these?"

She plucked a plate of scones from the depths of the Gladstone bag. With a flourish, she removed the dainty crocheted doyley from the top before setting the plate down on a small occasional table next to the armchair.

"And some jam would be nice, strawberry if you have any. It's my favourite. I imagine clotted cream would be expecting too much. Do hurry up, Edward dear, and do close the door. You're letting a draught in."

She caught the puzzled expression on his face as Eddie stood there, rooted to the spot, one hand still holding the open door. Pursing her lips, she sighed and shook her head.

"This is proving more difficult than I thought." More rummaging in her bag produced a well-thumbed, ribbon-tied notebook which she placed on her lap. She untied the ribbon and as she opened the book a photograph fell to the floor, face up.

Eddie stared at the photograph in disbelief, for the person smiling back was a much younger image of himself.

"Well," she smiled, "who did you expect? You didn't think I would keep a photograph of a total stranger close to my heart, did you? Oh, Edward, my dear, my darling, my Romeo, do buck up." Her smile grew wider. "Tea and scones, and don't forget the jam." Her tongue licked her red lips seductively. "Another log on the fire would be nice. It's cold out there without a coat in this weather, you know, and I've been waiting simply ages. Now be a love and help me off with these boots. They're new and pinch a little. Edward! Oh, don't just stand there, and do close your mouth."

"Who are you?" demanded Eddie, finally finding his voice. "How do you know my name? What do you want?"

"Oh Edward, darling," she teased, lingering over the final syllable. "Come, come, surely you don't need to ask. Least said soonest mended. I'm here now and not a moment too soon, it seems."

"What? Look, I'm sorry, but I really don't know who you are."

"Oh, sweetcheeks, do stop being silly. What would you like me to say? Talk about the first time we met? Walking out together on a Sunday afternoon, just the two of us, you and me? Drifting along, holding hands? That first kiss? Shall I continue, Edward?"

"No! I don't know you. We've never met."

"Oh, my Romeo, please. Do stop pretending you don't know." She gave a mock pout of indignation and folded her arms beneath her ample bosom. "Edward! How could you forget the lady of your dreams? That's what you called me. Remember?"

"Dreams? Lady of my dreams? You're not in my dreams. I don't dream of you."

"Oh, Edward, yes you do. Oh, yes, and so much more besides. Oh, so very much more. Every night you call on me and whisk me away to here and there, so many romantic and beautiful places; hand in hand until the dawn breaks, when you leave me. So now it is my turn. I have come to call on you, to stay with you, Edward, so we can be together once again. No longer just in your dreams until the dawn, but through your days, too, forever and ever. Now come here and give me a kiss."

She turned and offered her cheek.

By now Eddie had the front door closed and was leaning against it, the handle pressing into his back. The temporary discomfort felt reassuring. He closed his eyes and began to breathe deeply, his head spinning. He was surely dreaming. It had to be a dream. He had dozed off reading by the fire. None of this was happening. He opened his eyes. The chair by the fire was empty. He let out a deep breath, shook his head and began to relax.

"Edward, the teapot, where is it, darling?" The voice came from the kitchen. "And the stove? Everything looks so different now."

Eddie headed for the kitchen. This, whatever it was, had gone too far. He saw the photograph on the floor, the smiling face looking up at him. His face. Angry now, he snatched it up and flung it into the fire. It caught light immediately, curling as it burnt, black and silver amongst the orange and yellow flames. A cry erupted from the kitchen, a loud piercing wail which grew into a high-pitched scream that made him shudder. He was spun around as a figure brushed past him.

"You haven't heard the last of this, Edward, or the last of me."

The front door crashed open, cold, damp, mist-filled air washed into the room and the sound of footsteps was swallowed up by the darkness. Eddie slammed the door shut, locking and bolting it before returning to the fireplace. Heart thumping, he slumped wearily into his armchair and heaved a sigh of relief.

Then he noticed the worn Gladstone bag.

Over the following days, Eddie pushed the events of that autumnal afternoon to the back of his mind and put it down to an old man dozing in front of a warm fire. Preposterous though it seemed, he couldn't shake off the thought that the woman bore a certain familiarity to a young lady he had once known in his teens. He recalled she had worn red boots, too. But that was back then, a young girl in red boots, not the apparition of the other afternoon.

As for the Gladstone bag, he had thrown it back into the attic without even a second look. After all, he must have got it down from there in the first place, for some reason. The trouble was that for now, the reason escaped him.

Today, Eddie felt particularly cheery. It was a bright and sunny morning, the sky a deep blue flecked with fluffy white clouds, and though cold with a light breeze, it was just right for a brisk walk to blow away the cobwebs.

He would walk to the paper shop and then to the village coffee shop, to sit and read his paper over a large warming mug of coffee or even hot chocolate. He smiled to himself, adjusted his hat and scarf, buttoned his coat, locked the front door behind him and set off. The postman waved a cheery 'good morning' as he passed on his deliveries and the lady from number five called from the doorstep, to ask if he was well and what a lovely morning for a stroll. Everything seemed back to normal.

He crossed the road, turning right in front of the village church. A pretty sixteenth century church with a small squat steeple and a stone porch, set on higher ground and separated from the footpath by a dry-stone wall.

In spring the church yard was a mass of flowers, first islands of snowdrops and crocuses beneath the trees standing amongst the silent gravestones, then swathes of bright yellow daffodils. There were no flowers today, just a solitary figure on a wooden bench under the leafless branches of a tree. Unnoticed by Eddie, the lady, who was wearing a hat and gloves, a jacket, long skirt and a pair of red boots, watched him walk by.

Twenty minutes later, Eddie was seated at a table in the coffee shop, grateful for a rest. Buoyed up by the crisp sunny morning, he had walked a little further than usual, so by way of a reward he ordered a large piece of carrot cake and a mug of hot chocolate.

For the moment he was the only customer and the room was quiet except for the crackling of the log fire burning behind an old-fashioned fireguard, standing in front of a large fireplace. Several tables were set out with folded white napkins and blue and white crockery, waiting for the small group of ladies who met regularly for morning coffee and conversation.

Eddie glanced at his watch. The ladies were creatures of habit and it would not be long before the bell above the door would begin to tinkle and dance, announcing their arrival.

He pulled the newspaper out of his pocket and in doing so, accidentally sent a teaspoon spinning and clattering to the wooden floor. He bent down to retrieve it and that's when he saw the red boots again, one foot tapping impatiently. He straightened up, his eyes taking in the red boots and the long skirt till he saw her standing there, arms folded across her chest, staring at him tight-lipped. The blue eyes had lost their twinkle.

"Well, Edward, this is a pretty to do. I think we need to have a chat and set a few things straight. Did you really think you wouldn't see me again? I may have lost you once, but not again. Time for that pot of tea and a warm scone with strawberry jam, wouldn't you say? Now, where has that waitress got to?"

Eddie followed her gaze as she looked for the waitress. At the same time the bell above the door jangled to announce the arrival of two of the morning coffee ladies.

"Oh look, Agnes, it's that nice gentleman from Railway Cottages. And all on his own. We'll say hello, before the others arrive."

Eddie turned to see the two ladies smiling at him as they walked over to his table to engage him in conversation. Both were wrapped up in woolly coats, black boots, hats, gloves and scarves.

"Good morning, ladies, I'm afraid I must dash, I'm rather late for an appointment."

He hoped his perfunctory excuse and hasty exit from the coffee shop did not appear rude. Eddie just wanted to get home.

He needed to get that Gladstone bag from the attic. Something was stirring at the back of Eddie's mind, images from his youth of a few glorious weeks one spring, a young girl in red boots, a picnic with tea and scones.

Eddie reached his front door almost without realising he was home. He was confused, his head was spinning. He jiggled the key in the door, went inside, and noticed some mail on the floor.

He bent down to pick up the letters from where they lay face down on the mat, suddenly lurched across the room and sank into the armchair. As he stared at the envelopes, he realised his hands were shaking and stars were dancing before his eyes. He felt cold, chilled to the bone, colder than he had ever felt before.

A shaft of bright sunlight shone through the window, catching him in the face. There were tears in his eyes. The pain in his chest was excruciating now. Eddie closed his eyes and never opened them again. He did not see the face watching him through the glass, the blue twinkling eyes and ruby red lips, the hat with a feather.

The doctor ushered the middle-aged man into the room and gestured for him to sit.

"My condolences, I am very sorry. Your father passed away thirty minutes ago. There was nothing more we could do. I'm afraid he didn't regain consciousness. It was all very peaceful, he felt no pain. To be honest, I am surprised he fought for as long as he did."

"I wish I could have got here sooner, just that one last time, to be with him at the end." The son's voice trailed off.

"Oh," the doctor continued, "there was someone here. In fact, you must have passed her in the corridor a few moments ago. A lady in a long skirt with old-fashioned red boots. She dropped this photograph."

The doctor held out the photograph to him. He recognised his father, Eddie, much younger back then, sitting on a riverbank under a tree, beside a young girl wearing a high collared blouse and a long skirt slightly pulled up above her boots. He didn't recognise the girl or the riverbank, but they seemed to be having a picnic, drinking tea and eating scones. Turning the photograph over he could still make out the faded lettering and the words:

'Sweetcheeks, my Edward'.

Eddie's funeral at the village church was held a few days later, a small family affair with just a handful of people at the graveside. By the cemetery wall a man and a woman stood hand in hand, oblivious to the cold and the few snowflakes beginning to fall silently.

The woman was dressed in a jacket and long skirt with red boots and a hat with feathers, worn at a jaunty angle. Next to the man's feet was an old Gladstone bag. She was smiling, her blue eyes twinkling with happiness as she turned and kissed him gently on the cheek.

A New Start
Julie Bushell
Copyright © 2019 Julie Bushell
A work of fiction

We give our years a number
So they have a start and end
Set a framework for our life
And the time we have to spend

We see it as a challenge
Undertaking something new
Whilst deep inside admitting
That our plans are overdue

We should have started sooner
And not waited for a date
Set down by earth's rotation
Round a sun that does not wait

A task is so much harder
When left for fear to strengthen
As fears have special powers
For building apprehension

All the heroes of this world
Are the ones who dared to do
And shone their light for others
Hoping they might follow too

Not every step is massive
Sometimes smaller ones are fine
Why wait for fading carols
To herald your starting time

We give our years a number
A calendar birth and end
If you can begin today
I say bring it on my friend.

An early Group story where members took it in turns to complete the tale, and which was considered worthy off inclusion in this, our second anthology.

Prologue

'There is history and there is myth and somewhere, betwixt and between, lie the time-shrouded tales of legend.'

The words come soft and melodious to our thoughts and we, the members of ThirskWriteNow, are lulled into a soporific trance as we see, oh so clearly, the flickering candlelight caressing the deep lines of his weathered and ancient face.

With a stroke of the nib we clothe him in ragged frockcoat and fingerless mittens, endowing his frame with the stooping presence and the obsequious countenance of a stylised Fagin. Completing the picture, we add bulbous eyes and lank, thinning hair around his balding pate, all the better to create a sense of eager trepidation in our susceptible minds.

We glance, with nervous anticipation, at the highly polished double doors through which The Librarian, for so we name our creation, has appeared and, one and all, we wonder what awaits us.

Candle trembling slightly in his gnarled left hand, the Librarian extends his right arm in an expansive gesture and summons a toothless and humourless smile.

"Listen well, my friends," he entreats us. "For all will depend on the course each of you will take. Beyond these great doors lie the seeds of all of creation; tales yet untold, legends yet unimagined, and they are there for you."

The soothing voice quietens our beating hearts, preparing us for some gentle adventure.

"For those of you who choose to brave this endeavour, the rules are few but, I beseech you, break them not. Once named you must take the tale told unto a given point, then guide it on its way, each of you speaking not less than five hundred words nor yet more than one thousand and, as your part in the tale reaches its conclusion, write me into your lines and let me speak of the one who must follow. 'Tis simple, by all accounts, even for such a gathering as this."

His sarcasm is not lost on us. His smile broadens and then, in an instant, is gone.

"But be warned." Gentle voice no more, the new harshness of his tone sharpens thought and quickens the pulse and we look at one another nervously. "Only one at a time may enter and, once inside, the way out will be barred."

The toothless smile returns, his voice softens once more.

"Until, that is, through me, another is named, one to whom the creation may be safely entrusted, and thus, the tale continues."

His protruding eyes sweep across the faces of his audience.

"I know not what lies beyond, save there is one who waits for his story to be told, and all of you, each in turn, shall tell it."

His eyes slide from face to face and eventually settle on one of the gathered company.

"But for now, Julie," he says with a smile. "He waits for you."

Slowly, silently, as the name of the first storyteller falls from his lips, the doors begin to open and the Librarian reaches out in invitation.

"So, come now, gentle friend, take my hand and have the courage to share with us all there may be to see. Pass through the doors and walk with me now into The Library of Lost Souls and there, tell me your tale."

Chapter One

It was as I had been led to expect: dark, windowless and silent. Yet it carried an air of tranquillity, as of souls sleeping soundly within its shelves. They had plenty of space, for no books belonged in this library. Those who knew no better might easily assume it to be bare.

As I tried to recall my instructions, the flickering candle flame served more to dull my memory than to cast any light on my mission.

I began searching the room and found, the further in I travelled, the less I could remember. Which had been one of the warnings; for this library served only to remove knowledge, not enhance it.

Reaching the farthest wall, I was careful not to let my hands stray into any shelf space. Instead, I ran my fingers gently along the wooden edges. These were waxy smooth, no rough splinters but slightly sticky, as if containing a small build up of skin.

Four feet along, the oak felt much cooler. I held my breath and waited for the stooping Librarian to bring the candle closer.

His face crumpled into a frown, and his gentle whisper seemed too loud in there.

"Are you *sure* this is the one?"

His bulging eyes forced doubt into my mind. I hesitated. The moment grew, developed. I sensed a pulse which was not mine. My legs ached as though they had walked a hundred miles. Frozen there for what felt like hours, I felt, almost subconsciously, a soft caress upon my wrist. I turned in horror to see my right arm was now lying completely within the shelf. Something barely visible was stroking it softly.

The frockcoat swung out as the Librarian strode away.

"So! Now you have chosen, or been chosen, I don't care to quibble. Bring him over here lest we wake any of the others."

Our threesome proceeded to a small table in the corner, the figure at my side growing more distinct as we walked.

As we sat in nervous silence, I could feel the cold disapproval of the Librarian regarding my choice. I dwelled again on my instructions. Eventually he spoke, addressing the spectre, which now appeared to be almost human.

"You are not yet free, Whisker Twinrot, and you shall not leave without my authority. Should you desire anything other than an immediate return to your shelf you must prove your worth, and present such evidence before us now."

Twinrot cleared his throat before speaking.

"Sire, I beg you; I have dwelled here for so many years, I have no knowledge of the outside world as it is today. I need to be sure of the dangers before I offer explanation. I need answers to, how shall I put it, *certain* questions to ensure both my own safety, and that of...." He reached out and gripped my wrist "... and that of my saviour."

The Librarian shifted uneasily in his seat, as if the chair was causing pain.

"And whose council do you seek, my friend?" he asked. "That of the writer who craves no more than flighty imagination, or that of the keeper of all knowledge, who is wise and trustworthy?"

Twinrot dragged a bony hand over his lips, as if daring them to give away long held secrets.

"Only one with a head full of illuminating thoughts can understand such complexities," he said. "It is time the truth was told, suffocated no longer. I know your fears, Librarian. You would twist the facts to hold this tale down, you would place it on a shelf where it could not escape and become known, but now there is hope, for someone must know enough to have me freed. I am no longer alone."

The Librarian flew out of his chair and grabbed the almost-human by the throat.

"Speak not! For this person was only the finder, sent here under instruction to wake the chosen one. Now she must depart and leave her unfortunate decision behind her. We shall call the next in line. She is known to us as Cathy, and through her you may find your voice, and perhaps tell your tale. Come – we go to the door, but you, my friend, will stay this side of it."

Chapter Two

I, Cathy, am beckoned with a bony finger to follow the Librarian into the space vacated by Julie. The unknown territory of the Library of Lost Souls.

Once beyond the ancient doors, I do not speak but quickly

become aware of a silent invitation into the strange subconscious of Whisker Twinrot, to learn his story. For the time being, I am no longer myself, I am subsumed by his voice and thoughts.

"*Now listen 'ere, let us set the record straight. I never intended to be 'ere in this damned place at all. Never in a million years. I made a mistake yer see, I got trapped between 'eaven and 'ell. 'Eaven is where everything is luvverly, an' perfick an' 'ell is where you sink to when you take a wrong turnin'.*

"*I took a wrong turnin' all right, I got bloody married! 'Er name was Rosie and to start wiv she was 'andsome, buxom an' all loved up. But she turned; she turned into a ramblin' Rosie, wiv thorns and spiky bits. She rambled all over, pickin' up who she fancied whenever she fancied. It drove me nuts.*

"*She was on the gin a lot of the time, flouncin' 'erself about and gettin' into mischief. I wasn't 'avin none of it. One night I clobbered 'er, well and truly clobbered 'er till there weren't an ounce of breath in 'er body and I ran. Ran to the docks an' got meself on a boat out of London.*

"*I'd never been to sea, never even seen the sea, never been further than me own backyard, 'cept down the boozer and a few little 'olidays at His Majesty's Pleasure for minor offences. But I 'ad to escape, 'cos I knew I would 'ave ended up danglin' from a rope for what I'd done this time.*

"*Anyway, I got a berth on a boat what was going to places I'd never even 'eard of. Places the other side o' the world. I weren't alone, loads of others 'ad signed up all tryin' to escape their life's burdens.*

"*I 'ad no one to answer to, no one would miss me, Whisker Twinrot. I 'ad no livin' soul to call me own. I was as free as a bird.*"

I sense a change in Twinrot's persona.

"*Now let me tell you this. I set sail on that boat with expectations of a better life and I did better myself for, listen to my diction now. Improved is it not?*

"*I left London as Whisker Twinrot, a low-life, a waster and a criminal but fortune smiled upon me, thanks to a certain Captain Soloman Sly, who became my mentor and benefactor.*

"*Knowing nothing of my background, he took me under his wing for he had no son of his own. He tutored and nurtured me with his knowledge, expertise and kindness.*

"*How easy it was to rise to his encouragement and become the man he willed me to be. He adopted me and I took his surname. He saw me through all my service to rise through the ranks so that I too earned the title of Captain, Captain Whisker Twinrot Sly.*

"*But however hard you try, you can't change a man's nature. The nature he was born with. Sooner or later it will catch up with him. Sly by name, Sly by nature, you might say. This time I had slipped through the net by a whisker.*"

The candle has dimmed, I return to my place beside Whisker Twinrot, not within him. Our mutual gaoler is becoming anxious for me to name the next person to continue the unravelling tale of Captain Whisker Twinrot Sly, as we now know him.

I name this person as Antony and I wish him well, for this place is a hard place to be. I have said farewell to my lost soul and bid him salvation. The Librarian has now opened the door and leads me through to the present world and, I hope, sanity.

Chapter Three

Bookbynde shuffled uncomfortably on his stool and glanced up from his desk as the latest invitee – me, Antony - was ushered through the polished doors, into the foyer. The Librarian paused waiting while the newcomer's name was laboriously recorded in the '*Ledger of Visitors*'.

Black tongue jutting through crooked teeth, Bookbynde duly set about scratching the new name on to the surface of the vellum, placing an '*X*' with a bent quill in the column headed '*In*'. He paused, hovering over the next column and looked questioningly at the Librarian.

"Reading Room," barked the Librarian. "I'm taking this visitor to the Reading Room. Note it well."

"Oh, I shall Librarian, I shall. 'Tis an honour many seek and offered to few, to enter the Reading Room."

We passed on down the corridor. As the echo of our footsteps grew fainter and the flicker of the Librarian's candle dimmed, Bookbynde lifted the inkwell and sipped, smacking his lips with pleasure. Unseen, he toasted our departing shadows and I did not hear him whisper:

"Be careful, visitor. Not everyone who enters the Reading Room returns, as the pages in my ledger dutifully show. Whisker Twinrot can testify to that."

The Librarian led the way. "Follow me closely, and don't touch the books. Never touch the books unless instructed by me." *What books,* I wondered, but didn't say out loud.

"Oh, I hope you don't mind stairs," he said.

He stopped abruptly at a point where the corridor crossed a narrower passageway. Turning to the right, he swept aside a velvet curtain to reveal a door. Reaching beneath his frock coat and carefully selecting a key from a bunch tied to a leather belt, the Librarian unlocked the door and began to climb.

"Three hundred steps to the top, so keep up, keep up," he cried.

Neither of us saw the hunched form of Whisker Twinrot lurking in the shadows.

The stairs wound before us, round and round. The higher we climbed the lighter it became, the gloom of below replaced by a yellow light spilling from the doorway of the Reading Room above us.

We entered a round, windowless room, set with alcoves, in each of which stood a carved oak reading lectern in the shape of an eagle with wings spread.

High above, the walls ended in a glass domed roof, where light filtered through faded linen blinds.

"Behold the Reading Room," said the Librarian, spinning theatrically on one foot, his arm arcing round in a circle. He stopped and pointed to a lectern bearing a small closed book, bound in green leather.

"May I suggest," he said. "You step over and learn more of what you seek. The story of *Whisker Twinrot*. Please, place both hands on the sides of the lectern, but whatever you do and whatever happens, do not, do not touch the book."

I stepped forward and placed my hands on the sides of the lectern, as I had been told, noticing how the wood was smooth and polished beneath my fingers.

The book in front of me seemed to glow and let slip a faint sigh. A slight tingling sensation pricked at my fingertips, running up my arms and filling my senses with a haze of letters and words.

Slowly, a vision emerged, that of a woman with long dark flowing hair and the greenest eyes I had ever seen. Barefoot and dressed in little more than rags, she stepped towards me, touched her hand to my cheek and smiled. It was the sweetest of smiles and reached into my very being.

"Please, do not be alarmed," said the vision. "For I sense you are a good man and mean me no harm. Permit me to introduce myself and say 'good evening', my dear visitor.

"My name is Francesca, Francesca Sly, and this is my story. I am some years younger than my brother, Soloman, who as you already know, took in Whisker Twinrot and raised him to the rank of Captain.

"The time came when my dear brother could no longer manage the damp weather of his native Tyneside and so sought a more favourable climate, where he could live out his days.

"Twinrot helped my brother procure a modest residence on a former plantation in the West Indies. We sold our family home in North Shields and entrusted all our money and possessions to Twinrot, who would go before us to make ready our new home and life. We would follow on, taking passage on a slower vessel.

"Alas, what fools we were, but how were we to know the man raised by Soloman and Mary as their son would behave so? We disembarked to find there was no house purchased in our name and Twinrot had vanished.

"We were ruined, destitute, left with nothing but the clothes we stood up in and very little money in our pockets.

"So, I seek your help and of those who follow, to bring Whisker Twinrot to justice and eternal damnation.

"However, before I go, let me whisper these words of warning in your ear. Trust no one within this Library and, when you depart, make sure Bookbynde marks you '*Out*' in his Ledger.

"Now you must go, our time together is done. The Librarian approaches to take you hence."

Once more, I found myself standing in the foyer before Bookbynde, his quill raised in readiness, his head angled questioningly at the Librarian.

"You may mark him '*Out*', now, Bookbynde," said the Librarian.

No sooner had he spoken than a terrific hammering shook the Library doors and they crashed open.

"Ah, the next visitor appears somewhat anxious to cross the

threshold. Step forward, - Claire."

Chapter Four

"Come with me to the Reading Room," said the Librarian, beckoning. "Please take care along these dark passageways."

"Yes," croaked Bookbynde from behind us. "Your friend made it out of this place. You might not be so lucky."

As we entered the room, I saw the girl, just as Antony had described her. Her body seemed young with its long limbs and graceful movements, but her face told of the troubled life she had led, her green eyes clouded with horror and grief, filled with the weight of a tale needing to be told.

"Please," Francesca began before we were even fully in the room. "Please, hear the rest of my story. You must listen to me before you are fooled by him, by the man who called himself my nephew.

"Please, do not allow him to possess you as he did your friend. Do not allow him to fool you with his tales, to force you to speak with his voice. He is not who he would have you believe. His is not a soul which deserves to be saved."

"But my dear," the Librarian protested. "From what we have heard so far, this Whisker Twinrot Sly..."

"Whisker Twinrot!" Francesca cut in. "Just Whisker Twinrot! Do not honour that man with the name of my brother and my father."

"Very well. This man, Twinrot, has presented himself thus far as nothing more than a scoundrel and a murderer.

"Nevertheless, his soul is the one which has been chosen to be heard, so hear him we must. Now, please." The Librarian turned to me. "You must summon the soul of Mister Twinrot."

He grabbed me by the arm and led me to the lectern.

"No!" cried Francesca. "No! He is not a lost soul. I am the lost soul."

Just then I heard a hoarse whisper. "*We're all lost in here are we not, Aunt Francesca?*"

Even as the words were spoken I was aware that they were coming from my own mouth.

"*Every word my aunt speaks is true,*" the voice from within me continued. "*When the man I called Father grew sickly, when he* was coughing up blood enough to soak the bed sheets red every morning, I wanted to do something to repay the years of kindness. I wanted to take him and his own over the water to sun and warmth, to live out their days in a place of riches spun from sugar.

"This girl was always jealous of me and the place I held in the good captain's heart. First, she begged him not to send money with me. Said I weren't to be trusted.

"Then, when the captain did not heed her, she found out from a cousin of hers in London what I done to my poor old Rosie, and she told the captain that, too. But still he did not lose faith in me. 'The measure of a man is not in the mistakes he makes, Francesca, but in the steps he takes to redeem himself,' that's what he told her. Couldn't expect someone like her to understand that thought, could you?"

Francesca gave a scornful cry. "How dare you, you..."

The Librarian held up a hand. "Allow Mister Twinrot to speak."

"I worked my own passage across the water for four long months, up to Newfoundland then back down, through storms and pirates, half the crew dead of the fever.

"I spent every night half-awake, hunched over the chest that contained all my dear father's worldly wealth. One night the third mate came at me with his knife when he thought I was sleeping.

"I told the captain he'd gone overboard in some heavy weather around Freeport. But I brought the gold safe to the new world and I set about buying my father the house he deserved. Now..."

I could feel the man's voice growing fainter in my throat, his tones mixing with my own.

"You need to bring in the next seeker of truth to discover what happened to the gold, to the house... and to me."

A shudder passed through me and I felt the man's spirit move across the room until I saw him standing next to Francesca.

"Tell them to ask her," he rasped, a filthy finger pointing at the skinny, bedraggled girl. "Ask my Aunt Francesca. Because she knows the real story, she knows exactly what happened. Tell them to ask her."

"Tell who?" I whispered.

"Tell.... Steve."

Chapter Five

The Librarian took my hand with fingers of chilled iron.

"Follow me and remember what you hear, so you can carry it beyond the door."

My senses turned inside out. His words smelt of teal and rotten honey. Maybe all this parchment in one place was triggering a childhood allergy? Behind me the wax seal contorted, sliding back into place and sealing the library against interlopers.

The reading room didn't appear quite as others described. I shouldn't be surprised. Maybe we carry our own reading room inside? I stood, waiting.

The Librarian stayed silent and gestured toward the lectern. I could see it was fashioned from an upturned tree bole and I knew beneath our feet budded leaves pressed their way through abandoned animal setts and graveyard dirt.

"You will hear my story now, or at least as much as you can before you are compelled to leave."

The girl was older now, her hair lank and torn at the ends. Each eye shifted colour, first to blue, then hazel and then sand, never settling for more than a few seconds. She seemed elsewhere, her skin shifting like silk in a breeze.

"Twinrot tried to convince you with his elegant falsehoods that he arrived in the New World with the best of intentions. We do not need to listen to his lies today," she said.

From the corner of the reading room I heard a muffled sound. A man gagged with mandrake, and bound with green brambles, slumped against the damp plaster.

"We set about working to stay the right side of destitute, and found a house that would take us in. I went into service, while my brother worked as an overseer on the plantations," she said, her fingers playing with the hem of her dress.

"An overseer of slaves? But that is barbaric," I said, going to lift my hands free of the lectern.

The Librarian held up a hand. My throat closed and my words died a hundred little deaths.

"You are here to listen," he said. "Please do not interrupt. Speak too many words in these rooms and the empty pages will sense them." He turned to Francesca and nodded.

"It was a different time. Different morals, but my brother was a good man. He tried to treat the slaves well, minimise the cruelty of the plantation owners. Keep the female slaves away from the house when the sons had been drinking.

"After a while, Soloman was spending more and more time with the slaves, disappearing into the forests on a night."

She paused. When she spoke again her voice cracked like the Caribbean soil.

"He would come back in the morning, skin covered in dirt and eyes rubbed raw. Stumbling. His breath never smelt of liquor, just cochineal and soot, his lips stained black. I asked him where he'd been, of course. He would mumble words in no language I had ever heard."

She sat on the floor, her skirt spreading out on the chipped tiles.

"One night I followed Soloman. I finished my duties early and waited 'til he left his quarters. On the edge of the estate he met with three others. I stayed in the shadows, but they spared no attention for their surroundings. I followed them deeper and deeper into the undergrowth. Insects crushed under my feet, shards of carapace sticking in my heels.

"Soloman and his companions walked for half the night, making no attempt to quieten their movements. There was no need, no one else would be stupid enough to travel in these treacherous woods at night.

"I had to strain to hear their voices over the constant dripping of rain. Us English called this place the Elfin Forest; the slaves called it The Palace of Water Ghosts.

"The clearing was small, ferns crushed into the sodden soil. Soloman stood at one end, arms stretched to the clouded trees. I huddled by a pile of rotting branches, trying to ignore the cloying smell of mould.

"I watched my brother take out a silver inkwell, the one from the master's writing desk. Were we reduced to theft? He removed the stopper and threw it to the ground, lifted the container to his mouth and drank the contents. For a moment everything was silent, then Soloman spoke. His words ran into each other. I recognised bits of English, Dutch, patois, but none of it made sense. Soloman's companions stood, heads bowed. The clearing changed. Drops of water flew in from the surrounding undergrowth, first the size of mites, then growing and growing, wrapping around my dear brother like a shift..."

Francesca stopped speaking mid-sentence. I glanced up to see the Librarian standing in front of me with his hand out.

"It is time for you to leave," he said.

"But what about Soloman? And Twinrot?" I looked over at the forlorn figure still bound in the corner.

"All stories heard here are glimpses. Partial and tattered. Maybe one of your fellow visitors will find out the rest of Soloman's story. Maybe you will be the only one to carry this tale, frayed as it is."

Francesca was hollow now, her eyes like salt. I took the Librarian's hand and let him lead me back to the door. The wax seal slipped to the floor and a name appeared in the pool.

"David."

Chapter Six

"Follow me, lad! The Reading Room's just up here on the left."

The Librarian strode in an unusually forthright fashion for one so time-worn and bony. As I trotted dutifully along behind him, I began to wonder what else there might be to this unearthly place. Why were we all being lead by the hand, regaled with conflicting accounts of lives presumably once lived, from these so-called 'lost souls'?

What *is* a 'lost soul'? A ghost? A memory? Or something more sinister, perhaps? It was as these questions swirled around my head that I resolved to slip away from the Librarian and delve a little deeper into '*The Library of Lost Souls*'.

As the Librarian strutted along the old, dank corridor, muttering rules and regulations under his breath, I slipped into an unmarked door to my right, not knowing what marvels, mysteries or dangers might lie beyond.

It turned out to be a stationery cupboard.

"Well, that's disappointing," I said with a sigh. Moments later I heard the Librarian spluttering furiously.

"Bookbynde! *Bookbynde*! We've lost one!"

"I thought they were all lost, Mr Librarian, sir," Bookbynde replied from behind his ledger.

"Not the souls, you cretinous...cretin! One of the writers has given me the slip."

I had to think fast, or I'd soon be found out. Frantically, I rifled through the boxes of paper and ink, though what I was expecting to find I honestly couldn't say. As I heard two sets of rapidly approaching footsteps, I found an empty cardboard box, which in my panic-ridden state I proceeded to place over my head as a last-ditch attempt at hiding.

Amazingly, the box slipped right past my head, my shoulders and all the way down to my feet. Meanwhile, bit by bit, I rose up into what appeared to be a moderately busy Caffè Nero. None of the customers so much as glanced in my direction as I stood in front of the counter in a state of utter bafflement.

"Hi! What can I get for you?" the pretty, young barista asked genially.

"Um, where am I?" I mumbled.

"Caffè Nero," she said matter-of-factly whilst pointing at the large Caffè Nero sign above her head just to ram the point home.

"Yeah, I can see that, but... I mean, a minute ago I was in '*The Library of Lost Souls'* and now, I'm..."

"Oh man, what were you doing there? That place is *creepy.*"

"I know! But the point is, how come I'm here now?"

"Portals. You're pretty new to Limbo then, I guess?"

I stared at her in a manner which I hoped conveyed a sense of shock and bewilderment but probably just made me resemble a bearded cod.

"Why is there a Caffè Nero in Limbo?" I ventured.

"Why is there a '*Library of Lost Souls'* in Limbo? Limbo's a weird place. We've got all kinds of stuff here. I heard there's this one place where everything's made of meat and there's this other place which is just a room with a goose in it and it's like a test or something and some people kill the goose and some people learn to communicate with the goose and sometimes the goose gives you a bag of honey but if you try and eat the honey it steals your shoes.

"Personally, I'd take a cup of overpriced coffee in an inoffensive environment over that any day of the week, which in this case, and every other case for that matter, is eternity. So, what can I get you today?"

"An explanation of everything you just said would be nice."

"Sorry, we're out of stock."

"Pity. Well, how about a tip on how to get back to the Library?"

"Oh, well the portals here are pretty temperamental. However you got in here you're going to need to find another way out. Just try stuff, basically."

"Like, just shove my head into any nearby holes?"

"Pretty much. Though some people prefer to try an arm first. That way, worst case scenario you only lose an arm."

"Right."

"And not a head," she added with a cheerful grin.

"Yeah, I got that. Well, you've been very helpful," I said quietly, and retired to the gents. I looked at the three unoccupied stalls and sighed.

"Well, this is going to be fun," I said with a grimace.

I honestly couldn't tell you how long I spent leaping from one permutation of Limbo to the next - time doesn't work like that on this existential plane - but suffice it to say, when I finally re-emerged in the Library I had seen, eaten and been mauled by a lot of things I hoped to never see, eat or be mauled by again.

The portal I found eventually, exited via Bookbynde's lunchbox.

"He's back, Mr Librarian, sir!" yelled Bookbynde, as I clambered wearily out of the box and slumped against the wall. "I had better sign you '*Out*'," he added officiously.

The Librarian scowled darkly at me and pointed an accusatory finger.

"Where have you been, boy? Have you been tampering with my souls?"

"Oh, they're yours, are they?" I enquired innocently.

"Don't you put words into my mouth!" he snapped.

"I rather thought that was the point of this exercise," I mused.

"Enough! Send in the next one. I trust they shan't be as insolent as you, my lad?"

"I can't speak for Barbara," I said, "so I'll offer no such guarantee."

Chapter Seven

Nerves are slowly getting the better of me as I sit in the outer chamber, waiting for my name to be called.

I keep looking at my watch, trying to work out how long I've been here, but the bloody thing's stopped. I want to get up and go, however, the door we all entered by has disappeared, leaving only the heavy double doors the others have since gone through – but not returned.

A short time ago there was some sort of commotion on the other side. Raised voices. Things falling over. It did nothing to calm me.

Suddenly the doors fly open with such a force they vibrate on their hinges. Dust billows into the chamber from around the Librarian. He seems agitated.

"Barbara," he snaps, pointing a gnarled finger in my direction. "Come with me. Now!""

Unlike with the others, he walks behind me into the foyer. The place is in complete chaos. I stop, transfixed by the scene.

The Librarian pushes me further in and I stumble over an upturned stool. There's a desk lying next to it, paper scattered everywhere and, curiously, an overwhelming smell of freshly ground coffee fills the room. In the midst of all this mayhem, someone is scrabbling about on the floor.

"Get up, and mark this woman down in the Ledger," yells the Librarian.

"But my lunch, sir. First I must catch my lunch before it gets away."

Something scuttles over my foot and tries to hide under a fold in the moth-eaten carpet. But it's not fast enough. With a deft swipe of his hand, the Clerk catches the sandwich and lifts it to his gaping, black mouth. Sticking out from between two pieces of mildewed bread, are four pairs of legs, moving up and down in slow spider synchronicity.

"*Don't!*" The loudness of my voice surprises us all. "*That's disgusting.*"

The Librarian turns to me. He must be having a bad day – if indeed day it is – as his once bulging eyes are now nothing but narrow slits; his mouth two thin lines; his jaw set hard.

Without looking at his assistant, he says deliberately, in a voice too quiet for comfort.

"We are going to the Reading Room, Bookbynde. I want this mess cleared up before I come back."

Upstairs there is, quite literally, a storm brewing. Menacing, dark grey clouds rumble around the ceiling. Flashes of lightning streak from one corner to another. Large hailstones pitter, patter and ping off everything in the room. I've never seen anything like it, well, not indoors, anyway.

A weak, disembodied voice speaks from the shadows.

"Brought another one, have you, Librarian? What tales is she going to come out with, I wonder?"

Straining through the gloom between pulses of light, I see a small, frail looking man, bound up and half dead.

"Do not speak, Twinrot. You are here to be judged, not **to** judge."

The sight of this poor wretch puts the tin hat on it for me, and it all becomes much too much.

"What the hell is going on here? It's like the Mad Hatter's tea party. Just who do you think you are, treating people like this? You've no right........"

Before I have chance to finish, the Librarian is standing with his face six inches from mine. I can smell his maggoty breath. His iced-turquoise eyes now wide with anger.

"YOU would do well to remember who I am. YOU would do well to remember where you are and why you are here."

A massive clap of thunder shakes the whole building. Static electricity crackles in the air. Bright blue and violet plasmas run along the edges of the Librarian's frockcoat and leap into the room. I fear he is about to implode. Stepping back, I catch sight of my watch. It's working again but now it's going backwards.

Above the clamour I hear loud, almost hysterical laughter. Twinrot is up on his feet and is breaking free of his bonds. He is tall and upright. With every second that goes widdershins, he gets stronger. He appears to be feeding off the Librarian's discomfort. Which only serves to make the Librarian even more incandescent with rage.

"GET OUT." He shouts at me. "GET OUT NOW. You've broken '*The Rules*'. You and the one who went before you. Look what you've done, Twinrot is........."

I don't hear the rest of the sentence. I'm down the stairs, heading for the foyer. When I get back to Bookbynde, the place is calm, neat and tidy.

"Leaving are you, miss?" He grins, putting a half-eaten sandwich under the desk. "Did you tell the Master who is next?"

"No, I didn't," I say, expecting the Librarian to be hot on my heels. "Tell him it's Jackie. Now where's the door?"

Chapter Eight

Bookbynde greeted me with an obsequious grin, picking at what looked suspiciously like a spider's leg lodged between his teeth.

"I have taken the liberty of logging your arrival already," he said. "Follow me."

He hurried towards the stairs leading to the Reading Room.

"Come on, woman!" He glared back at me. "There's no time to waste!"

I clattered up the stairs behind him, wishing I'd kept up the gym sessions beyond the second week in January. Bookbynde paused to retrieve a mop and bucket someone had left at the top, then hastened on. At the door to the Reading Room, he became cautious.

"There has been ... an incident.' he said, indicating the cleaning apparatus.

We stepped inside. The room looked as though a hurricane had hit it. The massive reading table knelt wearily on its two smashed end-legs, seeming to lament over the sorry heap of items it had once held. These now resided in puddles of melting hailstones. The various lecterns were huddling in pairs, either comforting one another or enjoying a shocked gossip. The remains of the long, black curtains were still smoking. I could see a bundle of chains in one corner.

"Oh dear, oh dear," said my companion. "I fear the hour of reckoning is upon us."

"Why? What reckoning? Hey! No! What are you doing? NO! You can't!" I screamed as Bookbynde finished tightening Twinrot's newly discarded chains around my wrists.

He shook his head, shrugged, and scurried away.

I jerked at the chains. Immediately, they began to grow hot, uncomfortably so. At the same time, sinews of words seemed to grow in my head:

"The chains will burn - it's now your turn - now you will burn - the chains will turn," and a laugh grew and grew, like that of some demented genie, hammering me to the ground. Then, nothing.

"I had no choice, Sir." It was Bookbynde's familiar whine. "After the trouble we've had with the last two, and with Twinrot and the Librarian missing, I couldn't risk her wandering about."

Two strong, capable thumbs were massaging my wrists, easing away the soreness, the contamination. I opened my eyes. The face I encountered seemed somehow to flow: wise Native American melting into Latin Lothario, and back again; the first reassuring, the second definitely not. The voice matched the latter, the words the former

"Muy bien. That is good. You are awake. Can you stand?"

"I ... I think so."

"Good again. Bookbynde thought he had left you only for a few minutes. He had forgotten how time runs backwards in this room, so your ordeal lasted, in reality, much longer." He looked deep into my eyes, gently moving my head from side to side. "I think you have been fortunate, I cannot see any permanent damage."

He became brisk. "Come. We have work to do, my dear."

"What work? Who are you?"

He smiled. "Two questions, one answer. Longfeet DeLeche, madam."

I couldn't help it. I looked at his feet, and they were, indeed, long. Incredibly long. And they were encased in what looked like a pair of wellingtons made from a spotted-cow milk jug.

"Observe," he said, pointing an elegant toe.

A little stream of milk poured to the floor. Before I could say anything, spots of ultra-violet appeared in the stream.

"See," he pointed. "These spots are plasma-essence of Librarian, which appeared as he dematerialised. We must follow."

"But why do you need me?" I asked.

"You read in the human form, and sometimes the Librarian is human. Here."

While speaking, he had been following the trail of spots and now stopped by one of the quivering lecterns. He opened the book it contained with great care and took my hand.

"Hold on tight," he said, as we bent our heads to the text. "This portal could be uncomfortable."

It was. DeLeche slapped my back as I spluttered the last of the leaves out of my mouth. We had emerged from a less than salubrious teapot in a dingy room, which reeked of mud and midden.

"As I suspected," he said. "Twinrot reverts to type. A river-rat."

He spilled more milk from his right toe and once more we followed the spots. DeLeche kept up a steady commentary:

"It appears to have been a successful dematerialization, as Twinrot is unaware he is being accompanied. The Librarian has mastered his rage. He is thinking clearly, planning. But most importantly, he knows that he must somehow keep Twinrot away from anything to do with coffee. Twinrot's time in the West Indies... ." He broke off, frowned, pointed. "Read that."

I looked, amazed, as a word appeared in the spot he was indicating. "It says '*Creator*'."

"And these?"

"'*Obtains*' '*Necklace*', no, sorry, '*Necessary*'... um.... " The last spot was smudged. I squinted at it. "I think it says '*Souvenir*'."

"Madre de Dios!" DeLeche paled. 'You must go back, now. Tell the next one to hurry."

His last words were muffled by the fluff at the bottom of the pocket he was stuffing me into. Before I knew it, I was tumbling from the umbrella stand in the foyer of the Library, sending it clattering into Bookbynde's desk.

"Quick!' I gasped. "Tell Amanda to bring the Cafe de Paris!"

Chapter Nine

The crash of the slamming doors echoed around the entrance hall and for a moment I stood still, giving my eyes time to adjust to the flickering light of the candles. I was totally alone. Ahead of me was a dark sweep of stairs and, to my left, a broad expanse of desk, its surface a clutter of parchment, inkwells, books, quills.

I moved closer and noticed a large brass bell beside a chipped plate on which were a few curled crusts of dried bread and what, rather unpleasantly, appeared to be half of a spider.

Hesitantly I glanced around the empty room. I took a deep breath and tapped my hand sharply on the bell. As the sound echoed away a disembodied voice filled the air.

"*I regret to inform you that, due to unforeseen circumstances, today at 1800 hours precisely The Library of Lost Souls will close until further notice."*

Involuntarily, I glanced up at the large clock on the wall above and behind the desk and, much to my relief, it was only five fifty three, but the voice was still speaking.

"All visitors should make their way quickly to the exit and report to Bookbynde in time to be checked out before 1800 hours. Any person or persons remaining on the premises after that time will be condemned to a lingering death and an almost certain eternity as a lost soul. The Librarian would like to apologise for any inconvenience this may cause. Thank you for visiting The Library of Lost Souls."

The voice died away.

"Hello?" I called into the empty room. "Mr Bookbynde?"

Silence. I glanced nervously up at the ticking clock and then hurried to the doors and shook the handles but, as I feared, the doors were locked.

"You're very late," came a voice from behind me. I spun around to see Bookbynde sitting behind the desk, picking his teeth with an inky quill.

"Hardly," I protested, hurrying back to the desk. "I just came when I was called."

"Ah," said Bookbynde knowingly, "but who called you?" He smiled. "Not that it matters any more. It's all over. We're closing at six." He looked up at the clock. "Orders from the boss."

"You mean the Librarian?"

Bookbynde laughed unpleasantly. "Him, the boss? Hardly. Besides, the Librarian's gone... vanished. Ain't no one seen him." He looked up at the clock. "Two minutes."

"You'd better sign me '*Out*' then." I said hurriedly.

"I can't do that now, can I?" he sneered, "seeing as I haven't signed you '*In*' yet."

"Well, sign me '*In*' quickly and then you can sign me '*Out*'."

Bookbynde considered this for what seemed to me to be a very long moment and then he sighed with exasperation and opened his ledger.

"Let me see now," he mused, running a gnarled finger down the page, taking obvious pleasure in taking his time. "Ah yes. I see you now... Hmm, interesting..." he looked up at me. "It's you, isn't it?"

I wasn't quite sure what to say to that.

"You're the one... you started it." He gave me a sly smile and inked a heavy black cross against my name and, even as he did so, the clock began to strike the hour.

"Quickly, Bookbynde!" I urged him, "sign me '*Out*'."

Bookbynde laughed. "Oh, I couldn't possibly do that." He slammed the ledger shut. "The Library's closed."

"It can't be closed!" I protested. "You have to let me out!"

Bookbynde shrugged carelessly.

"Sorry," he said, not sounding it in the slightest. "It's more than my job's worth."

"Who's in charge here?" I demanded.

"I really couldn't say. Now, if you'll excuse me, that's my shift over. Good day to you."

He turned on his heel and vanished in the blink of an eye.

"Horrible little man!" muttered a voice behind me and I turned to see a young woman sitting on the bottom of the stairs. She stood up, wiping her hands on her long skirts as she came towards me. "Don't pay 'im no mind, luvvie. The Librarian will let you out."

"Where is the Librarian?"

"He's around... well, actually, if truth be told, he's hiding."

"Hiding from whom – or what? Do you know where he is? Will you take me to him?"

"Maybe...perhaps," she smiled and corrected herself. "Yes, of course I will... when it's time, but we have things to do first, if we're to save Twinrot."

"Why should we save him?" I demanded. "To be honest, he seems like a pretty unsavoury character, from what I've heard so far. Quite apart from everything else, he murdered his wife."

"Tell me about it!" She laughed and thrust out her hand. "I'm Rosie... Rosie Twinrot."

I took her hand uncertainly and shook it.

"You were married to Whisker Twinrot?"

"Married to and murdered by!" she confirmed with a broad grin. "But that was a long time ago. He ain't a bad old stick really – well, aside from the fact that he killed me, but that's water under the bridge, as they say. Truth is, he ain't a bad man... he made a mistake... a hell of a mistake, I grant you, but a mistake all the same, and he tried his best to make good."

"That's not what I heard," I muttered.

"No, but it's why you're here, ain't it? It's why you all come... to learn his story... but time is short and I don't think..."

she broke off, turning to look towards the desk where Bookbynde had just re-materialised.

"Hey, you!" He pointed straight at me. "The Library's reopened – orders from the boss! Your time is up. Over here, now!"

"They don't want you to know!" hissed Rosie. "They won't give any of you enough time. Listen to me... you have to help each other learn his story. You know where the truth lies."

"I said over here now!" shouted Bookbynde and I felt myself being tugged irresistibly towards him, as Rosie flickered and faded before my eyes.

"You know where you have to go!" insisted Rosie desperately, her voice faint now. "Find the portal to the Elfin Forest!"

She was gone and I found myself facing Bookbynde across his desk.

"I want more time, Bookbynde," I told him. "I *need* more time."

He shrugged and opened his ledger. "I can't help you. You're a rule-breaker, just like the ones who came before, except you're worse, because you set the parameters. So you, of all people should know better. You have to leave now."

He signed me '*Out*' with a scratchy '*X*' against my name.

"How did I break the rules?" I demanded as, behind me, the doors creaked open.

"You said no more than a thousand words... we're at one thousand, one hundred and thirty four... thirty six... seven... eight."

"Enough!" I muttered as I headed for the door.

"Wait!" Bookbynde scuttled round his desk and put himself between me and the doors, a grubby envelope held in his hands. "There's a letter for you."

"From who?" I demanded, taking the envelope.

"From whom," he corrected me, clicking his tongue loudly. "And you call yourself a writer. Now, out!"

I opened the envelope and pulled out the contents as I headed through the doors. It was unsigned but I knew, without doubt, it was from the Librarian. There was only one word scrawled across the cream paper. It said "Barbara."

Chapter Ten

"If I ever see that obnoxious little squirt again, I'll have his guts for garters," I swore to myself as I opened yet another door, only to find yet another brick wall on the other side.

I had been wandering around this infernal labyrinth for hours trying to find my way out. The delightful Clerk had obviously taken great pleasure in sending me on a wild goose chase. In my mind's eye, I could see him sitting there, feet up on his desk, leaning back on his stool, laughing his ugly head off.

Oddly, as I thought it, behind the next door there were no bricks. Instead, I found myself in the same room, the same obnoxious little squirt sitting there, feet up on his desk, leaning back on his stool, laughing his ugly head off.

When he caught sight of me, both he and his stool completed their precarious arc and landed with a rather pleasing 'thud' on the floor.

"I've got a bone to pick with you," I said, but was interrupted.

"Bookbynde!" The Librarian's voice echoed down the hallway.

The Clerk shot to his feet with a somewhat surprised expression on his face.

"I told you to get that Barbara person back here. Where is................Oh!" He stopped short in his tracks. "You're here." Spinning round to retrace his steps he added quickly. "Let us try again, shall we?"

As I set off to follow him, Bookbynde whispers behind me.

"Pssst, Miss, the way out – the portal – watch your watch."

Up in the Reading Room, things appear to be much the same as the last time I was here; only without the weather episode.

Twinrot seems calm, happy almost. Standing cosily close to him is a woman I haven't seen before and, yes, he has his arm around her. On the other hand, the Librarian appears to have physically and mentally shrunk.

From nowhere, I get an attack of *deja* vu. The air crackles and I fear more hailstones but there's not a cloud in the ceiling. Next to me, an image forms, disappears, forms again. A sea blue hologram of a short, stocky man, muscular and mermaid tattooed, finally flickers to life.

"Shwmai Idris Jones is the name, Chief Stoker on the SS

Carmarthen Bay. I've got to tell you this, boys. I sailed with Captain Cat there," he nodded towards Twinrot, "well, that's what the crew called 'im any'ow, 'Cat' as in 'whisker', see? – to places most people 'ave never even yeard of. 'E saw us right when we was crossin' the Atlantic, dew, rough ol' place that is, aye. But 'e 'ad a sense for it. 'E'd take us round the really bad storms see, and the icebergs, even if it meant we 'ad to go south instead o' north, like, y'know. Don't get me wrong, Captain Sly was a good man too, see, but 'e never 'ad the same nous as Cat. Sly always listened to 'im though. Thank God. And 'e'd change course to wherever Cat said. Aye, Cat saved all of us many times an' I won't 'ave nothin' bad said against 'im, see, nothin'. To me, the man's a ruby; a diamond." With that, Idris Jones, flickered and vanished.

For a moment nothing was said. Finally, Twinrot broke the silence.

"It would appear I have two people on my side now, Librarian. What do you make of that?"

The Librarian did not reply. Instead, with an icy, bony grip, he caught hold of my arm and unceremoniously pulled me to the door. Twinrot shouted after us.

"Since everyone seems to be breaking the rules around here, I think I'll choose the next witness, Librarian. Let's have Cathy back, shall we? She can help my Rosie, here."

He gave the woman a squeeze; she smiled up at him.

Once again, the Librarian said nothing but yanked me out into the hallway and back to the Foyer.

"Er, Cathy, then, is it?" Bookbynde asked in a small voice, seeing the look on his Master's face.

"It would appear so," hissed the Librarian. "Sign this one out."

"There's the exit, Miss," pointed the Clerk, once he'd finished writing in his ledger. With the same inky finger, he tapped his wrist and, with his back turned to the Librarian, mouthed the word. "Remember."

In the labyrinth, there was just enough light from the candles, heavily waxed on their iron sconces, to make out my watch. I walked from one door to another, not opening them this time, just waiting for some sort of reaction.

I'm not sure how far I'd gone, when the hands on my timepiece suddenly went whirring round and round in both directions at once.

"I suppose this must be it," I said to the door in front of me.

In the dim light it looked like all the others. Gingerly, I turned the handle to find - a brick wall.

"Nothing new there, then," I muttered in total disappointment.

But there was something; something different. I reached out and touched the masonry. My fingers disappeared. It felt like jelly and wallpaper paste and frog spawn. Instinctively, I jerked my arm back.

"Bloody hell." The reaction sounded off the walls. So, this was it. The portal. Much as I didn't relish the thought of being covered in sticky goo, I knew this was the way I had to go.

Closing my eyes and taking the deepest breath I could muster, I took a large step forward. Where would it lead? Who – or what – was on the other side? Time alone would tell.

Chapter Eleven

Well, this is all becoming most confusing. It sounds like pandemonium down there in the gunnels and people keep popping in and out of portals here, there and everywhere.

God knows where Barbara has been but you could hardly have taken her to see the Queen afterwards. Yuk!

Anyway, I am bracing myself for the next onslaught. The place sort of reminds me of Peter Pan's Playground at Southend, when I was about twelve. I was at a funny age. I went into the Crooked House that had all those distorted mirrors and it was pitch black and I remember going over a sort of spongy floor that completely disorientated me. I wasn't quite the same afterwards.

Mind you, I'm at a funny age now, so what's different? Anyway, better get on with the job.

Eh up, here comes old misery-guts again, beckoning me with his bony finger. Signed in by Bookbynde and on into the reading room.

Actually, if I recall correctly, I have never been here before and it all seems a bit quirky and there is poor old Twinrot with a look of expectant hope upon his face. Oh my God, am I supposed to be his saviour? Oops! Mr Librarian admonishing me for not paying attention. Yes, Sir, no Sir, three bags full Sir. Okay, got it.

Rosie has materialised and entwined herself around her beloved Twinrot, who by all accounts has been exonerated by his beloved Rosie for his crime of passion brought on by her behaviour and undue stress.

Twinrot supposedly did not fulfil his promise to purchase a retirement home for Soloman and Francesca Sly, who, by my reckoning sounds like a right old cow and is not being entirely honest in her account of events.

Eeny meeny miney mo, who's telling Porky Pies then? What we need to find out is what happened to Twinrot *en route* to complete his goodly deed and what the hell happened to Soloman, who seems to have gone a bit loopy and completely bonkers, in cloud-cuckoo-land; and Francesca, who seems to be the only eye-witness to her brother's strange behaviour.

Yes, Mr. Librarian I have got my head stuck in the plant pot. I am trying to find the portal to the Elfin Forest. Ah yes, here we go into the sludgy compost, comprising decomposed God knows what and entangled fern roots. I think Bookbynde must use this as his slop bucket.

Well, I was dying for a bit of good weather but this takes the ship's biscuit. It's hot, sticky and stinky and I've got compost everywhere, all up my nose and in my hair. I wonder if it has any rejuvenating properties. Anyway, I have a creepy feeling someone is behind me. Oh hello, Captain Sly, sir, bit sneaky to turn up like that. No, you don't look too well, actually, you look a bit like death warmed up but I suppose it's to be expected with all the gunge you were drinking.

What? The slaves duped you? So, they weren't that friendly after all, then, and you have suspicions that your dear little sister was in on it. Was she now? She fancied the plantation owner and wanted you out of the way because she didn't want to end up being a nursemaid to her old decrepit brother. Well now, that puts a different light on things, doesn't it? I thought she had funny eyes and a rather sharp tongue.

Well, I'm glad I found you but you do seem to have been a bit too trusting, it seems, bearing in mind how we are still researching Twinrot's involvement in all this stuff.

Oh, he was all right, was he? You feel confident about that, even though he didn't come up with the goods and appears to have mislaid a rather large amount of fortune in transit. You don't think he did it on purpose; he just got waylaid along the way.

Well, I rather think that needs to be investigated, don't you?

Look, I'm sorry, Captain Sly, but I have to go now back to the library, otherwise I might be stuck here with you and I don't relish the thought. I apologise if I have offended you but it's just the way it is.

See you later, alligator. Actually, I don't suppose you know the way out, do you? I mean, I did come via a plant pot but I can't seem to locate it in all this boggy stuff.

Oh right, thanks, I can slip into your stolen inkpot. Ouch, I've just been stabbed by Bookbynde's pen nib. Hey, let me out first, you moron.

Well, that's another little trip over, back to the drawing board. This is like trying to fit a jigsaw together. Oh sorry, Mr. Librarian sir, yes, I know I have to name the next investigator. What about Claire? Yes, let's have Claire again.

Chapter Twelve

"The Elfin Forest," I kept muttering to myself, as Bookbynde led me back into the library. "I have to get to the Elfin Forest."

I had heard what Captain Sly told Cathy and, remembering those icy green eyes of Francesca's, I tended to believe him. They were the kind of eyes which sometimes appeared innocent, like those of someone with nothing to hide but more likely, in my experience, belonging to someone with nothing to show. No human emotion, no conscience, no cares.

"In here," Bookbynde muttered gruffly, "you know the drill."

Old Whisker himself and the buxom, wart-faced Rosie were together in a corner and nodded amiably at me as I entered.

"Good luck to you, miss," Rosie said chirpily. "We're counting on you, dear, to get 'im out of here."

"Can I speak to Captain Sly?" I asked Bookbynde. "I would like to hear for myself how he tells his tale."

"Ahem." It was the horrible, slimy little Librarian, all phlegm and eye gunk and fingernails. I had not heard him creep up behind me. "I'm afraid that is not possible, madam. This is '*The Library of Lost Souls*'. Captain Sly has been redeemed and therefore is only available via special inter-library loan. Which is, as I'm sure you will appreciate, extremely costly. You lot have had your turn of the good Captain. You must do the rest of your research amongst the damned, I'm afraid."

"Fine." Nothing about this place could surprise me any more. "Then please tell me how to get to the Elfin Forest. Whatever happened to poor old Sly and Twinrot, that place holds the proof. Where is the portal?"

Bookbynde sniggered, snorting uncontrollably. "Sorry, sir," he said to the Librarian, holding up a hand in apology. "It's just that they're all so... naïve."

At this last word he descended into a fit of the giggles so long and deep that he slowly began to turn beige through excess oxygen.

"I'm sorry, madam," the Librarian said lugubriously, although I thought I detected the hint of a self-satisfied smile around his eyes. "We do not know which portals lead where. Which is rather the point of them."

"So, how should I ...?"

I glanced wildly around the room, trying to fix on something that might take me where I needed to go. The inkwell? Cathy had tried that. The waste-paper basket? The desk? The shelves? The umbrella stand? Bookbynde's upturned whale-skin umbrella? One of the pictures on the wall?

Aware of how fast time was running out, I made for the waste-paper basket, resolving to try anything and everything in the room until either I got what I wanted or my time expired.

After some seconds, during which I felt like an earthworm in a blender, I emerged blinking into daylight.

Bloody Caffe Nero again.

I went back through the earthworm process and when I emerged, ran headfirst towards the desk. As it turned out, the desk was not a portal and I now had a bruise on my forehead.

I tried the umbrella stand and the instant, vomity whooshing sensation told me this at least was going to take me somewhere.

It did; to Wakefield Municipal Bus Station. I tried each of the Librarian's framed portraits in turn and ended up in, respectively: a parish hall in Scotland in the middle of a child's birthday party; the car park of a shopping mall in Indiana during a hailstorm; an elderly Jamaican woman's front porch; and the Chelsea Flower Show pavilion on members' day.

Finally, in desperation and with thumb and forefinger pinched over my nose, I plunged into Bookbynde's brown, greasy umbrella.

Before I even opened my eyes, I knew I was in the right place. The cloying humidity, the damp, mossy smell, the guttural, tuneless chanting of slave voices. It could be nowhere else.

The singing, if such it could be called, was coming from a circle of muscular black men, naked from the waist up and daubed in paints and oils. I could not understand any of the words coming from their mouths.

The one white man among them, older and weaker and with a bleak, vacant stare, was silent, his face rapt as he swayed in time with their chants.

"*He weren't never a man for the church, you see, back home.*" The voice in my ear startled me. I swung round. There was no one there. "*Don't worry, love. I'm talking to you from the library.*" It was Twinrot. "*I can see what you see from up here,*" he explained.

"*My father,*" he went on, "*he never were much for any of the Jesus nonsense. But these lads here, when they was brung over from Africa, they brought their own religion with them. And my father, he were a broken man. He took some comfort in all this stuff. Can't blame him for that, can we?*"

Just then something caught my eye in the trees behind me – Captain Sly! And beyond him, a blur of movement, of women's clothes and long ringlets of hair. It was Francesca, and she was with a man – a young, white man with thick blond hair and the blunted, inbred features of a younger son of the aristocracy. They looked at each other and smiled an intoxicated grin of private glee, then turned and walked away hand in hand.

"Where are you, Twinrot?" I said quietly. "I see the Captain, I see Francesca. But where are you? Why did you not help him? Even I can see how lost he is here."

"Ahem." Him again. The Librarian. "Your time is up, madam. I am bringing you back now."

"No!" I shouted, though already I could feel the whirling pull of the portal, "just a minute longer! I need to know where Twinrot is!"

"Tell the next one to ask him," the rasping voice instructed me. "Tell Julie."

Chapter Thirteen

Bookbynde removed a gunk-encrusted finger from his left nostril when he saw me.

"Here's trouble, Librarian. This one's the finder, the one who sought out Twinrot."

Only the Librarian and I had been in the Lost Soul Storage Facility when I searched for the chosen one.

"Where were you hiding, then, Bookbynde?"

He smirked and jumped into his umbrella portal.

The Librarian glowered at me.

"Follow me to the reading room and see if *you* can find the answers from the Elfin Forest."

"No!" I stepped closer to him. "My instructions were to return to the Shelves of Lost Souls, because there is another to be released."

The Librarian's voice cracked dry.

"Very well, but tell me, who gives you this information? Who outside this Library knows so much?"

"They don't sign a name. My orders come through the post, with a stamp from the West Indies. Now, I need the shelf containing the soul of Mary Sly, Captain Soloman's wife."

The Librarian walked as slowly as he could along the shelves, holding the candle so it managed to hide more than it lit, but eventually we reached the far corner where he jabbed a bony finger

"She's here, but I beseech you not to release another untrustworthy source of drivel."

I reached my hand in and felt her firm grip. On pulling her out, I was surprised to see she materialised much faster than Twinrot had. We sat around the same table as before whilst she warmed up and drew strength, seemingly from the equal weakening of the Librarian. I turned to him.

"Tell me Librarian, are you made of the souls who rest in here? Others have noted how, as one develops substance, you appear to weaken."

His eyes dimmed a little and he drew a rasping breath.

"You ask too many questions of me. Your role is to bring Mary's words to life. You are wasting precious time."

We turned to Mary, a strong, muscular woman with a firm jaw and neat appearance. I quickly related how Twinrot had been re-united with Rosie, how questions remained unanswered about him and his deeds regarding Captain Sly's fortune, and how her sister-in-law Francesca was also under suspicion.

She took in all this information calmly and, upon my request, began her tale with care.

"My marriage to Soloman Sly lasted just fifteen years, a second one for both of us. Like Rosie, I was murdered but it was a greed-ridden killer who took my life.

"I had received a substantial inheritance and intended to spend it on retirement with my beloved Soloman, but I was poisoned before we got the chance."

I had to interrupt.

"Who poisoned you, Mary?"

Her face hardened.

"I don't know," she said. "But I have my suspicions. Francesca for one. She wanted her hands on the money and was certainly mean enough.

"There's my first husband, Longfeet De Leche, he was rather strange, I have to say. We divorced.

"Then there's that two-faced sailor, Jones. We had an affair, you see. There's a few others too, who would have benefitted by getting rid of me."

"What about Whisker Twinrot? Could he have been the one who poisoned you?"

Mary's mouth dropped open.

"Oh good grief, certainly not! He was our son and a fine young man he was, too. No, he worked hard for my Soloman and had plenty of money of his own. We were set to leave him all we owned, once we'd gone.

"He was another one who greatly irked Francesca.

"Anyway, he and Soloman were away at sea when I was poisoned. If you find out who killed me, you might find it's connected to what happened to my poor son; and the gold."

Clearly, all this was well worthy of further investigation, but I frowned.

"If you were innocent of any crime, how ever did you end up as a lost soul?"

She took on a cunning expression, accompanied by a small

upturn of her lips.

"Ah, I didn't say I was entirely innocent. Oh no, my dear. I killed a man, an evil man. Soloman knew about it, which is why he ended up here, as well, for helping me to cover it all up."

I was shocked. Mary hadn't struck me as the murdering kind. This was quite some learning curve I was on. I noticed the Librarian leaning closer to her, licking his lips slowly.

Mary continued.

"A slave trader came over on one of Soloman's ships; a weak and evil specimen, working for some secret master, he was. We heard tales about his terrible deeds.

"Anyway, when he found out we had a bit of money, and that Soloman owned his own ship, he tried to involve us with the wicked slave trade.

"Of course, my husband would have nothing to do with it and set sail without him to the West Indies, with his cargo. Unfortunately, the slimy creature decided to get friendly with me, if you know what I mean.

"We got into a fight and I bashed his temple with a heavy glass inkwell. He went dead, he did. Dead. Straight away, without a sound.

"That night, I dragged his body to the cliffs and shoved him over. So that's why I'm here.

"Now, if you'll excuse me, I'll just find my Soloman. He's got some explaining to do, regarding working as an overseer and getting involved with slaves."

Mary stood up ready to leave but the Librarian blocked her way.

"I fear you have missed something, my dear lady. You haven't told us who this slave trader was, or his master."

Mary shrugged. "What does it matter now, after all these years? I've no idea who the master was, other than someone very rich and powerful. The worm-riddled creature I bashed on the head was just his servant.

"He was a madman, you know, always ranting on about some place called The Palace of Water Ghosts. His name was Montgomery Swallowtail Bookbynde."

The Librarian made a choking sound, his protruding eyes unblinking. He leapt up, shouting.

"Get out, both of you! Find Antony. He'll know what to do."

Chapter Fourteen

There was something different about Bookbynde today.

His black hair was carefully parted down the middle, slicked down behind his ears. He was wearing a striped blazer, with cream-coloured trousers. He was sporting a silk cravat, tucked into a clean white flannel shirt.

A slender cigarette holder was clenched between his black teeth and he was carefully holding the stem of a tall fluted cocktail glass between finger and thumb.

The usual dreary, shabby and, in truth, disgusting demeanour I was accustomed to seeing on entering the library, was gone, replaced by what I can only describe as an air of joviality and of someone enjoying a few moments of stolen relaxation. Which promptly disappeared, the moment he saw me.

"How the hell did you get in? I thought the door was locked and, anyway, you're a day early," he grumbled. "And why are you staring, eh? The shock of encountering the Librarian's underling indulging himself? And why not?

"Week after week, you and your colleagues come poking your noses in here. Meddling. I'm sick of it. Literary voyeurs, the lot of you. You just don't get it, do you? Haven't a clue, not an inkling. None of you. No idea what it's like. None whatsoever."

"So, why don't you tell me, Bookbynde? Help me and the others to understand."

For a while he said nothing, his gaze distant, thin wisps of cigarette smoke escaping from the corners of his mouth and hairy nostrils and curling upwards, disappearing towards the distant ceiling.

"It's not easy," he grumbled. "Not easy at all. Being here, I mean, here in this place, the Library. This is my world, I exist in here now, not the world you and your friends know and love and inhabit out there. But it wasn't always so. I had a life once, too."

He stopped and poked at the olive in his glass with a long, dirt-ingrained fingernail, before lowering his voice until it was no more than a raspy whisper.

"Like you and your fellows, I entered this place to discover the truth of what lay within. And I did too, yes, and more, much, much more.

"Like you, I kept coming back until one day I knew too much and couldn't leave. Why do you think it's called '*The Library of Lost Souls*'?"

Bookbynde spat out the final two words, 'Lost Souls'. He crunched the cigarette holder between his teeth and swallowed hard. He let slip a sigh and used the back of his hand to wipe away particles of ash clinging to his upper lip.

"Can you imagine what it felt like, all those years ago? An impressionable and inquisitive young man, who had learned to read and yet never owned a book of his own, except for a bible?

"The wonders this place held. So many books. Stacked from floor to ceiling on oak shelves, the wonderful smells, of ink and hide, the soft touch of silk and the texture of paper and vellum, the Reading Room, the lives and stories buried within all those pages. A whole new world.

"Then I discovered I could be part of that world, a world I could enter, a world that for a few brief hours I could escape to, away from my miserable existence here.

"I saw life and opportunity beyond my wildest dreams and I was sorely tempted, blinded by lust and love, by greed and advancement. But I stopped short of slaking this thirst for at heart I remain a good man. My soul is not lost. It still resides within me, not on the shelves of this stinking library or under the control of the Librarian."

Bookbynde fell quiet. Tears welled in his dark eyes and rolled steadily down his cheeks, splashing on to the ink-stained surface of the oak desk. I proffered a handkerchief which he accepted gratefully. He gently dabbed at and dried his eyes.

A creature whom I had at first despised and detested, now cut a sad, lonely and forlorn figure, hunched miserably before me. He stuffed my handkerchief into a pocket and continued.

"You seek a satisfactory conclusion to a story and events I have journeyed long and hard to answer, too. So many twists and turns along the way, truths and half-truths, lies and deceit. Yes, even here among lost souls. And particularly those who fall under the spell of the Librarian.

"Some harbour a desire to return, for release from their damnation and believe it can be achieved by doing the Librarian's bidding. They will stop at nothing. Nothing.

"Some are misguided fools who do not realise, lost souls can never return, but there are a few who are not lost souls at all, merely trapped and unable to return.

"My beautiful Francesca, for one. We were sweethearts, betrothed and set to be wed, to live a life together, until she was taken from me. Kidnapped; stolen and held beyond my reach.

"My father did all within his power to find her and bring her back, for he felt responsible. For it was he who unwittingly met and introduced this stranger, the man who did this, this thief, into my life. But the thief was too clever and cunning by half and gradually the search drove my father mad.

"Montgomery Swallowtail Bookbynde was his name and you have now heard what became of him. And this man, the thief, I see him every waking moment and I loathe and hate him. He has made me what I have become. I hate all he is and everything he stands for with every fibre of my being. For 'he' is the Librarian. He has built this Library on ill-gotten gains, stolen from others and he will stop at nothing to protect the evil he has created here."

Bookbynde lurched forwards, grabbing my wrists and pulling me close so I could feel his rasping stale breath against my cheek. His eyes searched mine.

"Help me, sir," he pleaded. "Help me bring back my sweet Francesca. Let me gaze once more into her green eyes and take her to a place beyond his reach, where we can live our remaining days together."

After what felt like an age, he dropped his eyes from mine, released his grip on my wrists and rose from behind his desk.

"Go now," he said. "You must go before the Librarian returns. Your time here today is done. If Steve has the time, send him in next, for there is more to be told and more to be done."

Chapter Fifteen

In here it doesn't smell like a proper library. Proper libraries smell of dust and old paper. You can buy that scent bottled now. Maybe to inhale while you read your eBook, like some bibliophile solvent abuser.

No, this library smells of rotten rags with an underlying hint of dentures. Like a forgotten orthodontist's.

I can't help feeling we've only scratched the surface and we need to get beyond the reading rooms, down into the stacks, where the old papers are hidden.

I heard the Librarian's breath before I saw him.

"You might want to think twice before you go nosing around into the reference section, boy," he said.

"I've come prepared," I answered and emptied my bag on to the small wooden desk, scratched with the names of long divorced childhood sweethearts.

First, I took the library card and pushed jasmine petals and Valerian into the fold of cardboard, lighting the corner with moss and an old flint arrowhead. Then I rubbed the ash into a piece of Roman glass, its surface laminated to the colour of peacocks.

The Librarian watched, bemused.

My hands smelled of book burnings and midnight swamps. I muttered my words quietly so he couldn't hear me.

After a few moments the figure became visible. I reached down and held his hand, easing him from between the layers of glass. His grip was much tighter than I expected, fingers becoming more solid as he grew to full size.

"Do you have a name?"

"Not that I will tell you. You can call me RotTwin."

I peered at him closely. There was a passing resemblance, nothing more. As he moved, waves of perfume wafted from him, strangely at odds with his ash-smeared skin. On his forehead I could just make out the words 'Due and retur', the last few characters burnt away.

Over in the corner, arms folded and wreathed in smoke, the Librarian snored.

I wrote the instructions on a piece of old cardboard and passed them to RotTwin. He read them slowly, then again, before eating the words, savouring each mouthful. As he chewed, I could see a faint red glow.

With a sound like a bonfire collapsing in on itself, he loped away down the corridor, each footstep echoing back from the shelves of glass jars. As he disappeared into the stacks, the Librarian awoke.

"Have you been?" he asked, wiping sleep from his eyes and looking around the room, confused.

"Have I been where?

"The Reading Room. That's where you all seem to want to go."

"Not me. Not today. I think I'll just stay here. Design it yourself, did you?"

"Design what myself?"

"The Library. Well, in particular, this atrium. Very fine architecture. Inspired by the Austrian National Library?"

"The Zaluski in Warsaw," he said, standing up and walking across to a set of plan drawers in the corner. "If you want, I can show you the original plans."

"That would be great," I said, pretending an enthusiasm for architecture which I didn't really have.

I never realised how much planning is required to build a library, even one which exists in some existential plain between midnight and cock crow.

He explained how he dragged memories of different libraries from the dreams of sleeping readers, winding them around hazel sticks like drop bobbins, then planting them in the corpses of fictional characters, thus to grow the Library of Lost Souls.

I feigned interest, all the time waiting for some hint of the scent of flowers, over the stink of old teeth. I could have asked about the teeth-stink but really didn't want to know.

The Librarian was halfway through explaining the seasonal growth patterns of a Sumerian clay tablet library when he nodded off, head tipping forward to the desk.

RotTwin rested on the ground, limbs sagging on the hard stone floor.

"You did right, sending me to the reference section. That is no place for flesh," he said, a hint of fear in his voice. This confused me. As a rule, to the best of my knowledge, homunculi had no concept of fear.

"What did you find?" I said. He cleared a space on the old school desk and spread out an ancient document, edges held together with yellowed tape. I stared, unsure what I was seeing.

"I can't see anything," I said, peering at the stains on the paper, trying to make them turn into legible paragraphs.

"You won't," he said. Over the next few minutes he spoke in a tongue I couldn't decipher. As each sentence was spoken, he took a safety pin from his pocket and pinned it to the paper, the metal curls sitting proud of the parchment.

"Give it a few moments before you remove the pins," he said.

"Feral phrases need time to bed in."

I spent the time looking around the room. On a high shelf, tumbles of rotting teeth formed plaque-coated drystone walls.

"Borrowers who didn't renew their loans," RotTwin said.

"Lots of transgressors?" I asked.

He shrugged. "Should be fine now."

With a jeweller's hand, he removed each pin, hooking them into a garland which he draped around his neck. With ashen fingers he pushed the document over to me.

"These are the rules of the Reference Room: (1) Each reader must be assigned a seat by the attendant Librarian. (2) Only one book may be studied at any one time. (3) No pens, pencils, mirrors, etch-a-sketch or recording devices of any form, from any age, may be taken into the reference room. (4) The main collection should be referred to before consulting the reference collection. (5) Questions unable to be answered in the main collection should be directed toward the reference collection. (6) Questions unable to be answered in the reference collection should be directed towards the main collection. (7) Please allow sufficient time for the acquisition of new material. (8) Any queries or for further information please send a message to the Head Librarian's office, Room 708, using the Pneumatic Capsule Transportation system.

RotTwin looked at me, his skin coming apart like wet cardboard.

"Can you do anything with this?" he asked.

I shook my head. "My time is up, but maybe Jackie can."

Chapter Sixteen

In his new guise, Brookbynde dragged me through the double doors, past his desk, towards the stairs.

"You have to trust me," he whispered as we ran. "There's so little time left. I'm sorry I treated you badly when you were last here, but I wasn't myself - truly."

I assumed we were on our way to the Reading Room but, less than halfway up, Bookbynde staggered against the wall, creased with pain. His face was the colour of a snow-filled sky, and it sounded as though he was breathing through feathers.

"Ink ... with...drawal ... symp...toms," he mouthed.

"Drinking *ink* made you ... ?" I paused, not wanting to be rude when he was clearly distressed.

He nodded. "Libra...rian's ... quill ... scratched ... me, ... then ... reading ... words ... wasn't ... enough. Needed ... raw ... *ink* ..."

His hands twisted in longing. Minutes crashed by as he brought himself under control, and his breathing eased a little.

"Help me ... to ... the Reading Room. We can ... gain time there."

As time unwound in the Reading Room, Bookbynde regained his sense of purpose. He reminded me how Antony, following the Librarian's instructions, had watched Francesca come to life *from a book.*

"That wasn't the real Francesca, my Francesca. That one is an evil fiction created by the Librarian to weave shadows in the minds of those seeking the truth. By contrast, the lost souls of Twinrot and Mary are *real,* for Julie withdrew them directly from the shelves. You may trust them."

"Even though Mary killed your father?"

"Montgomery Swallowtail deserved everything he got," hissed Bookbynde. "Look at his initials: MS. A manuscript, scriven in ink. How could he be trusted?"

"Are you saying the written word can never be trusted?"

"There will always be space between the written word and the mind of the reader. Who knows what may fill that space?"

This was getting complicated and not a little scary. I changed tack slightly. "Mary's initials are also MS," I pointed out.

"Yes," agreed Bookbynde. "But only by marriage. She was born Mary Evans."

"And then de Leche." I blushed.

"Ah, yes." Bookbynde looked at me sternly. "Longfeet de Leche is a corruption, an anagram, if you like, of The Golden Fleece. The golden fleece was an ancient symbol of power. So, de Leche embodies the corruption of power, but since his surname translates as 'of Milk', he is cowardly and thus susceptible to someone stronger. In short, a perfect cypher for the Librarian."

"So, I should ignore everything he said?"

"Perhaps," said Bookbynde. "But in here, nothing is as it seems. Try a little reversal."

I struggled to remember.

"Twinrot isn't a river-rat, that's obvious." I paused. "There was something about coffee, about Twinrot's time in the West Indies. Yes! Twinrot had to be kept away from anything to do with coffee."

Bookbynde smiled. "Coffee is an antidote to ink. David, the first of you to break the rules, most opportunely found himself in Caffe Nero. He brought back the smell of freshly-ground coffee, which not only enraged the Librarian but also encouraged Barbara into further transgressions. Claire's little excursion around the portals brought back another dose of caffeine, to help things along."

"But Amanda didn't bring the Cafe de Paris. Surely that would have helped?"

Impatience scuttled across Bookbynde's brow:

"De Leche was referring to the nightclub, not the beverage," he said.

"Ah." Hastily, I shook my head to clear it of the miasma left by thoughts of de Leche. "And what about Rosie?"

"Hmm, little Rosie. One might think that being murdered has changed her ways, and she certainly seems to care for Twinrot now, but don't forget how she betrayed him, many times. That is a weakness and the Librarian ... loves ... weakness."

Snow-clouds were returning to his face.

I put my hands on his shoulders, looked directly into his eyes:

"Fighting ink addiction is anything but weak," I said.

"But it drains strength," he replied. "Dear Soloman has suffered ... for so many moons. You have all been witness to that. Think of the testimony you have heard, from Twinrot, from Idris Jones. Soloman is a good man. Claire saw how he was punished for talking to Cathy in the Elfin Forest."

Feathers were gathering in his voice. Time was catching up.

"Quickly! Tell me what to do."

"Go down forty-nine steps." His voice was faltering, becoming weaker as he spoke. "Find loose brick ... Key ... twist ... filing cabinet ... capsule."

His voice faded to nothing.

"Bookbynde!" I shook his shoulder. "Can you get to Caffe Nero? No, perhaps not. Imagine it, then. The barista making good, strong coffee. Smell it! Breathe in the dark, rich fragrance of it. Keep thinking of coffee and your sweet Francesca. We'll find her, I promise."

The second drawer felt like it was glued shut. The light was going. Blood ran from my knuckles as the bottom drawer came free with a screech and I fell in. Steve's reading of the rules of the Reference Room filled my ears.

"Room 708," I breathed.

I could feel time chasing me as I sped down the steps, counting as I went. I fumbled frantically with the loose brick and found the key. The filing cabinet was ancient and battered. I inserted the key. Twisted it right. Nothing. Left. A soft click and the smell of rotting teeth. Which drawer? A swishing on the stairs. I tugged at the top drawer. It wouldn't move. Second drawer. Cold air was wafting down my neck.

Nothing happened. And then the air was whooshed from my lungs, the world blurred, and I was squeezed and stretched, before being twanged painfully into the Head Librarian's in-tray.

There was a loud ping, and a bright voice said, "You have mail."

A small Pickwick-like man looked me up and down, disapprovingly.

"Oh, no. No, no, no," he muttered. "We can't send *you* to bring Soloman back into stock. You're not qualified to navigate the Mobile Library to the West Indies. It must be Amanda. She started all this."

Chapter Seventeen

I enter the Library for what I hope is the last time, armed only with my wits, a print out of the chapters that have gone before and - what I consider to be a basic and sensible precaution - a choice selection of coffee products, including a flask of strong black coffee, a pocket full of ground Arabica and a necklace fashioned from the finest Colombian beans.

"Bookbynde?" I call into the darkness.   "Twinrot? Librarian? Anyone?"

My voice echoes away into the blackness and the silence is all the thicker for having been broken. I can't pretend I'm liking this very much. Somehow, if I understand correctly, I need to reach room 708 in order to find the answers for which we have all been searching, but with no one to guide me and unable to see my hand before my face, my chances of going anywhere at all seem pretty remote. I really don't fancy blundering around in the darkness in the hope of falling into a helpfully placed portal, especially as, it seems to me, a large number of the portals seem to be anything but helpful.

I recall David's adventures which, after many false starts, only came good when he plunged into a urinal... it's not for me.

Perhaps the coffee... it's worth a try, I suppose. The worst that can happen is that I get a hot drink while I figure out what to do.

I unscrew the lid of my flask and immediately the strong smell of coffee permeates the air. Is it my imagination or, as I pour, is the darkness slightly less impenetrable? I take a sip and there's no mistaking it now. Something's happening; a swell of soft light swirls and strengthens before me, growing in intensity as I drink until finally, as I empty my cup, I am standing before a whirling vortex, of which even the special effects boys from the Dr Who studio would be inordinately proud. Forget the inkwells, urinals, drawers, umbrellas and other such detritus. This is the real thing, a portal of staggering proportions, a portal worthy of the final episode of any adventure.

In short, it's a portal to be proud of and I'm guessing it only goes to one place. Still, I take no chances, because time is running out (well, when I say time is running out, of course I mean my word count is running out).

I drop my now empty flask to the floor, take a mental deep breath and step into the portal, saying out loud, with as much command and clarity as I can muster:

"Room 708!"

Talk about an anticlimax. Nothing happens. The whirlpool of light chases around me but I haven't moved, I'm still standing in the foyer with the darkness pressing all around my small oasis of light. I try again.

"Room 708."

Again nothing, and then, as if from a great distance, a small voice instructs me to, "Say the magic word."

It's Twinrot's voice, or maybe Bookbynde's or perhaps even... oh, let's face it, I've no idea whose bloody voice it is or, come to that, what the magic word could be.

In the light of the portal I flick through the chapters, scanning each occasion on which one of our group has used a portal, looking desperately for the words they used to send them on their way but I find nothing.

"Quickly!" instructs the voice. "Say the words. There isn't much time. The portal is losing its integrity!"

Hmmph – losing its integrity? I ask you. Why do people always say things like that in sci-fi? They mean the bloody thing's about to stop working, so why not just say so? Sorry... just a little bugbear of mine, one of many... but I digress. Let's get back to it.

There I am, fumbling helplessly through my mind as the portal begins to 'lose its integrity', when quite suddenly, and rather sheepishly, I hit on the obvious answer.

"Room 708!" I bellow commandingly. "Please!"

The effect is instantaneous and gut-wrenching as the portal sucks me up into the vortex, only to deposit me, moments later, into the hard, grey confines of a cheap plastic in-tray.

I scramble out and find myself in a small, rather bare, office. There are just a rickety MDF desk with its single plastic in-tray, and a cheap, white moulded garden chair with a snapped leg, both of which stand upon a threadbare carpet which may, or may not have once had a pattern but is now a non-descript dirty brown. There are no windows, no discernible source of light (although it's not dark in the room) and a single door in one wall, a door on which I see the brass numbers 708.

"Well now," says a voice, the same voice, perhaps, as I heard in the portal, although I can't really be sure. "And who might you be?"

I look around but the room is empty.

"Answer in your own sweet time, I've nothing else to do today." says the voice, somewhat sarcastically. "Who are you?"

"I'm Amanda."

"Of course, you are." The voice sounds bored now. "You're very late."

"Late for what?"

"Whatever it is you're here for. You'd best go in, it's not good to keep them waiting."

"Keep who waiting?" I demand

"Them," says the voice unhelpfully. "The ones in there."

I step towards the door, then stop and look around again. "Who are you? And more to the point, where are you? Why can't I see you?"

"I'm no one," says the voice with an obvious yawn. "No one of any importance. Not in this story, anyway, although I should tell you, I'm quite the character elsewhere. In fact, if you have the time, I might point you towards a very fine novel called... what am I saying? Of course you don't have the time. To answer your question, you can't see me because I'm not really here. Just helping out, filling in, you might say. I don't belong in this tale but I was asked to fill in for a strange creature called Book something or other, so here I am... or here I'm not, if you get my meaning."

I don't, not really, but I let it go. "Just tell me one thing," I ask the disembodied voice as I put my hand on the doorknob. "Who asked you to help out? Was it the Librarian? Or Bookbynde himself?"

The voice laughs. "You know who brought me here,"

"I do?"

"You did."

"I did?" I query and, if I wasn't confused at the end of the recap then I certainly am now. "When did I do that? Why did I do that? I mean..."

"Oh, questions, questions, always so many questions! You don't have the word count so hurry along now and perhaps you'll find your answers. Good luck to you."

Although I've seen no one else in the room since my arrival, I am aware that the owner of the disembodied voice has gone and I am alone. Oh well, there's nothing for it. This is, as they say, 'it'; the end of the line, the grand finale, the answer (or so I hope).

I take a deep breath and open the door and find myself in what appears to be a slightly faded and dated drawing room. There are a couple of unremarkable pictures on the wall, a large fireplace devoid of fire, a couple of side tables and a dim, pedestrian chandelier, but what takes the eye is the large table in the centre of the room. Room 708.

I might have guessed it would be the Ryedale Room. How could it not be? But that doesn't matter now because seated at the table are nine figures, three across the top and three down each side. I cast my eyes slowly around the gathering. All nine sit in silence, hands folded on the table before them, eyes staring straight ahead and I don't need the written chapters in my pocket to recognise them all. Although some are more familiar to me than others.

Nearest the door, on the right-hand side of the table, sits Idris Jones, a character who, by his very presence, is perhaps more important in the scheme of things than is credited by his brief appearance in the library.

To his right sits Mary Sly and to her right her husband, Soloman. Across from Soloman sits Rosie Twinrot and to her right is Francesca, but whether she be the real thing or the Librarian's later fiction, I cannot tell.

On her right is a young man who I think may be the plantation owner's aristocratic son, whom we have met once away from the Elfin Forest, only then he called himself RotTwin.

That leaves the three at the head of the table, the ones around whom our story has unfolded. To the left sits Whisker Twinrot, to the right, Bookbynde, and in-between them, in the centre, as he has been in the centre of all things, sits the Librarian.

It is the Librarian, alone of the nine, who seems aware of my presence, a broad smile cracking his angular features.

"Welcome, welcome!" he says effusively. "Come in, join us. We've been expecting you!" he waves a bony hand and a single high-backed chair materialises in the middle of the unoccupied foot of the table. "Sit, please and all your questions shall at last be answered."

I feel reluctance and impatience in equal measure as I take my place in the chair and I can't stop my fingers from nervously twisting the coffee bean necklace at my throat. It's a gesture that doesn't go unnoticed by the Librarian. His smile widens.

"I see you have come prepared, but the question is, prepared for what?"

I can't answer that so I stay silent, as silent and still as the eight frozen figures flanking the Librarian, and that's how we stay, the ten of us, for what seems like an age, until eventually the Librarian clears his throat.

"So, here we all are," he says cheerfully, gesturing around the table. "A merry gathering indeed."

"What's wrong with them?" I force myself to ask as I look around the table. "What have you done to them?"

"What have I done to them?" he repeats, sounding slightly

puzzled. "Why, I've done nothing. They are just waiting, in limbo, one might say." He laughs. "In limbo... I made a joke. That's rather good, don't you think? Oh, come now, my dear, it deserves at least a smile, or perhaps you don't understand. The Library's in Limbo."

"Yes," I agree. "Like Caffe Nero."

"Quite," he acknowledges dryly, the smile fading from his face. "Oh well," he sighs. "I suppose we should get on, you're already a thousand words over your allocation, you know."

"Only a thousand?" I mutter to myself. It feels far more. "Can I speak to them?" I ask. "Can I ask them whatever I wish, without your interference? Will they tell me the truth?"

"Of course," he says without hesitation and, for my part, I believe him, but he hasn't finished. "However, what you have to understand is, every one of them has spoken only the truth up to this point. They have all spoken only the truth, their own truth. The problem is, you've been investigating the wrong story."

"I don't understand."

"No? From the moment Twinrot was plucked from the obscurity of the shelves, you have all been chasing the wrong tale. Twinrot this, Twinrot that. Did he or didn't he? Villain or hero? My dear, you've all been asking the wrong questions. This was never about Twinrot. He was nothing more than a device, a means to an end. That is all any of them have been. It is not their story."

"No," I agree as the light begins to dawn. "It's your story. No, not even that – it's the story of the Library."

"Ah." The Librarian sighs with satisfaction, his face softening to such an extent that, for a moment, he appears younger, almost handsome. "Finally, the mists begin to clear. Do you still want to talk to them, or will you be content to talk to me?"

"You'll tell me the truth?"

"It is not possible for me to do otherwise. You do understand that now, don't you?"

"I'm not sure." I confess.

"No matter," he says carelessly. "All will become clear, or, at the least, a little clearer. Now, where shall I begin? Let me see." He turns slightly to his left and pats the frozen Bookbynde on the top of his head. "There I was, a Librarian with no books, and there was Bookbynde, addicted to words and nothing to read. He came to me, you see, begging for books, but I had none to give so I gave him ink and quill and bid him write a world, a world in which we could raise the money to build a Library.

"Alas for Bookbynde. So engrossed in his tale did he become, he wrote himself into it and became lost to the real world, became a lost soul although, of course, he didn't know it. He thought he was just addicted to ink.

"Yes?" he enquired, raising his eyebrows at the look on my face. "You have a question?"

"I do. What exactly is a lost soul, and how does one become one? I mean, we thought maybe the lost souls were murderers, the ones in limbo, but Bookbynde never murdered anyone, did he?"

"The lost souls are characters, nothing more, nothing less, but they are the abandoned ones, toyed with briefly by their creators and then cast aside when something better comes along. They are the unfinished, the rejected, the prototypes, if you will. They are the characters you write and forget, the ones who never make it further than the first or second drafts. They haunt the 'Works in Progress' and are forgotten, their stories never told."

I look guiltily at Rosie, written on a whim, and think briefly of the nameless souls who have lived briefly and then expired on the nib of my pen.

"So," continues the Librarian, "as I was saying, Bookbynde wrote himself into..."

"No," I protest. "Hang on a second. That's not right. Bookbynde didn't write himself. He may be a lost soul but he isn't his own lost soul... he's Antony's... Antony wrote him into being!"

The Librarian claps his hands in delight.

"Oh, bravo, bravo! Do go on."

I shake my head trying to make sense of it all.

"Twinrot didn't steal the Sly family fortune – you did. You used it to build the Library except...no, that can't be right, because the Library came before Twinrot ... or did it?"

I get up out of my chair and pace around the room, glancing now and then at the silent lost souls around the table. I can't get to grips with this.

"The Library only exists," I add, deep in thought. "Because everyone around this table was written into existence to create a tale which would provide the funds to build it, and they only exist as lost souls within the Library. They can't exist without the

Library and the Library can't exist without them and... and.." Convoluted it may be but I can see the truth of it now. "And none of this, none of you exist without us."

I'm walking along the top of the table and the Librarian is turning to watch my progress. As I pass behind him, his hand shoots out and grabs the coffee beans around my neck, pulling me towards him with frightening strength and speed. Not just towards him but right into him. One moment we are two and the next we become one, except that's not strictly true. We are two but we occupy the same space, the same body and I can feel myself fighting to be free but, of course, I am fighting a losing battle. I wrote this creature and he is a part of me, even as I am now a part of him. I struggle to break free, knowing, if I fail, I am destined to remain in the library for all time, just another lost soul among so many.

I'm vaguely aware of the lost souls around the table beginning to stir. I see them with my own eyes and the eyes of the Librarian. I don't want to keep them. He doesn't want to let them go.

"Use the fairy dust!" urges a voice, Bookbynde, I think, and then Twinrot's strong voice joins in.

"The fairy dust – use the fairy dust. Quickly now, you're almost at three thousand words!"

"The fairy dust, the fairy dust!" They're all chanting it now.

"What bloody fairy dust?" I gasp. "I don't have any fairy dust!"

"In your pocket!" says Rosie. "Use the fairy dust."

"It's coffee grains!" I protest.

"Oh, don't split hairs," mutters Twinrot. "This is an emergency. Coffee grains, fairy dust, it's all the same! Just use it."

I grab a handful of the ground coffee. "I don't know what to do with it."

"Use your imagination – you're a writer, aren't you?"

I do the only thing I can think of, the only thing I can do. I fling the coffee up into the air and it showers down over the upturned faces of the lost souls. For a moment time stands still and I realise, I am alone in the chair and the Librarian, if he ever existed, is gone. Just like that; gone, and as I watch, the lost souls sink back into their seats as if in slow motion, silent once more.

I look around at their faces, eight lost souls, morphing slowly into their creators, the members of ThirskWriteNow.

And there we are, the nine of us, sitting around the table, at the end as we were at the beginning when first we conceived of this strange flight of fancy.

And why did we do it? Well, why not? We're writers. It's what we do, after all.

Footnote: About the Group

ThirskWriteNow is a group of like-minded souls, all with one big common denominator – a love of writing. Comprising both professionals and amateurs, the group welcomes all-comers. There is only one unbendable rule: No minors.

Meetings are informal. There is no committee. There is no chairperson. We select themes as 'homework', which we read out – or not – at the next meeting. Some members choose to just listen. Some elect to read out passages from their own work in progress. Opinions are only given if requested. Like we said, informal.

Assuming you have taken the time to read at least some of this anthology, then you already know the kind of work we produce.

Meetings are held 7.30pm to 9pm-ish, every second Tuesday, in the Rydale Room at the Golden Fleece Hotel in Thirsk's Market Place.

Charges are £5.00 per meeting. Room hire is £30.00 per meeting. As we usually see ten or more members per session, the kitty soon accumulates. Said kitty buys us an annual Christmas dinner from the Fleece and also pays for copies of our anthologies from Amazon Kindle.

Paperback versions of our books are available either from Amazon or from the White Rose Book Café in Thirsk.

Find us on Facebook at
www.facebook.com/groups/thirskwritenow
or you can email the publisher at
jamesjones950@sky.com

Or even, if you prefer, find out which Tuesday is hosting the next meeting and simply turn up on the night. Your first meeting is free of charge. Hotel reception can give you the relevant Tuesdays.

Whichever way you choose, we guarantee you will be made welcome – and we guarantee you will enjoy yourself.

Best wishes and thank you for reading our stuff.

James H Jones pp TThirskWriteNow

Printed in Poland
by Amazon Fulfillment
Poland Sp. z o.o., Wrocław

54495647R00162